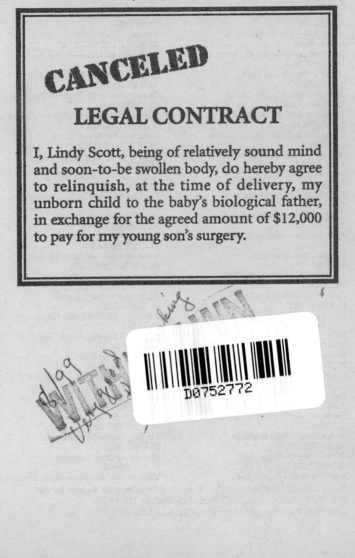

CANCELED

LEGAL CONTRACT

I, Lindy Scott, being of relatively sound mind and soon-to-be swollen body, do hereby agree to relinquish, at the time of delivery, my unborn child to the baby's biological father, in exchange for the agreed amount of $12,000 to pay for my young son's surgery.

Please address questions and book requests to: Silhouette Reader Service
U.S.: 3010 Walden Ave., P.O. Box 1325, Buffalo, NY 14269
Canadian: P.O. Box 609, Fort Erie, Ont. L2A 5X3

Born in the USA
ARKANSAS

BAY MATTHEWS

Bittersweet Sacrifice

Silhouette Books

Published by Silhouette Books

America's Publisher of Contemporary Romance

SILHOUETTE BOOKS
300 East 42nd St.,
New York, N.Y. 10017

ISBN 0-373-47154-8

BITTERSWEET SACRIFICE

This edition published by arrangement with Harlequin Books S.A.

® and TM are trademarks of Harlequin Books S.A., used under license.
Trademarks indicated with ® are registered in the United States Patent and
Trademark Office, the Canadian Trade Marks Office and in other countries.

Printed in U.S.A.

Dear Reader,

Bittersweet Sacrifice, a book I wrote under the name Bay Matthews, was begun when I fell in love with the character of Lindy and I wanted to show the reader that lots of men have as great a desire to become a parent as women. I also wanted to show that the healing power of love, whether it's between a man and woman or parent and child, can come when we least expect it, and often from the most unlikely places!

I chose Hot Springs, Arkansas, for the setting because I lived there for many years and it was familiar to me, but also because it's a place with a fascinating history and with lots of neat places to see and things to do.

I hope you enjoy your visit and getting to know Lindy, Zade, Josh and Butter.

All best wishes,

Penny Richards

Special thanks to Sherry Roche
whose freckles, red hair and effervescent personality
gave me the basis for Lindy.

****

For Susan C. Engle with many thanks
for the genuine interest in my writing,
for the gallons of coffee and the listening,
and the believing in me during the bad times.
For being such a special friend...
this one's for you.

Chapter One

"I'm not giving this baby up." The words, spoken in a low, trembling voice, were wrenched from the very soul of the woman who sat twisting a gold wedding band round and round a slender finger.

Dr. Amy Fedders, seated behind the massive, walnut desk dominating the book-lined room, glanced up sharply from the notepad on which she'd been busily scribbling indecipherable medical jargon. "What?"

Lindy Scott raked a fallen strand of flame-red hair toward the knot atop her head. Her voice held a stronger more determined note as she repeated her announcement. "I've decided not to give this baby away."

The blond physician, a prominent Little Rock gynecologist who'd moved to Hot Springs two years earlier in search of a smaller, more personalized practice, closed the folder and put down the pen she'd been using. She pulled off her silver-rimmed, half-frame glasses and placed them on top of the medical file. Elbows resting on the desktop, she propped her

rounded chin in her capable hands and simply stared at the
woman who had been her receptionist ever since she'd moved
her practice. "What happened to make you change your
mind?"

Lindy shrugged her shoulders and shook her head. "It's
crazy. Josh and I went shopping yesterday afternoon. When I
got home I was going through the things I'd bought." She
looked her boss squarely in the eye. "I bought white satin
shoes, Amy. I'd been trying to find the right ones for weeks."

"The right ones for what?"

"The dress." Lindy sighed. "Someone gave me a beautiful
little white dress at Josh's shower. I could never bring myself
to give it away. I kept telling myself that maybe I could use
it for my next baby. But this is my next baby, and..." her
voice trailed off in misery.

"And you're supposed to give it up," Amy said bluntly,
filling the lapse in the conversation with the uncompromising
statement.

Lindy leaned forward, her posture and her face proof of her
earnestness. "I really thought I could. When you came to me
suggesting I be a surrogate mother for that man, it seemed like
the answer to my prayers. You know how badly I needed the
money for Josh's surgery after the accident."

Amy's smile was filled with compassionate sorrow and her
head moved slowly up and down in affirmation as she remembered the tragic car accident a little over a year before that
had killed Lindy's husband, Randy, and severely injured her
son, Josh. She saw a lot of heartache ahead for two people.
"That's one reason I approached you. That, and you're a de-
cent, hardworking person. Not to mention the fact that you're
loving and caring, and I'd hoped you'd pass those traits on to
the baby." She paused, then asked, "What was it about the
dress that made you change your mind?"

Once more confronting the agony she'd faced during those
few heartrending seconds the previous evening, Lindy lifted
her troubled gaze to Amy. "I was standing there looking at
the dress and shoes, praying the baby would be a girl because

she'd look so beautiful in them, when it suddenly hit me that I wouldn't see it; I'd never even know whether the baby *was* a girl. I knew then that I couldn't go through with it.''

"What about your contract?" Amy asked. "You signed papers saying you'd let the man have the baby. You've accepted his money."

"I know. I don't want to cheat him out of anything. I plan to pay back the money on some sort of monthly basis."

Amy's blue eyes searched Lindy's face, noting the defiant tilt of her chin and the determination in her eyes. She meant it. Every word. After two years Amy knew her employee well enough to know that once her mind was set on doing something, she did it. There probably wasn't one chance in a thousand she could be persuaded to change her mind.

She had watched as the younger woman's love of life and mankind had enabled her to put herself together after the accident. Watched her face patients with a smiling face when her heart was breaking. Saw her face her son's operations with unfailing optimism and a confidence that somehow strengthened everyone around her. She had often marveled at Lindy's ability to face problems with such ease and wondered just what it would take to knock her off her stride. Looking back over the past few months, she realized she might have unknowingly witnessed it. Though Lindy was always pleasant, at times there had been a sadness about her Amy assumed had something to do with Josh's physical condition.

Now she knew it was more. Knowing what a good mother Lindy was, Amy should have put it together before now. Lindy Scott didn't have the personality to give up a child, nor was she the type to go back on her word. She must have gone through agony reaching this decision. With a feeling of helplessness, Amy wondered how Lindy would handle the repercussions. And, knowing the father of Lindy Scott's unborn baby as well as she did, she was quite certain that repercussions awaited. How strong the impact would be on both their lives remained the only question.

* * *

Zade Wakefield maneuvered the silver-blue Jaguar into a parking space behind the weathered, barn-gray professional offices and uncoiled his long form from the car's plush interior. He locked the door and made his way determinedly across the parking lot and along a narrow sidewalk that bordered a flower bed rife with the scent and color of half a dozen kinds of springtime blossoms. He paused just outside the office door that flaunted an ornately scrolled nameplate whose collective letters read: Amy Fedders, Obstetrics and Gynecology.

A quiver of apprehension pricked the back of his neck. Something was wrong. He'd known it ever since Amy had called an hour earlier. Always a woman of firm beliefs and opinions, his cousin had flatly refused to discuss the problem over the phone, insisting instead that he come to her office.

Zade knew it had something to do with "her," the unknown woman who was supposed to give birth to his child in three weeks and four days. Something must have happened. Several discussions with Amy revealed that having a baby involved many things. Things could go wrong. Things he had no control over. Things even now running through his mind and giving rise to frustration and helplessness and a rapidly escalating panic.

Perspiration dampened his palms, and a frown furrowed his forehead. What could be wrong? Was the woman having the baby early? If it was premature, that could mean... Unaccustomed nerves mingled with the cloying scent of peonies to knot his stomach in sudden nausea. His naturally dark complexion looked faded as he wiped shaking hands down the legs of his sharply creased slacks. *God...God, no! Let everything be all right. Let my baby be all right.*

He thought of the room waiting for his child. The bright, bold wallpaper depicted cavorting clowns with red and blue polka-dot suits and orange hair. There was an oak crib with patterned sheets and the blue gingham comforter he'd put on himself. A small, fluffy teddy bear guarded the room from its position on the bentwood rocking chair near the night-light... decorations that he chose after reading in some manual for prospective parents that babies liked bright colors. He'd decorated the room when the excitement and anticipation had threatened to overwhelm him.

And now something was wrong. He could feel it. Zade grabbed at the doorjamb to steady the shaking of his hands while images of a too still infant flitted through his mind and a low roaring filled his ears. He wanted this child so badly he could taste it. Worse, some inner sense told him he needed the things a baby would bring to his life.

"Excuse me."

He turned vacant, silver-gray eyes toward the sound of the nasal, feminine voice rescuing him from the unpleasant turn of his thoughts. A plump-faced woman stood just inside the partially opened door, her arms crossed over her jutting belly as she waited for him to move so she could leave the office.

When Zade neither moved nor spoke, she exclaimed louder, "Hey! Are you okay?"

The realization that he was blocking the doorway, and had been for some time, caused an uncharacteristic red to creep up the arrogant sweep of his cheekbones, returning the look of health to his face. He forced a polite smile, stepped aside jerkily and pushed open the office door for her. The half smile lifted the corners of a heavy black mustache bracketing a mouth that was more accustomed to frowning. "I'm fine. Sorry I blocked the door."

A knowing, complacent smirk replaced the woman's look of concern. She reached out a chubby hand and patted his arm comfortingly. "Dr. Fedders is excellent. She delivered my other one without a bit of trouble. Your wife will be fine. You'll see." Then, with a final, encouraging smile, the woman brushed past him.

Zade drew a deep, fortifying breath and stepped inside.

From her vantage point behind the opaque, sliding-glass window separating the waiting room from the office, Lindy watched the man standing at the door with one of their departing patients. Something about him looked vaguely famil-

iar, and even from where she sat she could tell he was scared
to death. She smiled. Must be a first-timer. The only men who
were comfortable in the office were the jobbers from the phar-
maceutical companies who came to hawk their wares, and the
men who had already accompanied their wives through at least
one pregnancy.

The woman moved on, and the man turned more fully into
the room. Lindy's auburn brows raised. *Not bad,* she thought,
liking the lean yet powerful build of the newcomer. And she'd
always thought there was something sort of sexy about a mustache. *Not bad at all.* But maybe she hadn't seen him before
after all. He was definitely in the category of memorable. Her
eyes made a survey of the room, doing a quick inventory of
the women present and wondering if she could correctly pick
out the one he belonged to. Instead, she found him the object
of instant curiosity as a sea of eyes lifted simultaneously from
the pages of the latest women's magazines. Surprisingly, no
one made any move to claim him. She watched as his gaze
swept the room. She felt a sudden empathy and wasn't sure if
he was looking for a chair or a way out.

A bloodcurdling scream of "Momma!" shattered the stillness and drew everyone's attention to the two small boys who
had spent the better part of the time they'd been in the office
wrestling on the lemon-yellow leather sofa they shared with
their mother. The six-month-old on the woman's lap gave up
her fretful gnawing of a tiny fist in favor of a shuddering wail
of surprise and fear. Nancy Collins raked her delinquents with
a look of exasperated patience. Her normally pleasant features
were drawn into lines of exhaustion. Lindy watched her sigh
disgustedly, toss the *Glamour* magazine she'd been reading
onto the table, and begin to work at the buttons of her blouse.

"I told you not to be so rough with him, Kevin." The words
were delivered by rote, and were guaranteed to be ignored by
the boy. Drawing a milk-plump breast from a nursing bra, she
turned the screaming baby whose mouth grasped the tip eagerly.

A sharply drawn breath drew Lindy's gaze from the nursing

woman to the man who stood rooted to the floor, his eyes shifting in embarrassment from the scene before him. The smile she'd felt before came full-blown, even as she sympathized with his predicament. As normal and natural as nursing was, she hadn't seen one man who wasn't absolutely mortified when confronted with it unexpectedly.

Lindy saw the man make another sweeping survey of the room's occupants and decided it was time to come to his rescue. Although it hadn't been more than ten seconds since he entered the room, he looked as if it had been eons.

"May I help you?" she asked, her voice reflecting the smile in her eyes and the pleasant attitude that made her so invaluable as a receptionist.

The man turned toward the sound of her voice, his eyes meeting hers in profound relief as he crossed the room toward her. "Zade Wakefield. I'm here to see Dr. Fedders."

"Dr. Fedders's cousin," Lindy said, suddenly remembering her boss had asked her to leave ten minutes free to spend with him. Her warm, sherry-colored eyes met his over the strategically placed pen and pad provided for the patients to sign in. "She's expecting you." The phone buzzed, and she flashed him an apologetic smile. "Excuse me a moment."

Curling slender fingers around the receiver, she nestled it against a small ear bearing a tiny gold stud. As she spoke into the phone she was acutely aware of Zade Wakefield's presence. Where in the heck had she seen him before? Listening with half an ear, she watched as he leaned one broad shoulder against the wall and waited for her to finish the conversation while he assessed her small domain with casual interest.

His gaze rested for several minutes on the picture of Josh sitting beside her humming typewriter, then moved to the black nameplate with the white capital letters that told the world she was Melinda Scott. Responding automatically to the woman on the phone, Lindy watched as he contemplated the bouquet of wild flowers Josh had proudly presented her—an unlikely combination of violets, dandelions, and dog fennel— residing with a certain dignity in a small, lead-crystal vase.

Lindy gave a soothing answer while covertly examining the casual elegance of Zade Wakefield's attire and handsome face. His chin was strong, aggressive-looking. The mustache was the same luxuriant black as his hair, and the mouth beneath it was sensually shaped, with a full lower lip. His nose was straight and could only be described as aristocratic, Lindy thought just seconds before his eyes, a startling, quicksilver hue, clashed unexpectedly with hers. If the eyes were the mirror of the soul, this man was in torment. She dropped her gaze from his and fought a sudden, irrational uneasiness that had nothing to do with being caught staring.

The new, frightened tone of the woman at the other end of the line pushed Zade Wakefield momentarily from Lindy's mind. She rolled her chair away from the desk and rose, moving with long-legged grace despite the protuberance of her abdomen that gently rounded the splashy yellow, purple and red of the maternity dress she wore.

She tilted her head to hold the phone between her cheek and shoulder as she withdrew a manila folder from a file cabinet and placed the folder on her desk. She cast another deprecating smile at Zade even as she murmured a sympathetic "I'm sorry" to the woman on the other end of the phone connection. A bit uneasy at the intensity of his gaze as he stared boldly at her body, she sank back down in the chair and raked one of several loose strands of vibrantly colored hair upward in a gesture that betrayed her nervousness. The hair slipped instantly back down.

"Just come on in as soon as you can. I'll work you in. And don't worry. It's probably nothing," she said, preparing to terminate the conversation. "Okay. See you in a little while."

She returned the receiver to its base and her attention to the waiting man. Thankfully, his face held none of the preoccupation of moments before. There was nothing to mar the perfectly sculpted masculinity of his features. "I'm sorry to keep you waiting, Mr. Wakefield, but it gets pretty hairy here sometimes." Another smile crinkled the corners of her eyes and straight, white teeth showed against her prettily shaped, carmine-colored lips.

"It's all right," he replied, with a smile that could only be classified as polite. Lindy thought he looked as if smiles might be foreign to his nature.

She explained how to reach Amy's office and, accepting his softly murmured thanks, watched as he disappeared through the door. She frowned, recalling the thorough way he'd looked her over. It was embarrassing to be scrutinized so carefully, but—and this was the kicker, she thought with a wry twist of her lips—something about him made her aware of herself as a woman, and physically aware of a man for the first time since Randy died.

Lindy stared at the picture of Joshua, her beautiful, blond four-year-old, that sat on her desk. Josh had been with his father when a drunk driving a pick-up truck smashed into the side of the car.

It had been a costly accident. It had cost Randy his life, thus depriving her of a husband and Josh of a father. And it had also exacted a toll of pain for the child not yet four who subsequently needed three operations: one on his leg, and two on his face to repair the ugly scarring left by the shattered glass on his once-smooth, baby face.

Lindy had quickly learned that surgery wasn't cheap and that her insurance was hardly adequate. It would barely cover the first two operations. She'd spent weeks wondering where she would get the money for the third, and then, out of the blue, Amy Fedders had come to her with the preposterous suggestion that she become a surrogate mother. It was a suggestion that seemed less preposterous the more she thought about it. Any qualms she might have felt about the morality of what she was considering and the possible emotional backlash were quickly smothered as Lindy worked at convincing herself that Josh was worth anything.

She told herself there was no way she could become attached to a baby conceived during a clinical act with no emotional involvement. There was no way she would feel anything for a baby who was fathered by a faceless, nameless man. So she'd agreed to the terms set up by the stranger's lawyer. She'd given Amy her power of attorney and said she would give up the baby at the time of its delivery. She had taken and spent the twelve-thousand-dollar check—one half of the total amount she would receive—on Josh's final surgery, which had taken place only two weeks before. She had done what she had to do and, given the same set of circumstances, she would have made the same judgment. She'd never been sorry. Until last night.

The baby inside her moved slowly, a tiny foot knotting her stomach. Mechanically, she rubbed the slight ache away. Her hand stilled on the spot, her usual thrill of wonder at the movement diluted by the recurring pang of guilt over the decision she had arrived at the night before. Her happiness and excitement over that decision cohabited uneasily with her culpability. Somehow, her promise to pay the money back didn't help much. She'd never been a person to renege on any sort of agreement, and her decision to keep her baby warred with her sense of fair play. Cheating wasn't her nature. But neither was giving up a child. How could she ever have agreed to such a thing in the first place?

Her gaze returned to the photo of Josh wearing his flannel pajamas with the feet. She loved every well-known detail of the photo taken on his third birthday. Before the accident. The remains of chocolate cake and ice cream were smeared on his laughing face and he held the stuffed blue body of Poppa Smurf that Randy's parents had given him. Suddenly, Lindy had the answer to her question. How could she have committed herself to such a thing? Easy. She would have dealt with the devil himself to make Josh well. Would have convinced herself of anything to help him.

And she had—to a point. Her eyes opaque with memories, Lindy remembered how eagerly she'd reached into her shopping bag the day before and pulled out the miniscule white satin shoes beneath the clear plastic covering, their tops adorned with a puff of something soft, pink and feminine.

She'd placed the shoes beside the dress and stepped back, her head cocked sideways in a considering posture, while she trailed a fingertip over the pastel ribbon attached to the front of the dress. The pale, baby pink was the only bit of color the dress offered.

Perfect! Absolutely perfect! The baby inside her stretched as if in some sort of silent acknowledgment while Lindy smoothed the mound of her abdomen in pleasured anticipation. She was seized with a sudden, almost tangible, longing to rest her cheek against the unparalleled softness of baby hair and warm baby flesh. She could almost see an infant with red-gold curls wearing the dress. *Let it be a girl. Please let it be girl.* She couldn't wait to hold the baby. Couldn't wait to rub it with sweet-smelling lotions...couldn't wait...

Even now she remembered how her hungry anticipation had faded with sobering abruptness, how reality had hit her with sudden, sickening clarity, taking her from happiness to hopelessness, from anticipation to anguish in a matter of seconds. There had been a roaring in her ears and the sudden throbbing of a headache—she'd never been prone to them before the accident—that she'd grown so accustomed to during the pregnancy.

Thinking back brought her fresh insight, and she realized the excruciating headaches weren't symptoms of a physical problem, but were tied psychologically to her agreement to give up her baby. The agreement was something she'd told herself was all right because it was for Josh, when in actuality it was unacceptable to her, if only on some subconscious level. Her mind had convinced her that making her son well was worth any sacrifice. Her tender heart dictated otherwise. Though the overnight change in her heart and mind was at odds with her sense of what was right, she would have to learn to live with it.

She knew Amy would tell the man sooner or later. Lindy hoped the announcement wasn't made until the last possible moment, after she had given birth and moved far away. She wondered how he would feel. Would he be sad as well as angry? A flicker of remorse flitted through her. It was his baby too. She hadn't forgotten that. But she had carried it for nine months. She had been the one who suffered morning sickness, the one who... She pushed such thoughts away. They served no purpose except to torture her. For the dozenth time, Lindy wondered what kind of man would buy a baby instead of marrying to get one? Beyond that, what kind of man would expect a woman to give away her child for money?

When Zade entered Amy's office, she rose from the leather chair and rounded the desk to hug him. He responded to the embrace with one of his own.

"How you doin', Doc?" He'd been calling her Doc ever since they were children and he'd sneaked Band-Aids and Mercurochrome from the medicine chest so she could doctor her dolls. A beautiful, sensitive woman who looked as if she should be on the cover of *Vogue* instead of delivering babies, Amy Fedders was the one woman in the world who held Zade Wakefield's complete trust.

"I'm fine," Amy said, releasing him and returning to her chair. "Sit down, Zade."

Zade complied with her request, resting the ankle of his right foot on the other knee. Then, typically, he came right to the point. "What's wrong, Amy? Is something the matter with my baby?"

He watched her face while she sat silently, almost as if she were weighing her forthcoming words. She raised weary blue eyes to his. They were surrounded by lines Zade had never noticed before. He was surprised, yet he shouldn't have been. She was his age. Thirty-eight.

Lacing her long fingers together, Amy rested them on the polished surface of the desk and favored him with a smile of encouragement. "There's nothing the matter with your baby, Zade. Everything is fine."

His relief was almost tangible. The fine tension holding him in its grip oozed from his body and left him feeling light-headed. He leaned forward, grasping his crossed ankle with both hands to still their shaking. "Then what is it?"

Amy drew a deep breath and plunged. "She isn't giving the baby up."

"What?" The word was spoken so quietly she barely heard it.

"The woman says she's changed her mind. She wants to keep the baby."

Suddenly the emotions buffeting Zade's mind for the past hour burst forth in fury. He jumped to his feet and leaned across the desk. His hands pressed the gleaming surface with white-knuckled fierceness. "What the hell do you mean?" he bellowed.

Amy regarded him soberly, well aware of his temper and its limitations. "Sit down and lower your voice. I'm running a clinic here."

Slowly he regained his composure, drawing in deep breaths to calm his boiling rage. "She took my money. Twelve thousand dollars, Amy. And she's spent it. The check cleared the bank long ago. And she signed an agreement. A contract. She can't do this."

"I know. I know." Amy rested her elbow on the desk and rubbed wearily at her forehead. "Look, Zade, she's a single parent. She's been through a lot this past year. A…member of her family has had a lot of medical problems. It's been extremely stressful for her."

"Stressful for her! Damn it, Amy, what about me?" He ran a hand down his face, pulling at his features in a gesture of frustration. "I've worried every minute of every day about this baby. My God! It's part of me. Doesn't she understand that?"

A sad smile tugged at Amy's lips. "It's part of her, too, Zade. And she's carried it for almost nine months. I've seen her so sick with headaches she could barely function, and she'd never take so much as an aspirin, not to mention morning sickness, backaches…"

"Whose side are you on, anyway?" he snarled.

Amy smiled slowly. "Would you believe I'd like to see the

best for both of you? Oh, Zade! This is hardly a unique situation. A lot of women think they can give up a baby, but when it comes right down to it, many of them can't. That's why I tried to talk you out of it in the first place. It would have been much easier to marry again.''

"Marry!'' Zade snorted, turning and pacing the length of the room. "Are you kidding! One Margot in anyone's life is more than enough! It was easy enough for her to give up her baby. Easy come, easy go.'' His arm swept before him in a wide arc.

Amy saw the pain etched in his features. Pain that the mention of Margot, his ex-wife, invariably brought. Margot Wakefield had single-handedly destroyed what little faith in women Zade retained after his mother had walked out on his father when he was thirteen.

As a wild and rowdy teenager without a mother to mediate for him, Amy had seen him face his father's merciless wrath. She'd seen him serve his time in Vietnam, pitting himself against an unseen enemy. Watched as he daily faced and overcame the many problems connected with running a ten-state hotel conglomerate. But none of that could prepare him for what he must be feeling now. This was something he couldn't overcome with sheer willpower or dogged determination.

She sighed. She'd like to tell him about Lindy. How sweet she was. How brave. How great a capacity for love she had. Love of all varieties, never received from Margot, nor from his mother or his father who'd taught him everything about corporate power, but nothing about caring.

Only she, Amy, had loved him. Only he had loved Amy. They had loved each other, but as they grew older she'd realized she couldn't give him the kind of love he really needed, just as he was unable to give her what her husband, Stephen, did.

"Is there a chance she'll change her mind again?'' he asked at last, the anger leveling off and a determined look entering his eyes as he straightened and thrust his hands into the pockets of his close-fitting slacks.

She shook her head, her blue eyes meeting his squarely. "I don't think so."

"Talk to her."

"I have."

"Okay, let me."

Her fair brows drew together. "Let you what?"

"Talk to her."

"I can't do that!" Amy rose from her desk and turned to look out the window. She crossed her arms, her hands agitatedly rubbing the raw silk of her jade-green blouse. "You know her name is confidential information. That was agreed on, too, Zade."

"Amy, I want that baby. I paid her for it."

Amy heard the steely note in his voice. Knowing it was useless, she tried again to reason with him. "She says she'll pay the money back in monthly installments."

"I don't want the money back! I want my baby!"

Amy whirled to face him. "Zade, listen—"

"No! You listen." His face was set, unyielding. He pointed his index finger at her accusingly. "I'll get lawyers. I'll subpoena the information. You'll have to give it to me then. It'll take time, but I can—and will—do it." He turned and stalked to the door. "Tell her that and see if she'll change her mind."

The door slammed shut behind him. Amy dropped into her chair, covering her face with her hands. What a terrible mess she'd made of things! She'd known from the beginning it wouldn't work. Or should have known, because she knew Lindy Scott.

Lindy was playing "this little piggy went to market" with the Collins baby's toes when Zade Wakefield stormed into the waiting room, covering the small area in quick, angry strides and leaving the outer office in the same manner he'd left his cousin's. She raised her eyebrows and shrugged. Amy and her cousin must have had some sort of a family argument.

Six hours later, Lindy tucked the light blanket around Joshua's shoulders and brushed her lips across his forehead, which still had a bandage over an area on the right side. Similar patches of white spotted his round face.

She straightened and smiled down at him. "Good night, Josh."

"Good night, Momma."

She flipped on the night-light and turned off the bedside lamp, leaving the room in soft, semi-darkness. She left his door ajar and went into the living room, massaging the back of her neck with her right hand. Darn headaches! She'd be glad when the baby was born. Perhaps she wouldn't be under so much stress once she, Josh and the new baby were relocated in another part of the country, somewhere far away. She smiled wryly. Even if the headaches didn't go away, at least she'd be able to take something for them once the baby came.

Lindy entered the small kitchen decorated in white, apple green and apricot. The colors were reflected in the white countertop, the ceramic apples sitting in a basket on the floor, and the copper pans hanging on the wall. She counted the days in her mind. Three weeks and four days. Less than a month. April thirteenth.

With a sigh, she opened the refrigerator door and took out a pitcher of ice tea. Maybe something cool would help ease the throbbing in her temples and the tightness of her neck muscles. Crushed ice was cascading into the glass from the icemaker when the phone rang. She poured the tea and moved around the bar to reach for the receiver of the wall phone.

"Scott residence."

"Lindy? This is Amy."

"Hi! What's up?" Lindy took a quick swallow of the tea and held the glass against her temple in an attempt to relieve the throbbing. A call from Amy wasn't unusual; she often called to check on Josh, the undisputed darling of the office who flirted outrageously with all the women, and was usually rewarded for his charm with loads of goodies.

"I called to see how Josh is doing this evening."

"He's fine. The babysitter said his appetite has picked up the last couple of days."

"That's great!" Amy commented. "And what about you? We were so busy I didn't have time to ask you how you're feeling."

"I have a heck of a headache, but that's nothing new."

"Lindy, you can take something now."

"No, Amy. I've held out this long, I can hang on a few more days."

Amy Fedders was silent a moment. "You're a stubborn woman, Melinda Scott."

Lindy laughed. "So I've been told."

The silence stretched to several seconds. Lindy began to get the feeling that something more than Josh's well-being was on Amy's mind.

"Amy, is something the matter?"

The sound of pent-up breath being released could be heard clearly through the telephone line. "I'm just wondering if you've changed your mind."

Lindy knew instantly what her boss was talking about. "No. And I won't."

"Look, Lindy, I know we went over everything this morning, but you're putting both of us in a very bad position. The man has the law on his side. He could make a lot of trouble for you. For both of us."

"I'm not giving this baby up, Amy."

"You signed a contract. You spent his money."

"For Josh!" Lindy cried, holding the phone between her neck and shoulder as she rubbed her throbbing temples with the fingertips of both hands. "You'd have done the same thing, wouldn't you?"

Amy sighed, the sound echoing wearily through the plastic receiver. "I suppose I would. But that doesn't change things."

"I know. Look, Amy, I'm sorry. Just tell him I'll pay back the money."

"He doesn't want the money back. He wants the baby."

Lindy gripped the phone tightly with her right hand. Shock made speech a momentary impossibility. Her voice, when she found it, was little more than a whisper. "You've already told him?"

"Yes."

"Wh-what did he say? I mean, was he angry?"

"What do you think?"

Tears filled Lindy's eyes and spilled over her suddenly pale cheeks. She pressed her fingers tightly against her lips to still their trembling. "What is he going to do?"

Amy heard the stark terror in the younger woman's voice. It was reminiscent of the look on Zade's face when he'd entered her office earlier that day. Her heart ached for them both, but she couldn't side with either. She was sorry to be a part of any of it. Being so closely involved with both parties made professional objectivity a near impossibility. Amy knew Lindy didn't need to hear anything to upset her any more than she already was, but she felt duty-bound to tell her what Zade threatened to do. "He says he's going to get a lawyer and subpoena the information—namely, who the woman is—then force her to give him the baby."

"Can he do that?"

"Probably. But it will take a while."

Lindy was silent, gnawing on her bottom lip in concentration.

"What are you going to do?" Amy asked.

"Pray that he doesn't get the job done until after the baby comes and we're long gone from here."

"Maybe I can talk to him—get him to let you sort of split up the time like people do in divorce cases," Amy suggested.

"No! I won't share this baby with a stranger. I—I couldn't bear to be around him, knowing that I'd had his child without even knowing his name."

Amy sighed. Further negotiating was impossible at the moment. "Okay. We'll play it by ear for a while. Just try to get some sleep and have a good weekend. I'll see you Monday."

"Sure." Lindy sounded discouraged. "Thanks for calling and warning me," she added.

"Sure," Amy said, her tone of voice mirroring Lindy's.

Lindy heard a click as Amy hung up. She replaced her own receiver and moved toward the light switch, exhaustion making her movements slow and clumsy, totally unlike the gracefulness that had unknowingly captured Zade's attention earlier. She carried her tea to the bedroom and sipped it while she got ready for bed.

She slipped between the cool percale sheets, lying on her back with her hands folded across her abdomen. The baby moved, stretched, and finally settled into a comfortable position. Lindy's hands recorded each sensation as her head pounded in rhythm with her frightened heart and she prayed for sleep. But sleep remained elusive as memories plagued her and tears stung beneath her closed eyelids.

Randy. Tall, blond, ruggedly good-looking. Randy's lips on hers. His hands moving over her body in gentle caresses that were so at odds with the tough-guy image his size and sometimes gruff manner projected. Randy whispering how much he loved her while their bodies strained to reach the ultimate level of physical human closeness.

She turned slightly, restlessly, trying to block out the memory of herself on the examining table. There had been no warm, hard body entering her during this conception, bringing aching, tingling sensations—only a slight discomfort as Amy performed the precisely executed ritual that would, with luck, ensure a pregnancy. And it had. She had conceived the first time.

But, unlike Josh's conception, there was nothing to make the memory sweet. No ragged breathing. No cries of joy. No recollection of sweat-dampened bodies tangled together afterward, and silken hair beneath her fingertips while Randy's hot lips moved restlessly over her, as if he were unwilling to relinquish the moment.

No love.

Tears continued to roll onto Lindy's pillow. The ache in her heart continued to battle the one in her head. It was a long, long while before sleep finally carried her to a temporary oblivion.

Chapter Two

Saturday morning dawned bright and sunny, and Lindy's disposition did the same. After sharing a breakfast of Captain Crunch, orange juice and toast on the apartment's porch, she and Josh set out to do their Saturday morning errands.

The old town wore springtime well, Lindy thought as she maneuvered her blue Pulsar through the streets of the residential section north of Hot Springs National Park, rounded the fountain near the Majestic Hotel and drove slowly down Central Avenue. Bath House Row was at her left, and already people dressed in shorts and summer tops paraded beneath the huge magnolia trees shading the sidewalks. The White Duck, a huge, amphibious vehicle, sat waiting to take a group of sightseers to Lake Hamilton, situated south of the city. There it relinquished the power of its wheels, and became a large, white boat that toured the inlets of the lake, showing off the homes and sights to the visitors who flocked to the spa from the first day of Thoroughbred horse racing at Oaklawn Park until the town that nestled among the famous Arkansas hills was set ablaze with vibrant color.

"I wanna ride the duck," Josh said, turning in the seat to see it better as they passed.

Lindy smiled. Every Saturday he asked if he could ride; every Saturday she said no.

"Not today, Josh. When it warms up a bit more, and the baby comes, we'll go."

She didn't have the heart to tell him they would be leaving after the baby was born. She appeased her conscience and his disappointment by promising him ice cream at the mall when they went to buy his new sneakers. For the moment, he was satisfied.

At the mall, they bought not only ice creams, but cookies and two Cokes—all on top of the hamburgers they'd had for lunch. Lindy knew she was spoiling him, something she was usually careful not to do, but she felt he deserved some spoiling for going through what he had the past year with virtually no complaint.

By the time they reached the supermarket, both were tired and out of sorts from a long day spent buying Josh's summer wardrobe. Her legs and back aching from so much walking at the mall, Lindy turned a deaf ear to her son's pleas for more junk food to take home.

"Put those back, Josh!" she commanded sternly as he held up a package of cookies. "You can have chocolate chip *or* peanut butter, but not both."

"Please..." he whined.

"Joshua Scott, if you don't put those cookies down, I'm going to blister you when we get home!" Lindy threatened.

With a disgusted sigh, he obeyed, then scampered on ahead of their heavily laden grocery cart searching out something else to beg for.

"Josh, slow down!"

Unheeding of her warning, she saw him career around the end of the aisle and heard the clanging of a buggy being hit, followed by his muffled cry of pain.

Her first thought was of his face. Fear pierced her heart. Had he bumped it? Hurrying as fast as her full buggy and her fatigue would allow, Lindy rounded the nearby corner and saw a young woman bending over and examining Josh's head. Struggling to control the apprehension building within her, Lindy abandoned the groceries and hurried to his side.

She dropped to her knees and, unmindful of the solicitous woman, whirled her son to face her. Her eyes scanned his bandage-spotted face for any sign of new injury before lighting on the small red spot on his forehead. Just a bump. Relief washed through her as she gathered his sturdy little body close. She lifted her eyes to the strange woman and a tired smile curved the corners of her mouth. "Thank you for helping. And I'm sorry he barreled into you that way."

The woman smiled in understanding. "I have two of my own. I know how it is." She ruffled Josh's hair and pushed her buggy on down the aisle.

Lindy held her son at arm's length, torn between relief that he was all right and anger that he'd disobeyed. "Josh, you've got to settle down. I know you're feeling better, but I'm tired and I can't keep up." She ran her finger down the bridge of his short nose. "Stay close until we get home, okay?"

He nodded solemnly.

"Is everything all right?" a deep voice inquired.

Lindy's gaze traveled from shiny leather loafers, up, up, the knife-sharp crease of wheat-colored slacks, past a casual, short-sleeved shirt to a tan throat...and on up to encounter the features of a man she'd seen at work the day before. Amy Fedders's good-looking cousin with the funny name. Zane something-or-other. He was staring down at her, a look of recognition in his eyes, and, if it weren't too ridiculous to consider, almost a look of pleasure. Maybe he liked seeing women in humble positions, she thought wryly, wondering how she could get to her feet without resembling a baby elephant attempting to roll over.

"Oh, hi!" She smiled, then quipped lightly, "Fancy meeting you here. Nothing serious. Josh, here, has just been cooped up too long, I think.'' She tried to push herself up and instantly felt the strength of his hand beneath her elbow as he helped her to her feet. She attributed her sudden breathlessness to her pregnancy.

''Thanks.'' She wished suddenly that she wasn't pregnant. Wished she was the kind of gorgeous, witty woman who knew all the things to say to snare the interest of a man like Amy's cousin. Shock at the turn of her thoughts flooded through her. What was this sudden awareness, anyway? Good Lord! Here she was, a widow almost nine months pregnant, and suddenly, for the second time since Randy's death, she was finding this man attractive. Talk about lousy timing, she thought. Then, two other thoughts hit her. First, she *wasn't* the kind of woman to interest a man so obviously wealthy, and so socially polished, and second, it was beyond the realm of possibility to believe that a man like this wasn't already taken.

The sight of Josh as he started to edge away from her brought her thoughts back to reality. Hooking a finger in his shirt collar, she said firmly, ''Oh, no you don't, young man. You stay right here.''

Josh wriggled and bent to climb onto the bottom level of the man's grocery cart. ''Josh, stop it!'' Why was he acting up, she wondered. Now, of all times? She glanced at the man who stood silently beside her. He was staring at her with the same disconcerting intensity of the day before. Feeling suddenly uncomfortable, she pushed a stray lock of hair back toward her jaunty ponytail. ''Well, thanks again, Amy's cousin.'' This time her smile was edged with embarrassment. ''I'm sorry, I can't remember your name.''

''Zade Wakefield.'' His attempt at a smile fell somewhat short, she thought, as if he hadn't had much practice at it.

She smiled again. ''I thought it was Zane. I was close.''

''Right.'' His mouth quirked slightly once more, and he looked past her. ''Did you have a buggy?''

''Yes. It's around the corner. When I heard the crash, I left it.''

"Wait here," Zade commanded in a tone of voice and manner that brooked no objections. "I'll get it for you."

In a matter of moments, he returned with her shopping cart. "Here you are." He glanced from Josh to Lindy. "Do you want me to put him in the seat for you?"

Lindy sighed in relief. "Would you? I can't lift him up there anymore."

"Surely." Without another word, Zade bent and hoisted Josh's slight body into the buggy.

"I don't wanna ride up here. It's for babies!"

"You'd better take advantage of it," Zade said. He glanced at Lindy's stomach, then raised his eyes to hers. There was an unexpected tenderness there that took her by surprise. Then, as if he'd been caught with his hand in the cookie jar, he jerked his gaze back to Josh. "It won't be long before your new brother or sister gets here, and then you won't ever be able to ride up there again."

Josh considered the advice carefully. "Okay," he said at last.

Lindy smiled up into Zade's silvery eyes. "Thanks, again."

"You shop here every Saturday, don't you?"

She nodded, wondering why he didn't just go on his way. Most men would never have stopped in the first place.

"I knew I'd seen you somewhere as soon as I walked into Amy's office yesterday."

Lindy laughed softly. "I thought you looked familiar, too."

"Have you worked for Amy long?"

"A little over two years," she said, pushing her buggy slowly down the aisle. She wondered if he was divorced or something and missed talking to a woman. Ha! That was a laugh! This man would never be short of feminine companions to talk to.

"How do you stand it?" he asked in a deep, pleasant voice.

She glanced back at him and saw that he was pushing his grocery cart along behind her, his brow furrowed in question. "Stand it? I love it! Amy's a wonderful person to work for."

Zade was silent a moment. "Yes," he said at last, "I guess

she could be." Then he added, "Isn't it hard on you to work…in your condition?"

Lindy stopped her buggy and turned toward him. "My condition? I'm only pregnant, Mr. Wakefield, not ill." She smiled and put a box of instant rice in the shopping cart. "But yes, some days it's hard. Especially if I haven't had much rest the night before."

"Do you have to work? I mean, how does your husband feel about it?"

Lindy's auburn brows drew together thoughtfully. What was with this guy? Why this interest in her and her pregnancy? Baffled by his questioning, she said softly, "He's dead."

Shock and pity leapt into his eyes. "I'm sorry."

"So am I. It was a car accident. Thankfully, Josh wasn't hurt any worse than he was. And that's why I'm working, Mr. Wakefield."

Lindy was aware her answer was a bit short and that she was leaving Zade Wakefield with the impression the child she carried was her dead husband's. She intended to. It was what most people thought. Only a few close friends knew what she was doing—and why. And they were still shocked.

Though she'd never been comfortable with lies and half-truths, and this one was especially hard on her conscience, it was much easier to let people think she carried Randy's baby than to have them believe she was carrying the child of some unknown man. Quite naturally, as now, any questioning about her pregnancy put her on the defensive.

Lindy saw Zade's shrewd gaze rake Josh's bandaged features and knew he was attributing the white patches to the accident.

"Josh just had plastic surgery on his face for the scarring," she felt compelled to tell him.

"It must be very hard for you." A frown drew his heavy dark brows into a single line.

"Yes."

Suddenly, Lindy felt very tired. The day and the reminder of what she was trying so hard to forget, combined to sap what strength was left after a restless night. She just wanted to go home and crawl into bed. But of course she couldn't. She forced another smile to her lips and looked up into the somber face of Zade Wakefield. "It's been very nice seeing you again, Mr. Wakefield," she said in a pleasant manner that nonetheless held a tone of dismissal. "Maybe we'll run into each other next Saturday."

"Zade."

"I beg your pardon?"

"Call me Zade. And you're Melinda. Right?"

"Usually just Lindy," she corrected, wondering when the necessity to call him anything might arise.

"Lindy," he said consideringly. "It fits you."

Too exhausted to follow his reasoning, and not really caring to as the throbbing ache in her lower back increased steadily, Lindy murmured a polite thank you, added a firm goodbye and left Zade Wakefield standing between the rice and the dried beans, a curious expression on his handsome face.

Zade put his groceries away, his mind filled with the picture of Lindy Scott. She'd looked tired, he thought. And with good reason. She shouldn't have to work when she was as far along as she obviously was. Still, he could understand why she had to, after she'd told him of her husband's death and Josh's operation. She had to be a strong lady to cope with everything, he reasoned, with admiration.

Finished with his weekly chore, he popped a frozen dinner into the microwave and filled a glass with tap water. He splashed some Crown Royal on top, added ice cubes, and pushed them down with one finger to mix the drink. Without conscious thought, he reached for silverware and ripped a paper towel from the roll in lieu of a napkin.

In a matter of moments the bell on the microwave signaled that his dinner was ready to be served, and he reached for the meat and potato entrée with a sigh of acceptance. God, but he was tired of this. Tired of eating out. Tired of cooking for himself. Tired of being alone. Still, being alone was better than the sham of a marriage he'd shared with Margot.

Zade slumped wearily into a chair and began to pick at his dinner, flipping through the messages left on the table by his cleaning woman. One of his workers had called. Damn! He silently reminded himself to return the call when he finished eating.

Why, why, couldn't one thing go right for him? Why was everything falling apart at once? The new hotel he was building in Arkadelphia hadn't met the building code. The electrical contractor had used an inferior grade of wire, and paid off the inspector. The sort of thing that happened to other people. Fortunately for Zade, he always had one of his own people check things out, and the problem had been discovered, preventing the possibility of a fire at some time in the future. That was the good part. The bad part was that he was now involved in a messy court case, and even worse, the building had to be completely rewired—a move that was costly in terms of money and time.

He really hadn't needed Amy's announcement about his baby the previous afternoon. And it *was* his baby. He had planned for it with all the anticipation of any father. He longed to hear laughter in this house, wanted to know a love that was returned unconditionally. Love that was honest. Zade seriously doubted that there was any woman out there who was capable of that sort of love. Intellectually, he knew his reasoning was presumptuous, but the residue of pain in his heart—the heart slashed twice in his life by two different women—only fueled the fires of his doubt.

His mother and Margot had taught him well. He could still remember the look on Margot's beautiful face when she had told him she was leaving him. That hadn't bothered him as much as it might have. Life with Margot had always been a series of roller coaster rides. What hurt were her parting remarks.

"I'm leaving you for Kyle Sinclair, Zade."

He still recalled his shock. A week earlier she had told him she was pregnant. His feelings about becoming a father were mixed because his marriage wasn't too stable, but after mulling things over for a day or two he had decided that a child might give the marriage something it needed. He had begun to look forward to the possibility of a son.

Trying to cover the hurt her announcement caused him to feel, he'd replied, "But what about the baby? Don't you think you should think about it? Regardless of how you feel about me, you should consider the fact that I'll want to father my child."

Margot had shrugged daintily before pinning him with her cool, blue gaze and delivering the calm statement that destroyed any remnant of feeling he might have harbored toward her. "That's no longer a problem, Zade. I had an abortion the day before yesterday."

Even thinking about it after all this time caused his stomach to churn uneasily. The beautiful, selfish bitch had made the announcement with all the insouciance someone would have used to announce he had just had his teeth cleaned. He downed a large swallow of the whiskey and water, clamping his jaws together and grimacing as the liquor burned its way down his throat.

And then there were the Lindy Scotts of the world. Women who would carry a child through all sorts of difficulties. He recognized the depth and unselfishness of her commitment to her unborn child even though her husband was dead. Of course there was the basic fact that Lindy and Margot were two entirely different types of women. Margot was shallow and self-centered, while from his two brief observations of Lindy Scott, he guessed she was just the opposite.

She intrigued him, and he didn't know why. She took life seriously, but didn't let it get her down; she seemed to be able to laugh at her problems and herself. There was an aura of serenity about her that he'd observed yesterday as she spoke on the telephone. From the moment he had walked into the office and been rescued by the sound of her voice, he had felt something drawing him to her. She exuded a calmness in manner and spirit that Zade found restful.

Pushing aside the tasteless dinner, he propped his feet on the chair opposite him and took another mouthful of his drink. Okay, he thought, let's analyze this attraction. Looks? No. Lindy Scott wasn't his type at all. Although her red hair, freckles, snub nose and wide mouth were attractive in a wholesome, little girl way, she was certainly not the kind he usually became involved with.

Her personality? Possibly. She absolutely bubbled. Zade couldn't remember when he had ever seen a person so alive. He'd already acknowledged her serenity as a part of her attraction. And her sense of humor was obvious, too. It was natural, not artificial and calculated as in some women he knew. But he realized that peacefulness and a sense of humor weren't enough to ignite his consuming desire to know more about her. He wanted to find out more about her as a person, as a mother.

Ahhh, maybe that was it, he realized with a flash of insight. Lindy Scott was more than a receptionist. More than a widow. More than a pleasant person. She was a mother. And would soon be one again. Zade suddenly knew that he had discovered a large part of her attraction. She was pregnant, and there was another woman out there somewhere who was pregnant with his baby.

It doesn't wash, Wakefield. There are lots of pregnant women out there who haven't made any impression on you, so why this one? He didn't know, and really didn't care. Maybe it was a combination of all those things. She was due at some time in the near future, seemed extremely capable with the child she already had, and was pleasant and calm...all the qualities he imagined it took to make a good mother. Perhaps that was the sum total of why he felt so drawn to her.

He sighed. He felt better for having worked things out in his mind. But he still had one problem: what to do about it. His feet crashed to the floor, and he shoved his chair away from the table, rising to his feet and grabbing the glass from the table simultaneously. Do about it? God, what was he thinking of? Trying to contact her? Ridiculous! The woman was recently widowed. She was probably still in mourning. What could he say to her if he called? What would she think? More importantly, what would he gain by trying to see her? Zade wiped a broad hand down his lean face and set the glass on the countertop.

He could be with a woman who seemed to epitomize what motherhood was all about. He could use her for a substitute until the courts granted him access to Amy's files and he could find the woman carrying his baby. But then, wouldn't that be unfair to Lindy Scott? Zade knew there was a streak of hard ruthlessness in him. He knew he could be calculating on occasion. But he could honestly say he had never deliberately used anyone before. The thought left a bad taste in his mouth. Still, the idea wouldn't leave him. He began to make excuses for his proposed actions. She could use help...not money, of course, but around the house. With the boy.

Suddenly, Zade's laughter filled the room. It sounded unused, rusty, the same way his smile looked. God, what did he think he could do? Become a surrogate husband? A surrogate father?

Lindy put away her perishable groceries and decided to save the rest for the next morning. She put her eggs in the compartment in the refrigerator, then added the empty carton to the growing stack in the bottom of her cabinet. As she warmed up some chicken noodle soup for Josh she peeled off the label on the can—one of many she was saving to pass on to his day-care center for playground equipment—and then made herself a sandwich before settling down with her feet propped up on the coffee table to watch a *Rifleman* rerun. Rather, Josh watched TV while she thought about Zade Wakefield.

He was an attractive man. Very attractive. So why had he hung around her and Josh so long at the grocery store? Lindy wasn't in the habit of deceiving herself. She knew she was passably pretty—if you liked blazing red hair and freckles.

She'd been told her smile was nice. Her eyes were her best feature though—large, round and, according to Randy, the color of sherry. She was usually slim and knew she wasn't too hard on the eyes. But now she was pregnant, so that didn't count.

She sighed. She could come up with no reason Zade Wakefield would go out of his way to prolong a conversation with her. Maybe it was nothing more than the fact that he recognized her from somewhere before he visited the clinic. Then, when he saw her at the market, he had made the connection and felt that that gave them a basis for a friendship of sorts.

That had to be it. There was simply no other explanation.

He was handsome. But too...too...uptight. It was as if his emotions were masked behind a carefully erected facade of polish and politeness.

Was he married? He knew about Randy, but she had no way of knowing if he was married or not. Besides, she chastised herself, what did it matter? She would only see him at the supermarket on Saturdays. Whether he was married was immaterial.

The following Friday evening, almost a week since her encounter with Zade at the grocery store, Lindy was on her hands and knees at the side of the tub while Josh wallowed in the shallow bathwater. By bending his knees and pushing against the tub with his feet, he was able to slide his eel-slick body back and forth along the length of the tub while dousing everything within two feet at the same time.

"C'mon, Josh, time to get out," Lindy coaxed. "Don't forget we have ice cream for a snack."

"Ice cream! Wowee!" he shrieked, flopping over on his belly and pretending to swim.

Lindy's tone sharpened perceptively. "Now, Joshua!"

"Aw, okay," he said, letting the water out and retrieving the washcloth and his plastic toys.

Lindy waited for him to climb out and then dried him off.

He was starting to look healthy again, she thought, starting to gain some weight. For a while there, he'd been so thin.

She wiped the beaded water droplets from the soft slope of his shoulders, the baby-fat tummy, the round, dimpled softness of his bottom, the sturdy legs—one with a jagged, still-red scar. Then, very carefully, she blotted the faint, pinkish scars on his face. Already she could tell that when the slight redness disappeared no one would ever know he'd been in an accident.

"Why are you starin' at me?" he asked.

"I'm looking at your beautiful, beautiful face," she replied with a teary smile and a bone-crushing hug.

He wriggled in protest. "Boys aren't 'posed to be beautiful. They're 'posed to be handsome," her son informed her in an aggrieved tone.

"Is that so? Well, then, I *'pose* you're handsome." Lindy dusted him with some of her own bath powder and swatted him on the backside. "Go get some underwear on, and I'll dish up the ice cream."

"Chocolate?"

"Um-hum. With marshmallow topping," she promised, fighting the lump in her throat. Dear Lord! She'd almost lost him, too. Sometimes that fact hit her with a force that was almost overwhelming.

"Mmmm!" Josh squealed, racing naked from the bathroom. Lindy swallowed hard and, grabbing the edge of the bathtub for support, pushed herself to her feet. She wiped up the majority of the water on the floor, pushing a damp towel around with the toe of her shoe, and vowed to make Josh come and pick up the wet things after he had had his ice cream.

She was on her way to the kitchen when the doorbell rang, stopping her in mid-stride and forcing her to reroute her course. She swiped loose tendrils of hair toward the knot coiled atop her head and wondered who would be calling at this time of evening, even though the springtime day still clung to a sliver of light.

Lindy unlocked the door and flung it open. A man stood

there. A man who had been taking up entirely too much room in her thoughts the past week.

Zade Wakefield.

Wakefield.

Chapter Three

Lindy's eyes widened in surprise, that was quickly followed by embarrassment as she realized she was wearing her oldest pair of shorts and a faded, scoop-necked smock that had seen better days. She gave a mental moan. No one should be caught dead looking as she did—especially by someone like Zade Wakefield. She watched in dismay as his eyes traveled a leisurely journey from her sandaled feet to the slender legs left bare by the shorts, past the water-spotted smock and on to the upswept hairdo that was suffering from the end-of-the-day straggles.

Embarrassed by her appearance and his slow survey of her, wishing she knew some sort of magician's disappearing trick, Lindy forced a smile to her lips and a glib apology to her tongue. "Hi. Bad timing, Mr. Wakefield. You caught us at the tail end of a bath."

Sensing her embarrassment, Zade had the grace to look a bit embarrassed himself. "I'm sorry. I should have called first."

"No. That's okay," she was surprised to hear herself saying. Looking down at the damp smock ruefully, then back up to the cool silver-gray gaze, she added, "It's just that you hardly caught me at my best. Although," she hastened to add with a self-deprecating smile, "sometimes I look worse. How did you find me, anyway?"

His mouth quirked into a semi-smile. He liked her slightly offbeat sense of humor. "You're the only Melinda Scott in the phone book, and you look just fine."

The words seemed to settle the topic under discussion, and any thank-you Lindy should have voiced was lost in the spinning of her thoughts. *What is he doing here?*

What am I doing here? The question surfaced to the top of Zade's thoughts as they stood staring at each other, neither knowing how to break the silence that bordered on uncomfortable. What in the world did he think he could accomplish by showing up on Lindy Scott's doorstep? Moreover, what did he hope to accomplish? Whatever his subconscious reasoning, he was making a first-class fool of himself. You just didn't show up uninvited at the home of someone you hardly knew.

He watched as Lindy attempted to tuck a loose strand of hair back into place. Watched as she rammed both hands into the pockets of the smock. Watched the hair slide back down.

"What—"

Both spoke simultaneously. Each offered the other a hesitant smile.

"What can I do for you, Mr. Wakefield?" she asked at last.

Zade cleared his throat. He couldn't remember feeling at such a loss for words since he was fifteen and asked a girl out for the first time. "I...uh...came to see how Josh was doing," he said, grabbing at the first coherent thought that came to mind. "I was wondering if there were any side effects to his accident at the store Saturday." *Way to go, Wakefield!*

"He's fine."

"Good." Zade plunged his hands into the pockets of his close-fitting slacks, unconsciously echoing Lindy's gesture of moments before. His gaze dropped to her bare shoulders. They were sprinkled with honey-colored freckles, the hue nothing more than the palest wash—more a reflection, really—of the red of her hair and the warm mahogany of her eyes. The freckles hadn't been discriminating, he thought. They seemed to be everywhere. He looked into her face. She could almost pass for a teenager. Almost.

A slow smile tilted the corners of Lindy's mouth as she took her hands from her pockets and took a step backward. Her voice was soft and pleasant as she asked, "Would you like to come and see for yourself?"

He stared at her for a moment, drawn by the warmth in her eyes and the soothing quality of her voice. Something about her called to something deep inside him…something he couldn't put his finger on. "You don't mind?"

"Of course not. He's just about to have his bedtime snack. He'd probably love some company. Anything for a reprieve from bed," she explained with another smile that Zade found himself almost reluctantly returning.

"Thanks. I'll just stay a moment," he promised, stepping over the threshold into Lindy Scott's home…into her life.

Zade had the feeling of entering an entirely new world as he followed Lindy through the living room. It was decorated in white wicker and bright tropical colors that spoke of a casual but vibrant life-style. Green plants hung from the ceiling in seashell hangers and every available nook and cranny of the room held more greenery. A chartreuse parrot squawked a grating, "Come hug my neck!" and rang the bell suspended from the top of his cage.

"Be quiet, Butter," Lindy reprimanded the bird who responded with an intelligent sounding, "Okaaay."

Josh, clad solely in Superman underwear and totally engrossed in television, was the picture of indolence. Resting on the floor with his legs crossed at the ankles and his arms folded behind his head, he seemed reluctant to tear his attention from the evening game show. Only when Lindy spoke his name more sharply did he roll over onto his stomach and prop his chin on his hands, giving Zade a very thorough once-over. "You're the man from the grocery store," he said at last.

"That's right. How did you remember?"

"You lifted me up in the buggy," Josh replied, as if the unrelated statement would answer the question to everyone's satisfaction.

"He doesn't miss much," Lindy said. She turned back to her son. "Ready for your ice cream?"

"Yaaayy!" Josh cheered, jumping to his feet and racing toward the kitchen.

Zade marveled at the unleashed enthusiasm of the child as he followed Lindy into the kitchen and seated himself.

"That's my chair!" The belligerent words were aimed at Zade who had unfortunately chosen the chair Josh claimed as his at the table.

Lindy turned from her job of dishing up ice cream with a look in her eyes that most children have seen on their mother's faces at one time or another. "Just sit somewhere else, Joshua."

Zade rose, apologizing instantly. A little of the diplomacy he employed at work might go a long way here, he realized. "I'm sorry, Josh. I should have asked. When I was little I had a favorite chair, too."

Josh claimed his chair and Zade pulled out another.

On his knees in the chair, the boy leaned his forearms on the tabletop and asked, "Where did you live when you were little?"

"On a farm not far from here."

Bright blue eyes widened. "Did you have horses and cows?"

"Just horses," Zade answered with a smile. "And a dog."

"A dog!" Josh whispered in awe. "I'd like to have a dog, but Mrs. Hancock won't let us have one."

"Maybe later," Zade suggested.

Lindy moved nearer and placed two bowls of ice cream on the table.

"You're not having any?" Zade asked, breathing in the scent of her fresh floral perfume that lingered in the air.

"I'm not fond of chocolate," she confessed. "Besides, Amy is a regular tyrant if I gain too much weight."

"You don't look like you've gained much to me. I mean, your arms and legs are thin. It's just your stomach..." His eyes met hers in shock and embarrassment and his voice trailed away as he realized he'd said too much.

Lindy felt the warmth as a soft primrose tint crept up over her cheeks. He ought to know, she thought. He had been staring at her ever since the first time she'd seen him in Amy's office. And, like Josh, he didn't miss much. She really hadn't gained weight all over. Every ounce seemed to have zeroed in on her abdomen.

To cover the awkwardness of the moment, she tossed him a saucy smile and quipped lightly, "All baby, Amy says."

"When is it due?" he asked.

"In about two weeks."

Lindy saw his eyes suddenly shadow to the gray of a storm-tossed sky and saw the momentary flicker of pain in their darkened depths, which was quickly replaced with what she could only interpret as anger and determination. She felt an involuntary shiver scamper down her spine. He wasn't a man she'd like to cross in any way.

"Zade?" she said softly, almost fearfully.

His gaze snapped toward the sound of her voice, his eyes no longer angry, but filled with a sort of bleakness.

Lindy stared at him, wondering what thoughts had filled his mind, what memories could turn him from a handsome, pleasant companion to a man who looked capable of all sorts of awful things. Things that were invading her mind with increasing frequency. Good Lord! Amy's cousin or not, she didn't even know this man! He might be a... She couldn't go on with the thought. What if he...

"I wanna straw..." Josh's unequivocal demand drew the attention of both adults from each other to him, just as he'd planned. In an effort to gain the attention of the two grown-ups who were ignoring him, he sat stirring the chocolate ice cream around and around, melting it to a thick slush.

"What in the world are you doing, Josh?"

"I'm making a milkshake," he announced proudly, lifting a spoonful to his mouth and dropping a huge glob of the softened dessert onto the table.

"You're making a mess!" Lindy retaliated, darting a look at their company as she rose and tore a paper towel from the roll hanging beneath the cabinets. Zade's mustache tilted in a lopsided manner.

Josh looked from his mother's face to Zade. "I need a straw," he said, with a child's inborn instinct of knowing who he could enlist in his aid.

Lindy saw Zade's smile widen a bit and, as she reached to wipe up the melted ice cream, he said, "I think Josh is right. He needs a straw."

Sherry-colored eyes challenged gray ones. "Oh, he does?"

"See, Zade thinks I'm right," Josh piped up, beaming.

"Mr. Wakefield to you, Josh," Lindy corrected.

"I don't mind if he calls me Zade."

Lindy started to tell him that she minded, but the eager look on her son's face stopped her. "All right," she acquiesced.

Zade and Josh exchanged glances that could only have been called surreptitious, then followed up with conspiratorial smiles.

"I can stand on my head," Josh bragged as Lindy sat down at the table with them.

"You can? Let's see," Zade encouraged, entranced with the boy's cocksure manner and the pure beauty of his smiles.

The next few minutes were spent watching Josh—his rear in the air—as he tried to balance on his head. In the end he had to settle for a series of somersaults.

"Great!" Zade complimented, his usually somber features slashed by the wide, white smile that caused wrinkles to fan out from the corners of his eyes and two deep grooves to appear in the sides of his cheeks. Lindy, whose attention was equally divided between the antics of her show-off son and the response of the man across the table from her, drew in a deep breath of air that caught in her throat. Zade was handsome at all times. But the smile that added warmth and life to his features could only be classified as devastating.

Josh's eyes were glowing with pleasure and pride at being the center of attraction. "I can break dance," he announced, immediately beginning his interpretation of a wave, following it up with his rendition of the moon walk, nothing more than the dragging of his feet backward slowly.

"Pretty good," Zade encouraged, thoroughly entranced with the four-year-old's cavorting and pleased that the child was showering him with so much attention.

"You're getting too wound up," Lindy interrupted. "You'll never go to sleep."

"Maahhm..." he whined, placing chubby hands on his underwear-clad hips.

"Just settle down a little bit, okay?"

With a deep, disgruntled sigh, Josh relinquished the limelight. Sidling closer, he leaned an elbow on Zade's thigh, looking up at the grown man thoughtfully.

Zade returned the child's steady gaze, noticing the faint scarring from his recent surgery.

Lindy watched the silent byplay, wondering what was going through both of their minds, wondering what Josh would say. She held her breath. He could really come up with some comments sometimes.

"Do you have a boy?"

Zade felt the slight tension in the plump fingers gripping his thigh. "No."

Lindy's breath trickled from her throat in a soft hiss.

"Would you like to have one?"

Zade's mind made a quick, mental journey to the room waiting for his child...perhaps his son. Would his son be as fantastic as this boy? Would he be as bright? Of course he would. He nodded. "I'd like that very much."

Josh didn't answer, but looked at the man for several more seconds before clambering up into his lap. Zade's strong hands helped him, and before long Josh was settled securely in the crook of the man's arm, cuddled snuggly against his broad chest. Small fingers toyed with the expensive, gold watch encircling a hair-dusted wrist, while Zade stared down at the top of Josh's blond head, wondering why the child was so accepting of him.

Lindy felt her throat tighten. Zade Wakefield probably didn't know what was going on. But she had a strong suspicion. A suspicion that was strengthened when Josh tilted his head back and said questioningly, "Zade?"

"Yes, Josh?"

"You don't have a boy, and I don't have a daddy anymore."

Zade, who suddenly understood, lifted his gaze to Lindy who was blinking rapidly to combat the moisture gathering in her eyes.

"I know," he replied at last, looking back down at the child in his arms.

"My daddy used to tuck me in. Will you tuck me in?" Wide blue eyes stared up in question and apprehension. Almost as if Josh was afraid the answer might be no.

Zade recalled the nights when he was small and his father had been too busy to bother with him. Remembered how he'd longed for some sort of attention, just as Josh longed for attention when he had been showing off earlier. He remembered how lonely he had been when his mother left...and he had been much older than Josh was now. He had received attention then by disobedience and rebellion. His mother's leaving had left such a void in his life, and there had been no one to fill it...especially not his father.

Looking down into the waiting eyes of Joshua Scott, Zade forgot he was only there to satisfy his craving to know more about the phenomenon of pregnancy until he could find the woman carrying his child. He momentarily forgot that his real interest was in the boy's mother. All he remembered was his own pain, and having no one to share it with. Pain, and his own loneliness that had grown greater each year of his life instead of lessening. He recalled needing someone to... Just *needing* someone. Did he dare to try to fill the vacancy Randy Scott's death had left in Josh's life even temporarily? More importantly, could he let Josh help fill the emptiness in his own life?

Yet, how could anyone deny those blue eyes filled with such trust and anticipation? How could anyone say no? There was a curious huskiness in Zade's voice as he spoke the words that committed him to at least try. "Of course I'll tuck you in."

Lindy watched as he rose with Josh in his arms. Watched as he settled her son astride his hip. Watched as Josh reached out to circle a stranger's neck with his short arms. Watched while her son—who obviously missed his father more than she had realized—bestowed the most precious gift a child can give on a man he hardly knew...and for reasons no one but he could fathom. Josh was giving his love and trust to Zade Wakefield.

The bedroom was bathed with the golden glow of the night-light as Zade eased quietly from the room, leaving Josh to his dreams. The child had allowed Zade to turn back his sheets, tuck them around his chin and sit at the side of the bed while he said his prayers—just as his dad had done. Then he'd wrapped his arms around Zade's neck and kissed him.

Zade stayed beside him until he had gone to sleep, not certain if it was the small hand chaining him to the bedside that kept him, or the utter peace he felt as he watched long eyelashes droop to cover sleepy eyes. He might have stayed because he felt needed for the first time in his life. Need that was proved by the hand clutching his and Josh's stranglehold around his neck as he had pressed a kiss to Zade's cheek.

A curious ache filled Zade's heart as he made his way toward the kitchen and Lindy—his real reason for being here. He hadn't counted on all this when he came knocking on Melinda Scott's door. He just wanted to be with someone close to having a baby so he could be a part of the anticipation, partake in some small way of what Margot had cheated him of and what he'd known he wouldn't get when he sought a surrogate mother to have his baby.

He had come to Lindy for selfish reasons, really. Selfish and self-serving. He hadn't thought that she might question his actions. Hadn't considered how it might hurt both her and Josh if he hung around as he had planned and then stopped showing up when he got possession of his baby.

But he thought of it now.

Joshua Scott had unknowingly shown him his selfishness by accepting him as he was and by giving him a portion of his father's place in his small world. And the strange thing was, Zade knew he'd done nothing to deserve it. Such was the wonder of a child's love. If he, Zade, became a part of Lindy and Josh's lives even for a short while and then left, wouldn't it hurt them in much the same way Randy's death had? Could he do that to a child willing to give his love so unconditionally?

Zade stopped in the kitchen door, one forearm raised and resting against the doorjamb, the knuckles of his hand rubbing thoughtfully at his forehead, the other hand propped at his waist as he watched Lindy take two cups and saucers from the cabinet and set them beside the dripping coffeepot. Her movements were unhurried, her manner relaxed.

The whole evening had taken on an unexpected aura of surrealism, but it was this very second that Zade knew would be indelibly etched into his mind. For it was at this precise moment that he realized that life had taken one of its curious twists by demanding payment for what he had hoped to gain from his association with the Scotts. Life was demanding the one thing he hadn't counted on, the one thing Zade had a short supply of. Emotional involvement. Could he—did he want to—pay the price for a few weeks with this woman? And what would happen when it was over, when he found the other woman and had his own child?

The answer eluded him as Lindy turned to see him standing in the doorway. Her eyes held surprise, then softened as she seemed to remember something. She turned and poured the coffee, then held the cup and saucer out toward him, a gentle, hesitant smile curving her lips…a titian-haired Eve tempting him with the promise of knowledge. The knowledge of inner peace, of laughter and a new joie de vivre, and the satisfaction of sharing himself. She and her son promised him a sense of belonging he hadn't felt in years—if ever.

There was a look of waiting, almost of apprehension, molding Lindy's features. Their eyes met. The promises flickered temptingly in the sherry-colored depths of hers and, like Adam, Zade felt no resistance within himself. His arm dropped from the door frame and his long strides carried him to within a foot of her. Only then did he return her smile, giving back a message of surrender and contentment. His eyes were no longer stormy as his hand reached out in acceptance of the coffee and…all she had to offer.

"I'm sorry Josh put you on the spot," Lindy said moments later as she poured her coffee and seated herself across the table from Zade. "He misses Randy. I don't think I realized just how much until this evening."

"It's all right. He's a fantastic little boy," Zade heard himself answering, still somewhat shaken by the emotions he had experienced only moments before.

Lindy nodded her agreement, her usual teasing nature surfacing as she said, "I think so, but then, I'm partial." She paused, looking askance at him from beneath her lashes before adding, "You were awfully good with him. Do you have children?"

Zade correctly sensed there was more to the question than the actual words implied. "No. I was married once, but we never had any children." A fierce look flashed briefly in his eyes once more.

Lindy was confused by the look. Surely if his wife had been unable to have children he would have been saddened, not angry. Zade Wakefield was a disturbing person—in more ways than one. There were things about him that made her uneasy, yet at times she sensed a vulnerability to him that made her want to "make it all better" as she did when Josh was hurt.

And other times, when Zade looked at her, she was all too aware of her own femininity, forgetting that she was a widow with a child. A *pregnant* widow with a child. Forgetting that her chances of making him equally aware of his masculinity were exactly nil.

Right this minute, though, it was the darker side of his nature that disturbed her. It was uneasiness that stirred within her now, not those half-remembered feelings of sexuality. Funny, Josh hadn't been afraid... What was it they said? That you could trust the instincts of dogs and children? Evidently Josh felt none of her misgivings about Zade Wakefield. He had wholeheartedly accepted him. Recalling her son's total capitulation, Lindy forced herself to ignore the unsettling emotion in Zade's eyes, asking instead, "You'd like a child, wouldn't you?"

He gave her a wry smile. "Does it show?"

Lindy's full lips widened into a derisive smile. "Well, you did say you came to check on Josh, and I hardly think you're hanging around to spend time with me."

Zade suddenly became engrossed with stirring a spoonful of sugar into his coffee. His eyes, when he allowed them to meet hers again, were bland, portraying none of the panic her innocent comment had evoked. "I think you're underestimating yourself."

Lindy's smile broadened. She placed her elbows on the tabletop and rested her chin in her palms, slender fingers creating a frame for her oval face. "I call it being realistic, Zade. I'm hardly the femme fatale type. Besides, it's natural for a man who wants a child to seek the companionship of one."

"Is it?"

"I think so. Before Randy and I had Josh, we spent as much time as possible with our friends' babies. We used to argue over who would hold them." She laughed, the sound light and airy, full of happy reminiscences. "We actually used to *beg* to baby-sit."

He took a large swallow of his coffee and set the cup carefully back onto the saucer, before raising his eyes to hers. "You loved him very much, didn't you?"

There was no hesitation in her voice as she breathed softly, "Yes."

Zade felt a curious ache in the region of his heart, a sadness that he had never experienced either the kind of mother-love Lindy showered on Josh and would extend to the baby she carried, or the kind she had given to her husband. The old fear—more a conviction that for some reason he didn't deserve love—surfaced. Perhaps he was lacking in some way. Maybe that's why he had never received any real affection from his father. Or why his mother and Margot had left him. He longed to know more about Randy Scott; he wanted to know what traits had spawned and held the love of a woman like the one sitting across from him.

"What was he like?"

"Randy?" A soft smile danced on Lindy's lips as her eyes grew opaque with memories. "Attractive. Big and husky. Funny." She giggled. "Clumsy, sometimes. And he had a temper that can only be compared to nitroglycerine—explosive. And when you combined his temper with mine..." She shook her head. "We used to have some real screaming matches."

"You have a temper?" Zade asked in disbelief.

"I don't have this red hair for nothing!" she quipped, picking up her coffee. She took a sip then held the cup between both hands, smiling with the merest trace of sadness. "He was just—" she shrugged "—Randy."

"Would you ever marry again?"

"Oh, sure! I think marriage is great! Of course, I'd have to meet the right person..." She paused, setting the cup down and propping her chin on her fist. "What about you? Why don't you marry again and have some kids of your own?"

Zade shook his head. "I tried marriage. It wasn't something I'm dying to try again."

Lindy saw the pain reenter his eyes, and the vulnerability

cloud his face. Her question held sorrow and sympathy. "Divorced?"

"Yes." The answer was soft and succinct. It was obvious he had no intention of explaining. Lindy was at a loss for something to say.

When the silence between them stretched uncomfortably, she finally broke it by asking, "Would you like some more coffee?"

He glanced at his watch and pushed back his chair. His eyes held an apology. "No. I need to be going. I really didn't intend to impose on you for so long."

Another easy smile arced her mouth. "It was no imposition. Actually, a little adult company is appreciated occasionally."

Together they rose and made their way to the front door. Polite goodbyes had been said, and Zade was halfway to the sidewalk when he turned back toward Lindy, who was still standing in the doorway, bathed in the soft glow of the streetlight on the nearby corner.

"I'd like to come again...to see Josh..." he hastened to add.

"He'd like that," Lindy said by way of giving her permission. *And so would I,* her heart added, much to her surprise.

"I'll see you soon, then." He turned and made his way down the sidewalk, his long strides carrying him with masculine grace around the hood of his Jaguar.

Lindy watched as he opened the door, slid inside and brought the engine purring to life. Then he put the elegant car into gear and pulled away from the curb. She was still standing in the doorway when he slowed down at the corner to make the turn, the taillights blinking brightly in the near-dark of the springtime evening before the car disappeared.

Spring peepers chorused a soprano serenade in the distance, with an occasional bass note from a bullfrog. A soft breeze carried the scent of faraway rain and trailed wisps of clouds across the paleness of the rising moon. A car door slamming shut down the street freed her from the spell Zade Wakefield had woven around her. She shut the door, shooting the dead bolt home from years of habit and wondering all the while just what was happening to her world.

He said he'd come back. Would he? Yes. She was sure of it. And then what? What did he really want? Time with Josh? It was strange, but then, what could it hurt? Lindy's mind went over every nuance of the evening: the brooding look on his face when he had told her his wife hadn't had any children, the smile that reached his eyes once or twice, finally resting with a bit more ease on the sensually shaped lips.

Lindy showered and dressed for bed, slipping beneath the cool crispness of the percale sheets, her mind on Zade Wakefield. She recalled the way his biceps had rippled beneath the short sleeves of his shirt and the heartrending sorrow she glimpsed in his silver-gray eyes.

What could it hurt if he came? Lindy had no sure answer. She only knew that somehow, without knowing exactly how it had come about, her heart—the heart that was only now beginning to mend from Randy's death—was responding to something within the man. Fight it, she would. Involvement with men like Zade Wakefield was futile for women like her. Yet something deep inside told her that even though she was bound to fight the attraction…the fight was useless.

Zade pulled into the driveway of his home on Lake Hamilton and crossed his arms on the top of the steering wheel, staring out over the huge expanse of the lake. Moonlight spilled onto the surface of the gently eddying water, like cream spreading across an ebony floor. Across the way, houselights glittered like jewels against the backdrop of the velvet night.

He'd told Lindy he'd be back to see Josh. Should he? Would he?

He wouldn't do anything deliberately to hurt the child who'd accepted him so readily. Nor would he deliberately hurt Lindy, the real power drawing him to the Scott house. The stiffness of his nature longed for the unpretentiousness of her. The restlessness inside him reached out for her serenity. Unhappiness had been his companion for the better part of his life and he longed for a bit of the joy radiating from her.

Oh, yes. He would go back. He couldn't help himself.

Chapter Four

It was three days later, a Monday, when Zade came to the conclusion that there was something lacking in the American judicial system. When he'd threatened Amy—and the woman carrying his baby—with due process of the law, he hadn't realized just how slow that process was. True, he had a lawyer. The same one who had drawn up the initial agreement between him and the unknown woman. An agreement so secret that the woman had given her power of attorney to Amy, who had in turn signed the contract for her. His lawyer, Paul Matthias, said that even if he knew who the woman was, he was bound by the same code of ethics as a doctor regarding the confidentiality of his clients. So Zade and Paul had started from the beginning by drawing up and filing the necessary papers and waiting....

Hell! Zade slammed the desk drawer shut with a bang and, heaving a disgusted sigh, leaned back in his swivel chair. Who could say how long it would take? According to Paul, who'd been in touch with Amy, the woman hadn't changed her mind.

So there was more waiting. And to top it all off, Monday was the first day of the lawsuit involving the crooked electrical contractor.

Swinging his feet to the gleaming top of the oak desk, Zade closed his burning eyes, settled back in his chair and folded his hands on his flat stomach. He hadn't been sleeping well. So many things going through his mind had made sleep a near impossibility. He was tired. Physically and mentally. He needed to get away somewhere and forget about business and the problem with...that woman.

A picture of Lindy moving around her kitchen eased his mind, bringing with it a sense of pleasure. He had told her he'd see her soon, but he hadn't contacted her since the night he'd intruded at the tail end of Josh's bath time. He wondered how she was feeling. Her self-sufficiency intrigued him. She was some lady, he thought, single-handedly supporting herself and her son and the child she carried. Actually, every facet of her personality intrigued him.

His feet dropped suddenly to the floor at the same instant his hand reached for the telephone. He wanted to see her, or at least hear her voice. He punched out the clinic number, then heard a series of beeps followed by a ringing at the other end of the line that seemed to go on forever before he heard a voice. "Good afternoon. Fedders's Clinic."

Zade leaned his elbows on the desk and exhaled a long sigh. "Mrs. Scott, please."

"This is she."

"Lindy?"

"Yes?" The questioning tone of her voice told him she didn't recognize his voice.

"This is Zade."

"Oh. Hi!"

Her voice sounded friendly and just a little breathless. And...relieved.

"Are you busy?" he asked.

"Not right this second."

"How have you been?"

"I'm fine."

"How's Josh?"

"He's great!" Her voice held a contagious enthusiasm. "He hasn't stopped talking about you since you tucked him in the other night."

It was the opening Zade had been waiting for. He closed his eyes and asked, "I was wondering if I could come over tonight?" He waited for her answer, his knuckles white as he gripped the receiver.

"I promised Josh I'd take him out for dinner this evening," she replied, causing Zade's heart to skip a beat. "But you could come over later, if you like." Tension oozed from him, and his heart recaptured its normal rhythm.

When she spoke again, he could almost see the smile on her generous mouth, the dimple in her left cheek deepening as her mouth widened and curved. "If you answer the next question correctly you might receive the dubious honor of giving him his bath."

Zade laughed softly and asked, "That sounds interesting. What time should I be there?"

"We'll be home by six-thirty. What time is good for you?"

"How about seven, seven-thirty?"

"You win! I'll see you then."

"Win what?"

"I told you you'd win the chance of giving Josh his bath if you answered the next question correctly. And you did."

"I don't even know what the question was," he countered one corner of his mustache tilting upward.

"I asked what time's good for you. You said about seven seven-thirty. That's the right answer."

"Says who?"

"Me." Her voice was threaded with amusement as she said "Look, who's running this contest, anyway? Do you want to bathe the kid or not?"

"I'll be looking forward to it."

Lindy's voice was skeptical as she countered, "Yeah, well

if you can say that after surviving the ordeal once, you're one of two things.''

"Oh?" Zade prompted, completely taken with her dry wit. "And what's that?"

"Crazy. Or one of those rare creatures…a born father."

A born father. Zade mouthed the words, liking the feel of them on his tongue, pleased with the way they settled into his mind. A father. Just what he wanted to be. Just what he was going to be. And by helping out at the Scott's he could start enjoying the experience early.

"Zade? You still there?" Lindy asked.

"Yes."

"Look I gotta go. My other line's bleeping. See you tonight."

She hung up before he could answer…a typical Lindy action, he thought, replacing the receiver. He sat staring at the phone for long moments before a smile lifted the outer edges of his lips. A smile that—to anyone who knew him well—could only be described as silly.

It had only been Zade. Lindy replaced the receiver and sat back with a sigh of relief, allowing her heart to slow its panicked rhythm. Every time she heard a man's voice on the line asking for her, her tension escalated. She lived in mortal terror that one day it would be *him*. She didn't know how much longer she could live with the increasing fear of discovery. It haunted her hourly, spilling over into her dreams in nightmares that woke her, leaving her with damp cheeks and a racing heart, thankful that in reality the baby was resting snugly inside her instead of being carried away in the arms of a stranger whose face she could never see.

She prayed for an early delivery and longed for the day she, Josh and the baby could be far away, away from everything threatening them and their happiness. The insistent ringing of the phone brought her sharply back to reality and the hard fact that though that day was somewhere in the foreseeable future, it hadn't arrived yet.

* * *

At eight o'clock that evening, Lindy turned on the coffeepot and took the cups from the cabinet. The scenario might have been an instant replay of Zade's first visit, had it not been for the fact that instead of worn shorts and a faded smock she was dressed in her most becoming dress, a teal-blue piqué with a matching eyelet ruffle at the hem. Its scoop neck and cap sleeves were perfect for the warm spring evening. And instead of smelling like Mr. Bubble she exuded a fresh, bold scent reminiscent of tropical flowers.

Her hair, freshly shampooed, was held back at the sides with white combs, its gleaming burnished-copper fullness tumbling onto her shoulders in curly abandon. Blush highlighted her cheekbones and a shiny red gloss glistened on her lips. Her large, round eyes were shadowed and lined and her lashes looked thicker than usual with two coats of mascara. She prided herself that the freckles hardly showed through her skillfully applied makeup. The extra time she'd taken was well spent, she thought, as she took some napkins from the drawer. Zade's look of appreciation when he surveyed her from head to toe had made it all worthwhile.

A smile hovered on her lips as she listened to the sounds coming from the bathroom where Zade was supervising the nightly bath ritual after Josh had consumed a scoop of all three of the different flavors of ice cream their visitor had brought. Her smile faded when a high-pitched squeal rent the air, followed by a thud that stopped her heartbeat momentarily before the sound of childish giggles mingling with deep masculine laughter normalized her pulse rate. In typical maternal fashion, her mind reconstructed the possibilities of what had just happened. She moaned softly and glanced at the clock, deciding that twenty-five minutes should have been enough time to turn one slightly dirty urchin into the semblance of a boy. She headed her footsteps resolutely toward the bathroom.

The scene that greeted Lindy as she entered the bathroom stopped her in the doorway. Josh was standing in the middle of the tub, coated with millions of iridescent bubbles. Zade, on his knees at the side of the tub, held a plastic bucket full of water, which he was sluicing down Josh's sudsy back. There were bubbles on the tile walls, bubbles spilling over the side of the tub and onto the floor and bubbles in the rich blackness of Zade's hair. Lindy's voice held a note of dismay as she groaned, "Joshua Scott!"

Two heads swiveled toward her. Two sets of eyes, one blue, one the tint of quicksilver, widened in surprise and, she could have sworn, guilt and fear. Zade recovered first, shrugging and saying in an apologetic tone, "I guess I put in too much of that bubble stuff." Josh, quick to see that his accomplice was going to shoulder the blame, pointed a verbal finger at him. "Yeah, Mom. Zade put too much Mr. Bubble in."

Lindy stood in the doorway, her arms folded across her middle. They looked for all the world like two little boys caught doing something wrong. Zade's face held the same waiting look as her son's. She fought to keep her face stern and struggled to hold back the giggles welling up inside her.

She cleared her throat. "You two have made quite a mess."

"I'll clean it up," Zade said, turning and pouring the last of the water on Josh's front before reaching for a towel and holding it out.

"Yeah, Zade'll clean it up," Josh chorused, darting a conspiratorial look at the man now enfolding his naked form with the large, blue towel.

"Don't you think you should help?" Lindy asked Josh.

Josh looked at the mess, then at the man holding him, then up at this mother. The woebegone expression on his face severed Lindy's tenuous hold on her mirth and sent her into a paroxysm of soft laughter. Zade and Josh looked at each other and broke into relieved grins.

"You aren't mad?" Josh asked, his expression relieved.

Lindy shook her head. "No. I'm not mad. You two look too pitiful for me to be angry. I just have one question. What was the loud thud?"

Josh leaned contentedly against Zade's chest, and began to wave his arms around as he demonstrated what he was doing.

"Zade was letting the water out and I stood up and slipped and fell on my butt!"

"Your what?" Lindy asked with raised brows.

"My bottom," Josh amended.

"All right. Go on and get ready for bed. I'll help Zade clean up this mess, then we'll be in to tuck you in."

Josh wriggled out of Zade's embrace and raced from the room, scooting between the door frame and his mother's legs with ease. Lindy stepped into the room and reached for a towel from the rack at the end of the tub just as Zade started to rise. She walked directly into him, her abdomen meeting the broad expanse of his back in a gentle collision.

"Ooops!" she said with a smile, her hands automatically going to the rounded protrusion of her stomach as she took a step backward. The citrusy scent of his cologne, whose fragrance was enhanced by the moist, steamy air, enveloped her senses.

Zade turned and grasped her upper arms, a concerned look on his handsome features as his gaze dropped to her hands, which were moving slowly over her abdomen. "Are you all right? You aren't hurt, are you?"

"I'm fine," Lindy said, thinking on one level of consciousness how strange it was that the bathroom seemed so much smaller all of a sudden, and on another, that the man was a chronic worrier. That second realization overrode the niggling man/woman awareness rapping discreetly at her dormant libido. She could tell the type. Always uptight. Always waiting for something to happen. Did he ever truly relax? She recalled the sounds of laughter during Josh's bath and decided that the times he did were rare, and therefore must be doubly precious.

Even his manner of dress reflected his reticent personality. His expensive loafers were always see-yourself shiny. He always wore casual yet obviously expensive slacks, and even his everyday shirts were probably hand-tailored. She wondered if he owned a pair of ragged jeans, scruffy sneakers or still had any old college sweatshirts.... A whimsical smile softened her lips. She doubted that he had ever loosened up enough to buy one in the first place.

Her eyes moved over the masculine planes of his face. She'd thought it from the first, and nothing so far had changed that first opinion, except the times he shared with her son: Zade Wakefield was a stuffed shirt.

"What are you smiling about?" he asked, loosening his hold on her arms.

Lindy spoke without thinking. "You."

A scowl replaced the perplexity in his eyes. "Me?"

Realizing what she'd done, she hurried to cover her error. Reaching up, she scooped up the blob of bubbles that perched on the top of his head, held them out on her palm and, pursing her mouth into an O, blew them up toward his face. At the startled look in his silvery eyes her full lips parted in a wide, teasing smile that wrinkled her freckled nose. Her lighthearted laughter bounced off the tiled walls and echoed softly through the small room.

Entranced, Zade watched as, unhindered by any self-consciousness, Lindy gingerly plucked the damp shirt away from his lean torso and pronounced in a pseudo-disgusted tone, "You came out of the ordeal in worse shape than Josh." Then she cocked her head sideways in consideration, looking him over from head to toe before qualifying the statement, "Weeelll, not quite."

Zade laughed, and Lindy's heart sprinted forward. The sound was different from any she'd ever heard from him, soft, deep, happy...and sexy. Suddenly the claustrophobic feeling was back. She stood less than a foot away from him, separated only by the gentle swell of her abdomen, and knew with a sudden overwhelming clarity that she was about to step in over her head. The discreetly knocking physical awareness she experienced earlier now battered at the door of her suspended sexuality with a force she knew she couldn't withstand.

She was attracted to this man. This stranger, this stuffed shirt. And she was *pregnant*, for goodness' sake! It was positively indecent...maybe even perverted! Where was her practicality? Where was her sense of decency? And where had all the air in the room suddenly gone? She took a deep breath and stepped backward.

A smile still arced Zade's mouth. The mustache framed his upper lip in sharp contrast to the even whiteness of his teeth, its softness inviting her touch. How would it feel if he kissed her?

Shocked and embarrassed by what she was feeling, Lindy turned on her heel and started for the door, tossing the words, "I've got to get Josh to bed," over her shoulder and praying that the foolish feelings invading her weren't apparent to him.

To her eternal thankfulness, when Zade joined her in the kitchen after tucking Josh in, he seemed unaware of her feelings in the bathroom. Taking the cup of coffee from her with softly murmured thanks, he sat down at the table.

Lindy sank into the chair across from him. It was going to be hard to act normally, she realized, with the memory of how badly she wanted his kiss in the bathroom still hovering in her mind.

"I'm really sorry about the mess," he said, offering her an apologetic smile. "Josh said he wanted a lot of bubbles and I wasn't sure just how much would make a lot."

"It's okay," she assured him, tracing the cup's edge with one fingertip. "I can get what you missed with cleaner any time."

Zade stirred in two spoonfuls of sugar and took a sip of his coffee. "Mmmm, tastes great. Although I shouldn't drink it. I probably won't sleep a wink tonight as it is."

Lindy raised her eyes from her coffee cup to his face. Her auburn brows drew together in a frown.

"Is something the matter?"

He shrugged, the action pulling the fabric of his striped knit shirt taut across his broad shoulders and causing Lindy's heart to speed up a bit. "Several things actually. Nothing that would interest you." He couldn't tell her about the problem with the woman who'd agreed to have his baby. That was one topic that definitely didn't qualify as an acceptable after-dinner subject of conversation.

"Oh, you might be surprised," Lindy said, thinking that at that moment everything about him interested her. "What do you do? I mean how do you make a living? You know all there is to know about Josh and me, but I don't know much about you other than you're Amy's cousin, and you seem to like kids."

"Where do you want me to start?" he asked, wondering what she would do if he told her about the mess his life was in.

She scooted her cup slightly to one side and, resting her forearms on the table, leaned toward him eagerly. "How did you get the name Zade? It's so unusual."

It was a common question for Zade, and one with no satisfactory answer. "I'm not certain where it came from. It's just an old family name."

She took a deep breath, realizing that if she wanted to learn more about him, she was going to have to drag out every tidbit. "So...what *do* you do for a living?"

"I own a string of motels."

"Oh?" Lindy said, impressed. She'd never known anyone who owned motels before. "Which ones?"

"The Great American chain," he said indifferently, taking another swallow of his coffee.

"But they're all over..." she began, hardly believing what he was saying. Great American was one of the most visible motel chains in the south.

"Ten states," Zade supplied into the sudden silence. "Mostly the mid-South."

Lindy's brows drew together as she digested this new, unexpected information slowly. If he owned all those motels he had to be loaded! Oh, she'd known he had money from the way he dressed, but he was actually *rich*. It made her wonder more than ever just what he was doing hanging around a middle-class, suburban, pregnant, working mother. Josh? So he said, but surely the people he knew—the rich people he knew—had kids. Why pick out a child he didn't know to shower with his attention? It just didn't make any sense.

And what would happen to Josh when Zade Wakefield tired of whatever game he was playing? For that matter, what would happen to her? The man had insinuated himself into their lives with relatively little effort. The realization came as something of a shock to Lindy. She was usually more careful. Maybe she had made it so easy for him because she'd sensed how much Josh liked him.

She frowned as a slight contraction tightened her abdomen. Piddlin' pains, Amy called them. They weren't too severe, and they always went away after just a few. Still, her palms found the hard roundness of her stomach in an automatic reaction.

"Are you all right?" Zade asked, concern etched into his features.

Lindy ignored the slight pain and his question. She lifted her limpid gaze to his, something akin to reproach showing in the depths of her eyes. "You're wealthy."

Zade was baffled by her seeming disinterest in her own welfare and shocked by the bluntness of the statement. He let the unspoken accusation he heard in the succinct deliverance of the two words sink slowly into his consciousness. "Yeah," he nodded after several contemplative seconds, "I guess I am. But no one ever made me feel guilty about it until now."

"I'm sorry!" Lindy apologized, rising with jerky movements entirely foreign to her usual easy grace. She snatched up her cup and refilled it with the hot, dark brew, than whirled back to face him. "It's just that it makes me wonder—" She broke off and tilted her head back to stare up at the ceiling, exposing the long, graceful column of her ivory throat.

"Wonder what?" Zade prompted.

She lowered her gaze to his once more. There was a question in her eyes, and a hint of fear. "What are you doing here with Josh and me? Why are you spending all this time with two people you hardly know, who don't fit into your world at all?"

Zade studied the earnestness in her eyes. How could he tell

her he was using them to fill in the time until he found the woman who carried his baby? How could he tell her that Josh was just a substitute until he got possession of his own son or daughter? How could he tell her that at this point in his life—and for reasons he couldn't disclose—he was fascinated with pregnancy and wanted to experience firsthand all the things he was missing by buying a mother for his child. He owed her the truth, but...

He started speaking, uncertain just where to begin, and was startled by the harsh, defensive sound of the words he heard coming out of his mouth. "I have money, yes. But that doesn't necessarily bring happiness. I'm here because I like being here. I like being with you and Josh."

"But surely you have a lot of friends..."

"Yeah. Loads." His voice was carefully bland, the words delivered in a stiff, offhand manner that itemized the facts, soliciting no pity—either from Lindy or himself. "They've all been married and divorced twice over. Their idea of a good time is a party where everyone chitchats about trivialities. No one ever gets close to anyone. And nine times out of ten if you ask them about their kids, they'll tell you they're off at some fancy finishing school so they'll be out of good old mom and dad's hair. That isn't my idea of a good time, or my idea of living. So I stay at home and watch a lot of cable television."

Lindy had a pretty good picture of the sort of life he was portraying, but never having experienced it made it hard for her to believe that it was as bad as he painted it.

"Poor little rich boy."

Zade's shrug was stiff, his eyes stark. "If you want to put it that way."

"I'm sorry," she said again. "It's just hard for me to see how that sort of life-style can be so hard."

"The grass is always greener..." he quoted with the barest trace of sarcasm lacing his tone. "That's why I like coming here. Believe it or not, this house feels more like home to me than my own. And I feel more welcome here than I do with any of my so-called friends." As Zade spoke the words he was startled to realize they were true. He felt better. He hadn't had to lie after all. His voice grew gentle as he said, "That's all there is to it, Lindy. There's no dark, ulterior motive for my coming around. I just like being here with you both. Can you understand that?"

"I suppose," Lindy said, still feeling uncomfortable. It wasn't that she didn't believe him, it was just that there was still the problem of what would happen when he stopped coming around. She had no answers to the problem, and probably wouldn't find any tonight. What they needed, she thought, was a shift in the conversation. She held up the glass urn. "Would you like more coffee?"

"Please."

She refilled his cup and sat back down.

As if sensing their current topic of conversation was steering them into troubled waters, Zade said, "I go to court tomorrow."

Court. The words took her by surprise since he'd been so reticent about his life. They also filled her mind with all sorts of thoughts she'd rather not pursue. She forced herself to answer calmly. "Oh?"

"Yeah," Zade answered. "I'm in the middle of a lawsuit. I subcontracted the wiring of a new motel in Arkadelphia, and when I had one of my own people go and check on it, we found out the contractor had used an inferior wire."

"What will you do?"

"I have to go back and pull everything already done and do it to specs. I'm suing the company for loss of time and money. And criminal negligence. That wiring could have started a fire and caused hundreds of people to be killed." His face was grim as he added, "He had a contract. He was supposed to live up to it. Since he didn't, he'll have to suffer the consequences."

Suffer the consequences. Just what she would have to do if her baby's father found her. The words pierced Lindy's heart and conscience. They seemed to trigger another slight abdominal cramp. She tensed in the chair.

"Are you all right?" Zade asked again as his brow furrowed in concern.

Lindy gave him a wan smile. "I'm fine. Just a little pain. Nothing to worry about."

"But you got so pale for a moment," he told her.

"I'm fine," she insisted. "As a matter of fact, the baby is doing gymnastics right now. Uncomfortable sometimes, but not really painful."

"Do you mean it's moving?"

"Yes."

"And it doesn't hurt?"

"No," she said, laughing softly. He was so curious and so concerned. Maybe if he knew more about what was going on, he wouldn't be so jumpy over every little thing. "Would you like to feel?"

Zade's eyes widened in surprise at the offer. "You don't mind?"

"Of course not. Come here." Lindy scooted her chair back slightly and indicated that Zade move to the chair next to her. She reached out and took his big hands, forcing him to lean forward as she placed them on the gentle swell of her stomach.

His eyes flew to hers as he immediately felt a series of fluttery movements, then a hard jab against his palm. "That didn't hurt?"

"No," Lindy said with a smile.

"But it felt like a kick!"

"It probably was. The feet should be up—" she moved his hands higher, to a spot just below her breasts, rewarding Zade a triumphant smile as the baby gave another vigorous kick "—here."

His hands began to move of their own accord, seeking places of movement. He felt his throat tighten slightly with suppressed emotion. This was life he was touching. This woman held within her the miracle of creation. A miracle of love. He lifted his eyes and sought her gaze, a rapt expression on his handsome face. "This is unbelievable!"

Lindy's eyes glowed with tender emotion as her lips curved upward in a smile of singular sweetness. Without thinking, she placed one hand over his.

Zade's attention shifted suddenly from the miracle at his fingertips to the one before his eyes. He'd never seen such a breathtaking smile. Never known a smile could change anyone so drastically. Yet the simple action magically transformed her from a wholesome, attractive woman to one of unbelievable beauty. Maybe it was the way the light fell on her face... maybe it was the way he knew she moved. But in that moment, Zade realized he'd never before seen anyone as *alive* as Lindy Scott.

The overhead light spilled onto the vibrant red of her hair, glittery gold splintering off the bold, vivid color...like a swath of raw silk shot throughout with gilt threads. He found himself wanting to touch the soft froth of curls on her forehead and, without realizing he was doing it, found his hand lifting...

Breath was suspended. Time paused. Coherent thought was an impossibility as their eyes clung, searching out the feelings burgeoning between them, feelings as old as time, as lasting as eternity. The floral scent of her perfume mingled with the clean soap smell of her, sending a single message to his brain: Woman. Her lips were parted and her breasts rose and fell with each quickened breath. A pulse hammered in the hollow of her throat as he lifted his hand and she waited...

Her hair was soft, yet seemed to have a life of its own as the flame-colored curls twined willfully around his strong, masculine fingers. Lindy's breath rushed out in a soft sigh; the finely honed tension gripping Zade eased its hold. Her long, thick lashes drooped to cover eyes darkened to the hue of port wine. A soft, agonized moan escaped her lips before the hand that rested on his tightened.

His other hand slipped down from her hair, his fingers tracing the edge of her exposed ear and the small gold heart studding it before moving down to her neck. His fingers slid beneath her hair and were instantly surrounded with warmth. Body warmth? Or heat from the fiery tendrils of heavy red hair? He exerted the barest pressure against her neck, drawing her nearer, his gray gaze fastened on the moist redness of her lips.

"I'm thirsty." The sound of Josh's voice cut through the quiet, emotionally charged room with the same effect as cold water being thrown into the face of a fainting person. Whatever might have happened was forever lost. Lindy's eyes flew open, her head snapping toward the sound of her son's voice and then back to Zade, guilt chasing away the tender emotions of moments before. Her hand moved from his.

Zade recovered more slowly, moving away from her and straightening in his chair. He raked a trembling hand through his dark hair, watching as she rose, shocked by the heat of the desire that had held him captive.

The woman was a widow. And she was carrying her husband's baby. So why had he suddenly felt the need to see if her mouth was as soft and giving as the rest of her seemed to be? His brooding gray eyes followed her movements as she got Josh a drink of milk and ushered him back to bed, while Zade's mind sought to straighten out the confusion inside him.

Things weren't working out as he'd planned. And they hadn't from the very beginning. He had accepted the tender ties Josh demanded the other evening, but becoming emotionally involved with Lindy would never do. He sighed. Right now he needed to go home and think things through—needed to revamp his game plan one more time. He had to figure out why he'd felt as he had with Lindy a few moments ago, and just where he wanted to go from here. Lindy and Josh Scott didn't play according to the rules he had devised in his mind.

He rose as she reentered the kitchen, suddenly eager to leave the house and all the conflicting emotions behind him. "I'd better be going," he said in a voice husky with remorse. "I'm supposed to be in court early in the morning."

Lindy stood near the door, her hands clasped together beneath her chin in a contemplative gesture. She nodded, her eyes not quite meeting his, and let her hands fall to her sides.

Zade stood before her, his eyes lingering on the freckle-dusted face that seemed pale beneath the rose tint of her blush. He reached out and lifted her chin with one finger, forcing her eyes to meet his. Eyes that seemed to ask, "What's happening? What do you want from me?" Zade's held no answers. Still, before he moved away, his thumb brushed the rounded curve of her chin in a gentle caress he couldn't have stopped if he'd tried.

He brushed past her and headed toward the living room. The parrot squawked, "Butter wants a kiss," as he passed. The bird wasn't the only one, Zade thought, still surprised that the thought had even entered his mind. He let himself out of the Scott house with the feeling that he'd somehow lost control of his life. And he didn't like the feeling at all.

Chapter Five

Lindy's troubled gaze followed Zade from the room. Her heart ached with a curious pain, and her usually smiling mouth turned downward at the corners. What was happening to her world? Was it possible he was feeling a little of what she had experienced in the bathroom? It seemed farfetched under the circumstances, but what other reason could there be for what had just happened?

And it had happened. Though there had been no actual kiss, the emotions leading them both in that direction had been vividly real. For the first time since Randy's death almost a year ago, Lindy found herself experiencing a definite feeling of sexual awareness, and there was little doubt in her mind that Zade felt the same. It might have been a while, but she could still read desire in a man's gaze. She hadn't forgotten how to chart the building of sexual excitement by the quickened sound of breathing and the slumbering promise of passion that reposed in masculine eyes just waiting to be fully aroused. He *had* felt it.

A deep, tremulous expiration of breath rippled through her, underscoring her inner unrest. While she couldn't deny what had passed between them—and she didn't think Zade would be able to, either—she wondered just where it was all leading. He claimed no interest in marriage and, she thought with a weary smile, she could hardly see herself involved in a torrid love affair in her condition...assuming of course, that what transpired between them was more than a moment's madness.

Lindy found it all exciting, frightening and just a tad ridiculous. She also found herself fighting a sense of guilt. She'd always had a healthy sexual appetite, and sex between her and Randy had always been good. Her husband had been dead for almost a year, and she had felt no real sexual urges until she'd come across Zade Wakefield...which made her feel afraid and guilty. Afraid, because her life was already in such a mess and she certainly didn't need another complication. Guilty, because she was pregnant with a stranger's baby and had no right to the feelings Zade ignited within her. She was hardly in a position to become involved with anyone.

Okay, she reasoned, so she was physically drawn to him. Was there more? While three meetings were hardly a sufficient amount of time on which to base any strong judgment, he had shown her several likable personality traits during the time he'd spent with her and Josh. He was prompt. And bringing the ice cream to Josh showed he was thoughtful. He had proved he was helpful by giving her son his bath and putting him to bed. He was obviously successful and very handsome. Lindy couldn't be sure, but she thought there was a definite chance that prolonged exposure to his particular brand of charm could lead to something more lasting, at least on her part. Was it leading somewhere?

No.

The ruthless answer came to her immediately, and without pretense. She had to be honest with herself. The man was gorgeous. Movie star material—the stuff dreams were made of. And she was just plain vanilla Lindy Scott. Clean. Neat. No frills, no fuss. Attractive, certainly—if you liked the wholesome, girl-next-door type. And she certainly couldn't think of any traits she might possess that would snag more than a moment's interest of a man like Zade.

So put it out of your mind.

She moaned. Easier said than done. What did he intend to do? He'd left in such a hurry. Would he be back? The thought that he might not come again threw her into a new frenzy of worry. It didn't matter, she told herself. But what about her son? Zade was quickly replacing Randy in the child's life. If the mysterious Mr. Wakefield didn't come back what would she tell Josh?

"I want some action," Zade growled, pinning Paul Matthias, his long-time friend and personal lawyer, with a look that could only be called a glare. His index finger pointed at the center of Paul's chest. "And I want it now!"

Spinning on the heel of shiny black dress shoes, Zade turned and started an agitated pacing. Head down, and hands thrust into the pants pockets of the charcoal-gray suit he wore, he walked a deserted hallway of the courthouse, listening with half an ear to the excuses for why things weren't moving faster in finding out the name of the woman who carried his baby.

He'd heard them all at least twice before.

After another sleepless week, he'd decided the safest course for him would be to concentrate on finding out who she was, and leave Lindy and Josh Scott alone. There was too much danger there. Emotional danger.

He was already crazy about the boy. Who wouldn't be? And he was afraid that much more time spent with Lindy would be his undoing. Though her actions clearly told him that she was different from the other women who had shared his life, he still held back. The old, haunting fears of hurt and rejection were too strongly ingrained in his heart and mind for him to put much faith in the positive signals Lindy transmitted.

Zade stopped suddenly and planted his hands on his slim hips, the action splaying open his unbuttoned jacket. His heavy, dark brows drew together in a dissatisfied frown. Only someone who knew him well could detect the emotion lurking in the shadows of his gray eyes. "How much longer do you think it will be?"

Paul had known Zade a long time. He could see the feelings beneath the hard, gruff exterior. Worry. Fear. He'd been there when Margot walked out, and had seen firsthand the destruction she'd left behind. A square, well-manicured hand came up and scrubbed at a freshly shaven jaw. Paul's voice, when he spoke, sounded as discouraged as Zade felt. "I don't know. All I can tell you is that I'm hurrying as fast as the law allows."

Zade swore. "Well, while we're waiting, put a little pressure on her through Amy." His softly spoken words were all the more dangerous-sounding for their quietness.

Paul's brow furrowed in perplexity. "What do you mean?"

"I mean get in touch with her, and you, personally, talk to her. Tell her that if she knows what's good for her, she'll go through with what we planned."

Paul sighed, knowing it was no use trying to reason with Zade once he had made up his mind about something. "Okay. You're the boss. I'll see what I can do." Pushing back the sleeve of his striped shirt, Paul gave a cursory glance at his watch. "Look, I've got to go. I'm supposed to be in the judge's chambers in a few minutes."

Zade was silent, wrapped up in thoughts that had nothing to do with the case involving thousands of dollars that would soon be coming to trial.

Paul slapped him on the shoulder. "Come on," he encouraged with a heartiness no deeper than the tone of his voice, "Let's go in there and win this one. The other will turn out okay."

"Sure." Zade's hands dropped to his sides.

Paul gave his friend's shoulder a comforting squeeze before bending to retrieve his briefcase from the floor. "See you in court," he said as he moved past Zade and headed down the long marble hallway.

Zade watched him walk away. He felt as though he stood

at the edge of a precipice with the ground slowly crumbling away beneath him. God, how much more could he take? He swore, fighting the enticing image of full, cherry-glossed lips that insinuated itself in his mind every time he closed his eyes. He wouldn't contact her. He wouldn't.

And he didn't. Not until later that night.

Lindy was barely in the door that afternoon when the phone began to ring. She handed a small grocery sack to Josh and reached for the receiver with a command to her son to put the milk away.

"Hello?"

"Hi," came the familiar, feminine voice of her boss. "This is Amy."

"Oh, hi! What's up?" Lindy said with a smile.

"I...uh...have someone here who wants to speak to you." She paused, almost, Lindy thought, as if she were choosing her next words with extreme care. "He's the...the attorney who drew up the contract for the baby."

Lindy's heart plummeted, then began to race with fast, heavy beats. Her stomach churned with sudden nausea, and her head began to throb an agonized rhythm, pounding in cadence with her wildly beating heart.

"Amy..." she began.

"I'm sorry," Amy said softly before the scrambling sounds of the phone being exchanged from one hand to another came across the wire.

"Hello." The voice, pleasant and richly masculine, reached across the space of the city and fell ominously on Lindy's ear. A voice with no name and no face. Just like the man whose baby she carried. "I'm calling in regard to the statement by Dr. Fedders that you've decided not to give up the baby after all," he continued.

"That's right." Lindy was surprised to hear that her reply held none of the fear crawling up her spine inch by numbing inch.

"Do you mind telling me why?" The stranger's voice now

held a soothing note that begged, "Trust me...trust me..."
But she knew she couldn't.

The words came out in a rush, betraying her nervousness.
"I can't explain why. I just know I can't go through with it,
that's all. This baby is a part of me. I can't give it away."

"It's part of the father, too," Paul said in a reasonable tone,
resorting to a ploy already tried unsuccessfully by Amy.

"I know."

"Don't you think he has any rights, especially after he's
paid you for the child?"

"Y-yes. He does have rights," Lindy said falteringly. Her
hand went to the back of her neck where the tension was
tightening ever so slowly. *Zade, where are you? Why aren't
you here when I need you?* "I know he gave me some money,
but I told Dr. Fedders I'd pay him back, and I will. Did she
tell you? Have you told him that?"

There was an edge of desperation in her voice that was
clearly apparent to Paul. He began to feel just a bit uncomfortable with his assignment, but hell, Zade was paying him
to do what he could. "My client knows you've said you'd pay
him back, yes. But you must understand that by receiving the
money in small installments he'll never realize anything from
it. Besides, money isn't the real issue here except that it was
chosen as the basis for this transaction. One baby for twenty-
five thousand dollars. And you've already received the first
half."

Lindy remained silent, her mind searching for something to
say that would sway this man to her side, and coming up with
nothing. How could she make this man—or any man—understand the unparalleled closeness between mother and infant?
A closeness begun at the instant of conception.

Paul listened to the silence and decided it was time to play
his trump. With the keen instincts that made him a successful
lawyer, he realized that if ever there was a time to get her to
change her mind, it was now, while she was low. And she
was low. Her voice told him so. "You do understand that

failure to comply with the agreement can lead to severe consequences?''

''Yes.'' Her voice was hardly more than a whisper.

To the man across town her voice came through the wire sounding lost and without hope. He cleared his throat, his discomfort with his assignment escalating in tandem with her despair. ''My client just wants you to know that if you'll agree to go through with the terms of the contract, he'll stop the legal procedure to subpoena the information of your identity, and things can progress as planned. If you don't agree, we will eventually find out who you are and you'll be wide open to a breach of contract suit.''

Lindy swallowed, and her eyes filled with tears.

Paul reached up and tugged at the knot of his gray silk tie. *Damn you, Zade!* ''Do you understand what I'm saying?'' he asked, silently vowing never to get involved with this sort of deal again. There were some things you should just never touch. And this was one of them.

''Yes.''

''And what shall I tell my client?'' *Please go through with it, lady...for your sake and Zade's.*

Lindy's voice was thick with unshed tears as she said, ''Tell him...tell him...I can't.'' Her voice broke. ''I'm sorry.''

The phone suddenly went dead in Paul's hand. He cradled the instrument thoughtfully for a moment, then hung up, his heart heavier than it had been for a long time. Rubbing his eyes with a weariness born of a sense of futility, he ached with sorrow for the unknown woman. But he felt sorry for Zade, too. He knew how badly his friend wanted this baby.

One thing for certain: whatever else this woman was, she was a fighter. And knowing Zade as he did, he thought that fact just might stand her in good stead during the next few weeks.

After Lindy hung up the phone, she sank onto the sofa and buried her face in her hands. Bitter, scalding tears seeped between her fingers and spotted the bright purple smock she wore.

Josh stood in the doorway, watching as his mother curled into one corner of the living room sofa. He wanted to cry himself, but felt that would only make her feel worse. Slowly he made his way to her and crawled up beside her, leaning against her and wrapping his arm across her burgeoning stomach in a fierce hug. His limited vocabulary offered no words of solace, but one hand smoothed and patted her comfortingly while he whispered, "I love you, Momma...I love you."

Zade had just finished another of his solitary dinners and was stashing the dirty dishes in the dishwasher when the doorbell rang.

He picked up the scotch he'd been drinking and crossed the living room to the front door. The bell pealed impatiently once more.

"I'm coming!" he called irritably. He threw back the dead bolt and flung open the door. Paul Matthias stood there, his shirt wrinkled, his tie off and the top buttons of his striped shirt undone. His graying brown hair looked as if he'd been running his fingers through it, and his face was etched with lines of fatigue.

"What did she say?" Zade asked without preamble, standing aside so the lawyer could enter the flagstone foyer.

"My God, Wakefield, do you mind if I get in the door before we start the third degree?"

Zade had the grace to look embarrassed. "I'm sorry. Would you like a drink?"

"Just a cold beer if you have one," Paul said, flinging himself into one of the blue-and-ivory striped chairs flanking a floor-to-ceiling fireplace made solely of Arkansas crystal.

"Sure. Be right back," Zade said, turning and disappearing into the kitchen.

The few moments he was gone gave Paul ample time to survey the room. *Not bad.* Zade had recently bought the sprawling house on Lake Hamilton, and Paul hadn't had an opportunity before now to visit.

The floors were all polished flagstone, their glossed surface covered at strategic intervals with Persian rugs. The walls of the living room were ivory, and the lovely but stark oriental decorating throughout did nothing to alleviate the feeling of coldness. There wasn't one touch of greenery to add life to the surroundings, only bare branches arranged decorously in a large urn standing in one corner. It was a beautifully decorated, unlived-in room that held not one ounce of welcoming warmth. Just like its owner, Paul thought cynically.

Zade returned and silently handed over the beer and a glass, which Paul promptly set on the black lacquered table. Zade sank into a chair and watched as his friend popped the ring on the can. A soft hiss broke the room's silence; Paul put the can to his lips and tilted his head back, letting a long draft of the cold, yeasty brew slide down his throat. "Ahhh," he said with a discreet belch. "I needed that."

Zade was silent, waiting for Paul to make the first move.

"You know, a guy could go bananas working for you," he said at last.

"Yeah?" Zade queried.

"Yeah. That court case is turning out to be a bigger deal than I thought." At the look on Zade's face, he continued, "Oh, not that there's any problem. We'll win it, but the guy's got a damn good lawyer on his side."

"To hell with the motel case," Zade said, getting down to what mattered the most to him. "What about the woman?"

Paul sighed and crossed his leg ankle to knee, grasping the ankle of the crossed leg with one blunt-fingered hand. "You want it straight, Zade? Okay. You got a tiger by the tail." Paul felt a sense of satisfaction at the announcement. For some reason it pleased him that the woman wasn't folding as easily as most would.

"What do you mean?"

"I mean we're dealing with one cool lady. I put it to her straight, and she didn't budge an inch."

"Did you tell her she could expect a lawsuit if she doesn't comply?"

"I did."

"And?"

"And she said she was sorry, but she just couldn't do it."

Zade muttered a harsh expletive, took a large gulp of his scotch and made a face at the potency of the drink. He cradled the glass in his hands and appeared to become inordinately interested in the pale amber contents. "How did she sound?"

"She was scared. I could tell that much. Scared to death." Paul uncrossed his legs, took a long pull of the beer and rested his elbows on his knees, dangling the beer can between his thighs. His troubled blue eyes looked askance at Zade. "She was crying, man," he said softly. "But she didn't fold. And I felt like a low-life bastard for putting her through that little piece of hell."

The woman's plight obviously didn't faze Zade as he clarified his question. "I mean, how did she sound, what kind of person do you think she is?"

Paul leaned back in the chair, his eyes focusing on a floral watercolor gracing a far wall. "Young. She sounded young. Scared. Hurting." He cut his gaze abruptly to Zade. "She sounded *nice*. Is that what you want to hear? She sounds like a nice woman who made a mistake." He gave a shrug, and added, almost as an afterthought, "She had a pretty voice."

"Do you think I could talk to her?"

Paul snorted and shook his head. "No way! It takes an act of congress to get through to her. I went to Amy's office. She dialed the number; I turned my back and everything. Amy told her I wanted to talk to her. No names...nothing. Besides, it wouldn't do any good. She isn't going to change her mind. The best thing we can do is just what we've been doing—wait for the subpoena to go through."

Zade drained his glass; Paul killed the can of beer. They set down their containers simultaneously. An uncomfortable silence stretched between the two friends, each lost in his own world.

Finally, Paul glanced at his watch. "Tammy's gonna give me hell when I get home. I was late two nights last week." He rose and stretched.

"I'm sorry," Zade apologized. "You should have just called."

"I wanted to come by. I needed a few minutes to unwind before I go home and face the rug-rats," Paul said affectionately of his children. Then he realized he could have chosen his reasons—or at least his words—more carefully. His blue eyes held contrition as he mumbled, "I'm sorry."

"It's okay," Zade said with a wry twist of his lips. "I'll see you in court tomorrow."

"Sure." When Zade started to rise to walk with him to the door, Paul held up a restraining hand. "Don't bother. I'll see my own way out."

Zade watched the portly figure of his friend leave the room. Heard the soft latching of the door, and soon after, the sound of an engine revving to life and finally fading into the distance. Only then did he rise and go to the glass doors that opened onto a flagstone patio.

He stepped out into the twilight and perched his hands on his slim hips. Far out on the lake the droning of a ski rig pulling a lone skier toward some faraway shore trailed off into a muted thrumming. A fishing boat, silhouetted against a pink-and-mauve sky, bobbed gently up and down. The sounds of laughter and the scent of charcoal drifted on the evening breeze from the house next door. Trish and Dan Rowel were barbecuing again, he thought randomly. The utter tranquility of the evening and the sounds of their happiness filled him with a feeling of frustration—and worse, a feeling of sorrow—as he realized that his house never rang with laughter the way his neighbor's did. Zade's shoulders drooped. Even his mustache drooped over the down-curving turn of his mouth.

She sounded nice. Paul's words came back to haunt him. *She was nice...she was crying...Crying. She had a pretty voice.*

Zade groped eagerly in his mind for the memory he'd denied himself for four days...the soothing sound of Lindy's voice. Now, in a moment of indulgence, he let his mind be filled with her. The way she talked. The way she moved so easily and gracefully. The clean, wholesome look of her. The way her freckle-dusted nose wrinkled when she laughed. The happiness in her eyes. The way life never seemed to get her down.

A sudden squeal of laughter drew his eyes to the Rowels's yard where Dan Rowel was chasing his wife. While Zade watched, he lunged at her, and they both fell to the ground. The laughter stopped abruptly. Zade turned and went inside so he wouldn't have to witness Dan lowering his lips to his wife's in a long, lingering kiss.

The sound of the doorbell ringing roused Lindy from a light doze. She lifted her head from the sofa cushion and glanced at the wall clock above the television. Darn! She shouldn't have moved her head so quickly. She struggled to focus her pain-glazed eyes on the slender brass hands. Nine o'clock. Nine, and the television was still on.

A sudden thought threw her troubled mind into a new panic. She had cried for hours, it seemed, and Josh had been right beside her. How long had she been asleep? Where was he now? She pushed herself up on one elbow and made a hasty survey of the room. Where had he gone while she slept?

Fear clutched her heart. She started to rise just as the doorbell pealed again. In her concern for Josh, and in her sleep-befuddled state, she'd forgotten what had awakened her. Her eyes automatically returned to the clock, even though she knew the time. Who could be here at this hour?

She struggled to her feet, torn between answering the door and looking for Josh. Josh won. She started toward his room, but halted when whoever was at the door began pounding. Her head throbbed with every thud of fist against wood. Nausea clawed its way up her throat. She closed her eyes and massaged her temples in a futile effort to stop the pain.

"Lindy!"

Her lashes flew upward at the sound of Zade's voice coming from the other side of the closed door. She sobbed, a feeling of thankfulness washing over her. Her feet began moving automatically toward the door. Zade was here. After the long, lonely days of hearing Josh complain of his new friend's absence, and wondering if he ever intended to return, Zade was back. He would help her find Josh. She unlocked the door, but before she could open it, she felt the knob turning beneath her hand as he pushed his way inside.

He stood in the open doorway staring down at her with a frown. "What took you so long to answer the doorbell?"

"I—I was asleep on the sofa."

He noticed the dull pain in her eyes as she stared up at him. A feeling of anxiety tore through him. "Are you all right? It isn't the baby, is it?"

She shook her head and groaned. "It's Josh. He's gone."

Strong hands grasped her shoulders. "Gone!" Zade barked. "What do you mean, he's gone? Is he lost?"

Lindy's eyes filled with tears. She was so tired. And her head hurt so badly. She needed someone to take care of her...like Randy used to do. But there was no one anymore. She gazed up at him, her long lashes sticking together in damp spikes and her bottom lip trembling as she accused softly, "You're yelling."

Zade's eyes closed, and he prayed for patience. What was going on? Lindy wasn't making much sense. His hands moved from her shoulders up to cradle her pale cheeks. "Lindy," he said softly, "Where is Josh?"

"I don't know." She saw something flare in his gray eyes and begged, "Please don't be angry." She drew a deep breath. "I—I had a bad headache, so I stretched out on the sofa for a few minutes. The next thing I knew, you were at the door. The TV was going, and I don't know how long I was asleep, and I was just going to see where he was, but you were banging on the door..." she babbled, stopping long enough to drag in another lungful of air. "Oh, Zade, I'm so worried!" Her fragile hold on her composure slipped, along with two crystalline tears that tumbled down her cheeks unchecked by the random spattering of honey-colored freckles that stood out more noticeably than usual against her unusual pallor.

Zade brushed the tears away with his thumbs, her misery tugging at his heartstrings and fanning the embers of feelings he thought were as cold as last week's ashes. "Don't worry," he told her huskily. "We'll find him. Do you think he's in his room?"

She shook her head. "I don't know. That's where I was going when you started pounding on the door."

"Let's go look," he suggested, placing his arm around her shoulders and drawing her against his side. Lindy's arm automatically circled his slim waist; her thumb hooked without conscious thought in the belt loop of his slacks.

Josh's bedroom light was on and his toys were scattered around the room, but he was nowhere to be seen. Lindy's horrified gaze clashed with Zade's. The tears she'd managed to get under control only moments before, started afresh.

"Come on, babe. Don't cry," he pleaded, unaware of the ease with which the endearment slipped from his tongue. He reached out and brushed the ever-wayward tendril of hair from her damp cheek, fighting to keep his voice worry-free as he said, "Let's go and check the rest of the house before we get too upset." He offered her a comforting smile. "Okay?"

Lindy nodded and tried to smile back as she followed him from the room. Forcing himself to move quickly yet with a deceiving nonchalance, Zade struggled to keep his own fears from surfacing. The bathroom was empty. They moved to Lindy's bedroom, and he prayed they would find Josh curled up on her bed, but they didn't. Silently, he led her toward the kitchen. He approached the doorway with warring emotions— hope and misgiving. The light was on, but then, Lindy might have left it on earlier.

The scene that met Zade as he entered the room halted him just inside the door. He hadn't realized he was so wound up until he felt the tension draining from him, leaving him limp with relief. Then a slow smile lifted the corners of his dark mustache. He turned to Lindy and held out his hand. She placed her hand in his and he pulled her into the curve of his arm and into the room.

Josh was on his knees in a chair at the table, which was cluttered with a loaf of bread, a jar of strawberry jam and a jar of peanut butter. A glass of milk sat in a white puddle near a paper plate. Unaware of the silent approach of the two adults, he was digging into the peanut butter with a table knife, a frown of concentration on his face.

Relief flooded Lindy as she realized he was all right. A relief that was quickly supplanted with anger that he had caused her so much worry. Trying to ignore the ache in her head, she started to move toward him, but Zade's hand and the look of warning in his eyes stopped her. He shook his head slowly. He was right, she thought. Now wasn't the time to scold him. She nodded in acknowledgment of his silent message.

"What are you doing, Josh?" she said when she could finally trust herself to speak.

The boy started guiltily, his blue eyes round with something akin to fear before he decided to brazen out the situation. "I'm makin' you a s'prise. I was hungry, and you were feelin' bad. So I'm makin' us dinner." He reached for a completed sandwich and held it out. The bread looked as if it might have soaked up some of the spilled milk, jam oozed from the edges and a fat strawberry plopped onto the table. Josh looked at Zade, his eyes brightening at the sight of his friend. "You came back," he said. "I told Momma you'd come back. Do you like peanut butter?" he asked hopefully.

Zade was having a hard time with the unexpected obstruction that had climbed its way to his throat. He could only nod.

"Do you want me to make you a san'wich?"

"I'd love one," he told the boy in a voice that held a curious huskiness. He turned to Lindy, a smile lighting his face. He was surprised to see that although her expression held a profound relief, pain had etched lines between her eyebrows. "Are you all right?"

She clamped her teeth onto her bottom lip, shaking her head with a grimace. "My head...it hurts so..."

"Go on back to the living room and rest," he commanded gently. "I'll take care of Josh."

Her eyes searched his questioningly. "Are you sure?"

"I'm sure. Go on." He caught her by the shoulders and spun her gently around to face the door.

A feeling of dizziness swept through her. Her knees gave way and she murmured a soft, surprised, "Oh!" Zade caught her as she crumpled and, swinging her up into his arms, he carried her toward her room. Lindy struggled in his embrace. "Put me down!"

"Be still," he said sternly.

"I'm too heavy," she argued, her eyes swimming with tears of pain and mortification. "Put me down."

"You fainted, dammit!" Zade growled. "Now be still."

"I didn't faint, I was just dizzy," she clarified.

"Sure."

She looked up at him. His face was shadowed with a day's growth of beard. He looked handsome and tough and...safe. She hadn't felt safe in a long time. Her arms slid around his neck in a totally unconscious gesture of acquiescence. "You'll get a double hernia," she whispered, her usual teasing coming to the surface in spite of her pain.

"I always wanted one," he quipped back, marveling that she could joke at a time like this.

"Yeah, well, you're about to get your wish. *Please* put me down?"

He pushed open the bedroom door with his shoulder and carried her to the side of the bed. Lowering her feet to the floor, he steadied her with warm, strong hands at her shoulders. His silvery-gray eyes met hers. "Did anyone ever tell you that you're stubborn, Mrs. Scott?" he asked, his breath fanning her face in a gentle caress.

"Occasionally."

"I'll bet," he said with a grin. "Can you get ready for bed, or do you need some help?"

"I can do it."

"Okay. Where do you keep your gowns?"

Lindy pointed to an oak chest of drawers. "The third drawer from the top."

Zade pulled open the drawer. His olfactory senses were instantly assaulted by the floral fragrance he had come to associate with her. It was sweetly erotic, conjuring up images of his face buried against the soft fullness of freckle-dusted, ivory breasts. Appalled at the turn of his traitorous thoughts, he snatched up the first gown and carried it to her. It was all he could to to keep from burying his nose in the soft fabric. "Will you be okay if I go take care of Josh?"

She nodded.

"I'll get him fed and ready for bed, then I'll come and check on you." He turned to leave the room.

"Zade?"

He turned. She looked terrible, her face pale and hollow-eyed. She also looked...forlorn...lonely. She looked, he thought, like he had felt earlier while watching the Rowels at play. She looked like he had felt since he left her last Monday night, and until he'd walked through her front door a few minutes ago. It was astonishing how quickly the loneliness fell away under the feelings of concern and tenderness she ignited within him.

There's more, Wakefield. Some part of him acknowledged the truth of that thought, but right that second, his mind couldn't accept it. But his heart did, and it reasoned that since the love had been so long coming, it could wait a while longer before the reckoning that would change his life. Zade's eyes and his heart absorbed the picture of Lindy clutching the gown to her breast and he offered only a single word. "Yes?"

"Thank you. You're fantastic to do this."

Fantastic? Him? Zade smiled slightly and left her standing near the bed. A redheaded sorceress who was somehow magically leading him to believe that love wasn't an illusion after all.

Chapter Six

An hour later, Zade tucked the sheet beneath Josh's chin, pressed a kiss to his cheek and left the room. It had taken him a long time to convince the boy that his mother was going to be all right, to share a soggy sandwich and to clean up the kitchen before tackling the nighttime bath, which was this time, of necessity, short and quiet.

Zade closed Josh's door to a mere crack, allowing a sliver of light from the hallway to partially illuminate the darkened room. He stood indecisively for a moment before running a hand through his already tousled hair and moving quietly toward Lindy's room. The knob turned noiselessly in his hand; the door opened without a sound.

A small lamp on the bedside table cast a golden glow throughout the bedroom that was decorated with a sea theme. Soft blues and grays, seascapes and more wicker furniture gave the room a natural feel…just like Lindy.

He tiptoed nearer the bed. Lindy lay on her side, the soft incandescence of the lamplight skimming the planes of her pale cheeks and pooling dark shadows beneath her closed eyes, mute testimony of the pain she suffered.

During their peanut butter and milk, Josh, near tears himself, confessed that his mother had cried for a long time before falling asleep on the sofa. Zade tried to console the boy and wondered if the headache was the reason for her tears, or if she was finally succumbing to the considerable weight of her cares? After all, it was less than two weeks now until the baby came. Knowing her as he was beginning to, he knew she must be concerned about all the added responsibilities caring for another child would bring. He sighed, the sound loud in the stillness of the room. He didn't know how she did it.

Lindy, floating in the realm somewhere between sleep and wakefulness, had been aware of the hushed sounds coming from the kitchen and bathroom, but was completely unaware of the passage of time. She was content to lie in bed unmoving, willing sleep to claim her and ease the pain and the worry, however temporarily. The sound of a sigh alerted her to a presence in the room, causing her lashes to lift and her sherry-hued gaze to fall on Zade. The depths of her eyes held a strange combination of sleepiness and confusion. He stood by the bedside, a frown pleating his forehead and dragging at the corners of his beautifully shaped mouth. His dark hair was mussed, and his once-immaculate shirt was unbuttoned halfway down his chest, revealing a mat of thick, black hair. The shirt, pulled free of his slacks, was wrinkled and water-splotched from Josh's bath and had a red stain on it, as if it might have been the recipient of a blob of strawberry jam.

In spite of the lingering headache, Lindy couldn't help the upward curve of her lips. She'd never seen him this disheveled before. And, with her heart quickening at the sight of his blatant masculine virility, she realized she'd never seen him this sexy-looking before.

"Feeling better?" His voice was a low rumble.

She moved her head tentatively and found the pain much better than it had been an hour earlier. "I think so," she murmured softly.

"I'm sorry I woke you," he apologized.

"You didn't. I wasn't really asleep." She scooted up into a sitting position, careful, for modesty's sake, to keep the sheet pulled up over her breasts. "Is Josh okay?"

"He's fine. I got the sandwich down him, and gave him his bath. He conked out the minute his head hit the pillow."

"He isn't used to staying up so late. Eight-thirty is usually tops for him." Lindy lifted a hand to her forehead and massaged her temple.

Zade shoved his hands into his pockets, a curious pain in his heart because she hurt and he could do nothing to help her. "Can I get you anything? Pain pills? Aspirin?"

"No, thanks. I don't like to take anything because of the baby, even though Amy assures me it's okay now. The pain is just a dull throbbing now." She offered him a smile, adding, "I can handle it."

"How about something to eat, then? I know you didn't have any dinner."

Lindy sighed. "I am a little hungry. But I'll get up and fix something." She started to rise, but one hand came out of his pocket, reaching out and grasping her shoulder, forcing her to stay where she was. Her eyes dropped quickly to the hand that lay warm and heavy on her bare shoulder, then moved up the hair-dusted forearm revealed by the rolled-up sleeves of his shirt, over the bold thrust of his broad shoulder straining the bounds of the shirt fabric and on up to his eyes. Was that a glimmer of what she was feeling reflected there in the dark depths of his eyes? She wasn't certain, not in the dimness of the room.

His hand fell from her shoulder. "You stay put," he commanded. "I'll bring you something." He perched his hands on his lean hips. "What'll it be? Grilled cheese? Scrambled eggs?"

"I don't know..."

"You'd better choose," he said with a sudden smile. "That's about all I know how to fix besides frozen dinners," he confessed. "Of course, there's always the specialty of the house."

"And what is that?" Lindy asked, intrigued by the way the grooves in his cheeks deepened when he smiled.

"Peanut butter and jelly à la Joshua."

Lindy felt a deep pleasure spread warmly throughout her. Zade Wakefield was actually teasing! It was hard to believe. He seemed to have done a considerable amount of softening in the short time she'd known him. "And what makes it different from a regular peanut butter sandwich?"

"Why, it's soaked in milk, ma'am," he told her in pseudo-serious tones.

Lindy laughed softly. "Did you have one?"

"You bet! I couldn't hurt his feelings, could I? I ate it with a fork. It's an experience I'd recommend to everyone."

"I think I'll pass," she said, thinking how nice it was of him to humor Josh by eating the disastrous meal he'd fixed. A lot of men would have dumped it and fixed something else. The fact that Zade recognized how important the sandwich fixing was to her son said a lot about his sensitivity where others were concerned.

She must have been staring at him while thinking how nice he was to Josh, because she suddenly became aware of the brooding intensity in his eyes and the silence stretching between them. "How about some chicken noodle soup?" she asked in desperation.

"Great!" he replied with a fervor that belied the seriousness of his expression only moments before. He turned to leave the room, then turned back. "Don't get up, I'll bring it in here."

"I can come to the table."

"Maybe so, but let's not push our luck. The headache's on the run, so let's not do anything to bring it back...okay?"

She sighed. "Okay." He turned to leave. Once again her voice halted him just outside the bedroom door. "Zade."

He poked his head back around the door frame. "Yeah?"

"Peel the paper off the can and put it in the top right-hand drawer, will you?"

He looked puzzled. "Sure," he agreed.

"I'm saving them for Josh's day-care center. They send them in for playground equipment," she explained.

"Okay," he said, acquiescing with a shrug of wide shoulders, not understanding why they just didn't go out and buy some equipment, but willing to do as she said anyway. He flashed her another devastating smile. "I won't be a minute."

His minute was more like fifteen. He returned with the tray, placing it temporarily on the bedside table while he fluffed Lindy's pillows and arranged them behind her back for support. The helpful gesture threatened to get out of hand as his eyes feasted on the expanse of creamy back with its light sprinkling of whiskey-colored freckles bared by the low cut of her gown. Her hair was up, though straggling; one curl rested lovingly against her ivory nape. The tantalizing scent of her perfume, enhanced by the heat of her body, wafted up to him much as it had the night in the kitchen...as it had from her drawer of nightgowns.

Zade found his reaction much the same. He was suddenly acutely aware of Lindy as a woman. A desirable woman. He fought the urge to press his mouth to the beckoning curve where her neck and shoulder joined. Whoever said pregnant women had no sex appeal was crazy. And he felt the stirrings of the physical evidence to prove it. This time, the realization didn't frighten him. After the way he had been unable to keep from coming over tonight, he knew he had very little choice about what was happening to his regimented life. He just wondered what to do about it.

Tearing his gaze from the lure of her satiny skin, he gave the pillows a final pat. "There," he said in a voice that held a curious huskiness as he straightened and moved away from her. Their eyes clashed briefly before he began to busy himself with situating the dinner tray just so.

Unable to locate a real tray, he had improvised, covering a cookie sheet with a clean towel. Steaming soup and crackers, a few slices of cheese and a glass of iced tea comprised the meal. With a rumbling stomach Lindy thought it looked hearty and filling, and it smelled delicious. Next to the pale green paper napkin was a spoon and a solitary pink dogwood blossom.

She picked up the delicate flower and held it to her nose. Its soft smoothness felt cool against her. "Thank you," she said, returning it to the tray and picking up the napkin. "This looks delicious. And the dogwood blossom is lovely." She wasn't certain in the dimness of the room, but she thought a slight red crept into his face.

He cleared his throat and gave a smile that looked forced and a bit uncomfortable. "Amy and I used to play doctor when we were little. She was the doctor. I was always the patient. She'd fix me up a tray of pretend food and always put some sort of wildflower on it." The usual intensity in his eyes was banished with the remembrance and replaced with a look of tenderness.

"That sounds like Amy," Lindy said, dipping into the soup and carrying a spoonful to her mouth. "Mmmm…good," she murmured as she closed her eyes momentarily in delight.

He smiled.

"Sit down and keep me company," she offered, indicating the chair sitting beside the bed. "Unless you have to go," she tacked on hurriedly.

"No. I'm in no hurry." He sank into the chair with an easy grace and stretched his long legs out before him, fiercely glad she'd asked him to stay. He hated going back home. Dreaded the emptiness he knew waited for him there. The sandwich he'd shared with Josh was the best food he'd had lately, solely because of the boy's company.

"Were you and Amy close growing up?" Lindy asked, jarring him from his disquieting thoughts as she tackled her dinner with hungry enthusiasm.

Zade laced his fingers together and rested his hands on the flat planes of his stomach. "She was more like my sister than my cousin. We did almost everything together. She was friend, sister and mother, all rolled into one."

"Mother? Did your mother die?" Lindy asked with a natural curiosity.

He was startled by her question, unaware that his straightforward observation of the role Amy played in his youth had been so revealing. Though he was usually loathe to talk of his mother's desertion, he found himself saying, "No. She left my father when I was thirteen."

Lindy saw the hardness enter his eyes as he stared at a spot across the room and realized that even though his mother had deserted him years ago, the scars of her betrayal were still an angry red. "I'm sorry," she murmured softly. "It must have been hard on you."

His smile was edged in bitterness. "You could say that."

"Are you and your father close?"

His rueful gaze returned to hers. "Are you kidding? No one gets close to my father. Least of all me. You see, I had the misfortune to look like my mother. I was a constant reminder of her." His mouth twisted in a crooked mockery of a smile. "Oh, he did the right thing and taught me the corporate ropes so I could climb the ladder of success he built, but he never once showed me any love. And Amy was in the same boat, so we just gave our love to each other." He laughed shortly. "That was okay until she met Stephen. And then I was right back where I started."

Lindy was silent, unsure of what to say when confronted face-to-face with his hurt.

Suddenly Zade was aware he'd said too much. "I'm sorry," he blurted into the silence, sitting up straighter. "I didn't mean to burden you with my problems. God knows, you have enough of your own."

Lindy put down her spoon and dabbed at her lips with the napkin. She had the sneaking suspicion that Zade Wakefield seldom, if ever, opened up as he just had. "It's all right. I've talked a lot about my problems to you, too. That's what friends are for, isn't it?"

He looked at her for a long time, their eyes meshing while unanswered questions flowed silently from mind to mind. He leaned forward, resting his elbows on his knees. His voice was soft as he asked, "Is that what we are? Friends?"

He sounded unsure, she thought. Almost as if he didn't believe it, or as if he wasn't certain she'd given whatever it was between them the right name. In a moment of truthfulness with herself, Lindy acknowledged that she wasn't certain what it was either. Her voice was breathless as she countered, "Aren't we?"

His eyes devoured her face. He seemed to be weighing something in his mind. His smile, when it came, was wonderful—wide and white against the black brush of hair framing his upper lip. "I guess we are at that." The slight tension of the moment passed, and he indicated the almost empty bowl of soup on the tray. "Are you finished?"

She nodded. The tension-filled moment passed. She was helpless to change the feelings that had somehow taken root in her heart, and she was afraid to hope that they might be reciprocated. It was easier to ignore them—when she could. "I think so. It tasted delicious."

He stood up and reached for the tray. "I'll clean up the kitchen and check on you one more time before I go."

Her smile was grateful as she folded her right hand over her left, twisting her wedding ring around and around, suddenly at a loss for what to do with them. "I appreciate it. I'll have to make dinner for you some evening to pay you back for all you've done."

"Pay me back? Don't be silly. Josh already fixed me dinner." He couldn't tell her he would willingly pay her cold, hard cash just to be able to spend all his free time with her and Josh.

Lindy watched him leave the room, a tall, handsome man just learning to laugh. A man of position and wealth who would never fit into her coupon-clipping life-style. But when he left, he left behind a feeling that was both wondrous and frightening as it unfurled within her. He left her facing one irrefutable, laughable fact.

She was falling in love with him.

Her troubled gaze fell to her hands. Slowly, but with a sense of purpose, she drew off Randy's ring. After pressing it to her lips in a brief farewell, she placed it in the drawer of the bedside table. When she closed her eyes to sleep, she couldn't conjure up Randy's face. She didn't even try.

Zade lingered over the few dishes, wanting to make them last as long as possible. He didn't want to go home. Home. The house on the lake was anything but that. It was just a beautifully decorated house on the lake. Not home. He hadn't had a home since Margot. And even that had been a poor excuse, now that he was learning from the Scotts what a real home was like.

He folded the damp towel and left it to dry on the partition between the double sink, then left the room. Butter roused as he passed through the living room on his way to check on Lindy one last time. As Zade passed the cage, the bird gave out the gritted warning, "Joshua Scott! You stop that, right this minute!" Zade smiled. He had a feeling that phrase had been easy for the bird to learn.

Lindy's closed eyes and the rhythmic rise and fall of her breasts beneath the light covering of the floral sheet proved she was asleep. She had taken down her hair and it made a bold splash of color against the pastel print of the pillowcase. Drawn in spite of himself, Zade moved silently into the room and squatted beside the bed, gently tracing the arch of one winged, auburn brow with a fingertip. She stirred slightly and mumbled something in her sleep.

He gazed in tender musing down at her freckle-spattered face with the tilted little nose and the too wide mouth that was seldom without a smile. Funny. He couldn't remember how many women there had been in his life. Dozens, certainly. Yet he couldn't ever remember feeling this uncertainty before... this sense of indecision over how to handle things.

He knew by now he couldn't stay away from her, even though every instinct warned him that if he wanted his life to go on as it had been, he should run away from involvement with her as fast as he could. He agreed, with a bit of surprise, that they were friends. He didn't have that many friends, and the knowledge of her friendship pleased him. But still, he was unsatisfied. He was in limbo, waiting for an event that would make some course of action crystal clear. Maybe it was his baby he waited for—and the life he'd mapped out for their future.

He dragged in a deep chestful of air. The wait had been so long. Long…and lonely. One lifetime and nine months was a long wait for love. And now, to add to the already complicated mess things were in, there was Lindy and Josh. A woman and a boy who were filling the last weeks of waiting, filling the aching void in his life as no one ever had.

He was suddenly acutely tired of waiting. Never a quitter, Zade longed to throw away all the plans, all the months of anticipation that were turning sour as the woman who would have his baby stood by her threat to keep it. He waited daily for word that the possibility that was never far from his mind had become reality…the possibility that she might leave before he found her, and he would never get his child.

His eyes moved in gentle surveillance over Lindy's body. The promise of the life within her was manifested by the mound of her stomach, a sweet certainty. A certainty with infinite possibilities that teased Zade's mind, urging him to forget the unknown woman and his baby and settle for the reality within his grasp. Urgings that wouldn't leave him alone, despite his efforts to maintain a reasonable distance between himself and Lindy Scott, who, after all, was no different from any other woman.

Ahh…but she *was* different. He reached out and plucked a bright, bronze curl from the pillow, crushing it in a tender bondage of masculine bone and flesh. She was sunshine personified, bringing a radiance into his dull, work-oriented existence he'd never known before. She was whimsical magic as she teased him into loosening the laces of his life. She was joy—laughing at herself and teaching him to laugh. She was Lindy…just Lindy…and as his hungry gaze lingered on her lips, he knew without a doubt he could wait no longer to taste the other treasures he instinctively knew she had to offer.

He'd lost every battle he'd fought against her. Every ploy he'd tried to use for his own gain had backfired. He was tired of fighting the yearning growing inside him…the yearning to be filled with the wonder of her love. The yearning to know what it was like to be the core of Lindy Scott's existence and to have her as the hub of his. And the yearning that grew each time he was with her to fill her with himself. He was tired of fighting whatever it was that drew him to her. At this moment, all that mattered was the need to see if the taste of her mouth was as delicious as its tempting pink promise.

Action followed thought as Zade leaned nearer.

It was a light kiss, the merest brush of mouth to warm mouth. Like the promise, hers was warm, sweet…and soft… so soft…

Lindy felt a pressure against her mouth. A touch so light she might only be imagining it. Zade. Kissing her in a dream. She knew it was Zade because she could smell the tangy scent of his cologne. She knew it was a dream because only in a dream would he kiss her.

In the dream, she lifted her hand to his face, caressing his whisker-stubbled cheek with tentative fingers. He felt warm, real. She found herself responding the tiniest bit to the gentle pressure of his kiss. A tremor originating at the point where their lips touched began to ripple through her in wave after wave of pleasure.

Zade's hand moved between them to circle her throat, and he deepened the kiss in an involuntary gesture, transporting the gentle meeting of their lips from the testing stage to a state that definitely bordered provocation. As his mouth parted slightly over hers, demanding more, a low moan welled up from deep inside him as he felt her immediate response.

The sound, somehow too raw, too intense to be part of a dream, loosed Lindy from the tenuous bonds of sleep still binding her. Her eyes drifted open. She was in her room, her bed… Dear God! It wasn't a dream. Zade Wakefield's mouth covered hers; her hand rested against his face. Even as a fragile ribbon of need curled throughout her, a whimper—the prisoner of a building passion warring with a sudden surge of guilt—escaped her throat and was swallowed by his hot, searching mouth.

She turned her head away from him, causing his lips to brush against her jawline. Her breath came in quick bursts of air as she fought a feeling of panic, a sensation aided by the frenzied palpitation of her heart and abetted by the touch of his mouth resting in gentle torment against the spot just below her earlobe. Tears clogged her throat and burned beneath her tightly shut eyelids.

For long moments they stayed that way, both afraid to move. Both afraid that to say anything might be to say the wrong thing. Both desperately wanting the moment to end, yet needing it to go on forever. Both afraid to come to terms with the emotions ravaging their hearts, minds and souls.

Finally, Zade lifted his head, then, unable to help himself, dropped one last kiss to the sweetly curving line of her jaw. His long fingers moved from her throat to her rounded chin, forcing her to face him, to meet his eyes. His gray eyes were as bleak and desolate as the frozen tundras of the Arctic.

Her composure was fragile, held together by nothing but her will. A will no stronger than a dew-spangled spiderweb tossed by capricious breezes. Her eyes held the glimmer of tears and a question she vocalized with a single, softly spoken word. "Why?"

Rising from his squatting position, Zade sat down on the edge of the bed, uncertain if he could explain something he didn't fully comprehend himself. She didn't object when he took her hands, holding them in the nest of his large ones. Almost incapable of thought, let alone fabrication, he answered truthfully, "I don't know."

Her eyes, shot throughout with ruby shards from the glow of the lamp, begged for an explanation. She drew a tremulous breath. "You've told me you come over to be with me and Josh because you feel at home here, because you don't feel that way anywhere else. Okay," she nodded, "I can buy that. You don't have anyone at home, and everyone gets lonely sometimes. I get lonely myself...especially this past year. But a kiss...that's different. It's a loneliness for a different kind of companionship." She took a deep breath, bracing herself for her next statement. "I can't deny that I miss kissing... touching..." Her eyes fell from his in embarrassment at the stumbling concession.

"Making love." His voice, low and husky, sliced through her rambling efforts at rationalization to the very core of the matter. Her lashes flew upward, and her eyes, wide with shock, collided with the gray of his.

"Yes." The word was the barest thread of sound.

"I miss it, too," he told her.

Her brow furrowed in disbelief. "Oh, but *you*, I mean, surely you..."

Zade's mouth slanted slowly upward in one corner, in pure mockery of a smile. "Oh, yeah," he nodded. "I do. Sometimes." He raised one of her hands and pressed a kiss to her knuckles. His voice was a soft rasp as his eyes mated with hers. "But it isn't making love. It's having sex. There's a difference, Lindy, believe me."

She swallowed and freed her hands from his, lifting them to her hot cheeks and shaking her head slowly from side to side. "I can't believe we're having this conversation!" she told him in a mortified whisper.

Prying her hands from her cheeks with gentle insistence, Zade confessed, "Neither can I."

"Then why are we?" she asked, completely knocked off stride by his almost brutal honesty about his sex life.

He smiled, his eyes caressing the blush-stained curves of her face, finding unending delight in the fact that she was so easily disconcerted by talking about sex. She actually blushed. Entranced by each new, unfolding layer of her personality and the pattern of whiskey-toned freckles marching across the bridge of her nose, Zade answered somewhat distractedly, "Because you wanted to know why I kissed you, I think."

She nodded and moistened her lips. "Right. But you never did say."

"You looked so beautiful, I had to," he said with a half smile.

The answer caught Lindy by surprise. "I what?"

"Looked so beautiful," he repeated.

"I'm not—"

"Your hair was spread out over the pillow," he interrupted, raking his fingers through the vivid strands and brushing a fiery tendril away from her temple. The backs of his fingers stroked the upward sweep of a cheekbone. "Your skin...it's so smooth...so soft..." His voice trailed away and his silvery gaze found the surprise in hers as he confessed, "I've been wanting to kiss you for days now. Surely you know that."

"I thought so...the other night in the kitchen," she admitted, "but I still don't know why."

"I honestly don't know either, Lindy," he said with a sincerity she couldn't doubt. "That's why I stayed away so long this time. But I came back because I couldn't help myself. And I kissed you for the same reason. I can't remember wanting to kiss anyone as badly as I wanted to kiss you just now."

"You can't find me attractive," she said bluntly.

He lifted one black brow in question. "I can't? Why not?"

"Open your eyes, Zade!" she said a bit shortly, giving him a glimpse of the temper she claimed to have. "Look at me!"

He nodded slowly. "I have looked. And I've never seen anyone so vibrantly alive in my entire life. You glow, Lindy Scott. With health, happiness and a love of life that's contagious. And contrary to what you might think, it's very attractive. No, it's more than attractive. It's gorgeous. You're gorgeous."

Her anger fizzled out in the face of his directness, and Lindy was momentarily stunned into silence. "I'm not gorgeous," she came back at last. "Passably pretty on a good day, maybe. Besides, do you kiss every woman you think is gorgeous?"

Zade shook his head, and grinned. "Nah. Only the red-headed, pregnant ones."

"You're making fun of me," she said a bit sharply.

Zade saw the hint of anger once more. He was tempted to tease a bit, to provoke her, just to get a glance of yet another facet of her personality, but knew that it wasn't the time. He lifted her hand, turned it over and placed a moist kiss to the warmth of her palm. Their eyes clung as he said softly, "Never."

"But, Zade, I *am* pregnant," Lindy pointed out unnecessarily.

"I had noticed," he said, placing her hand on her abdomen, and resting his on top of it. "But you won't always be."

"No," she said, wondering what he was alluding to, "I won't always be." She waited for him to continue. When he didn't, she prompted, "So...what?"

Zade wasn't certain. But he had to answer her. And he had to be as truthful as he could. He smiled, a sexy flash of very white teeth against a blacker than black mustache. A smile that stole Lindy's breath. His thumb rubbed her hand in soft circles. "Sooo..." he drawled slowly, "I think I'll hang around for a few weeks."

"You wouldn't just..." she shrugged against the pillow, "just stop showing up one day, would you? It would kill Josh." *And me.*

Zade's face showed his surprise that she'd put into words the very thoughts he'd considered at first, back when he planned to take from them what he could without giving anything in return. Back before he learned that everything had a price...especially selfishness. He didn't know what tomorrow would bring in his strange relationship with Lindy and Josh Scott, but he knew he definitely wanted to be around to see. He couldn't promise he wouldn't leave, but he could tell her he wouldn't leave without explaining why.

"I'd never do that to you." He smiled again, stiffly, a smile like the ones he had tried the first few times she'd seen him. "I'm not going anywhere, Lindy, unless you don't want me here. I'd just like to be here with you for a while. To help you out these last few weeks. You could use the help with Josh, couldn't you?"

"Yes," she said, nodding slowly, her eyes stinging with the threat of tears.

"You don't mind if I still come over, then?"

Mind? She had almost gone crazy without him the past few days. "No," she said slowly, "I don't mind."

"Good," he said with a nod, rising from the bed and glancing at the gold watch on his wrist. "Do you think you'll be okay now?" he asked.

Her voice trembled the slightest bit. "I'm fine."

She didn't look fine, he thought with some concern. She looked beat, and somewhat sad. He didn't want to leave her. He wanted to go to her, stretch out beside her and hold her until she fell asleep. He wanted to draw the scent and sweetness of her into his very soul, the beauty of her cleansing his old hurts. Wanted her warmth to fill the coldness in his heart.

And, God help him, he wanted to kiss her until she couldn't breathe. Wanted to feel her naked beneath him as he possessed her and in turn became her possession. He wanted her—heart, body and soul. The realization came to Zade so strongly that he felt the blood drain from his face. He was even willing to pay the price.

Zade felt the need to get away, not to run from what his mind told him, but to revel in it. He wanted to sift through the past and let his newly found security rid him of the old hurts. Wanted to open his heart to the feelings she brought to his life. His smile was crooked as he said, "I'll see you in the morning, then."

Lindy nodded and murmured a soft, "Good night." Josh, she thought as she watched him leave the room. He would stick around because of Josh. Not because of her. A tiny, bittersweet smile lifted the corners of her mouth. She'd be a fool to think the kiss meant anything. A pregnant fool whose life was in such a mess she couldn't afford emotional entanglements with anyone—let alone falling in love with a man who could have anyone he wanted. Lindy knotted the sheet with her hands, damning the driver who'd killed Randy, damning herself for taking a stranger's money, and damning her heart for falling so easily for Zade Wakefield's charm and vulnerability.

Zade entered the living room and sank onto the sofa, resting his elbows on his knees and burying the heels of his hands into the burning sockets of his eyes. He hated to go home. Sleep had been illusive lately. Butter rang his bell and squawked, "Come here, Josh! Talk to me!" Zade, usually fascinated by the bird's pithy comments, barely heard. How long he stayed bent beneath the responsibility that came with the realization of his changing feelings, he couldn't have said. Nor could he have said just how many minutes were spent examining the tender shoots of feeling springing up in his heart. Exhausted at last by his mind's meanderings, he kicked off his shoes and stretched his long frame out on the plump sofa.

"Good night, Josh," Butter called, swinging upside down, and ringing his bell again.

Zade laced his hands beneath his head and crossed his ankles.

"Good night, Josh! Sleep tight!" the bird called more loudly.

Zade sighed and smiled slowly. "G'night, Butter," he said lowly, yet loud enough for the bird to hear. "Sleep tight. And don't let the bedbugs bite." He repeated Josh's nightly ritual with the bird, knowing he wouldn't shut up unless he was answered. Strangely, the small formality made him feel even more like a real part of the family. And he was beginning to think that becoming a real part of the family was exactly what he wanted to be.

Chapter Seven

"Momma...Momma...wake up!" Josh's soft, urgent command was accompanied by the insistent patting of his small fingers against Lindy's face. She lifted her lashes slowly and encountered her son's excited blue eyes so near her own that she could see the black rings around their irises. Smiling lazily, she reached up, threaded her hand through his silky blond hair and pulled him nearer for a good-morning kiss. "Morning, sweetie," she murmured through a yawn.

"Momma! Come into the living room. Quick!" Josh whispered loudly, ignoring both the salutation and the kiss.

The desperation in his voice finally penetrated Lindy's fog of sleepiness and alerted her to the fact that something was wrong. She sat up quickly and threw back the light covering. Butter. It had to be something wrong with the bird.

"Is Butter okay?" she asked as nonchalantly as possible as she swung her legs to the floor and stood up, searching with her toes for the terry-cloth slippers that were kept beneath the dust ruffle.

"Yeah!" Josh said, tugging on her hand. "It's Zade!"

Lindy's heart plummeted to her toes. "Zade? What are you talking about, Josh?"

"Zade's on the couch. I talked to him and he didn't move." The boy's sapphire eyes grew round and wide and his mouth dropped open with a sudden thought. "Do you think he's dead?"

"Of course not!" Lindy scoffed, grabbing up her robe from the foot of the bed where she'd thrown it the evening before. Her movements, as she tugged it on and tied it around her middle, were jerky, and her heart beat a staccato tempo of concern. Why was Zade on her sofa? Was he all right? She followed Josh quickly from the bedroom and into the living room, her slippers whispering across the floor.

She paused at the door, taking in the scene before her. Zade lay sprawled on the sofa, his feet dangling over the fat, stuffed arm, his hands folded and resting on the flat plane of his abdomen. His shirt, left partially unbuttoned from the night before, revealed a large portion of his chest, a chest that—along with the cloud of curly black hair covering it—thankfully moved up and down with the rhythm of his breathing. The even rise and fall of his chest and his discarded shoes beneath the coffee table were evidence that he had apparently spent the night right where he was.

Lord! He was beautiful, she thought, moving farther into the room. Magnificent. So wonderfully male that he stole her breath away. Before her senses could recover, Josh was bounding across the room, launching himself onto Zade's chest. His hands cradled either side of the sleeping man's unshaven face. Almost nose to nose, he began to shake Zade's head.

"Zade! Wake up!" he cried loudly. The effect was immediate as Zade's eyelids flew open, revealing a startled gray gaze with all vestiges of sleep wiped away by the worry in the child's voice. He sat up quickly, grabbed Josh by the shoulders and snapped out a terse question with wild-eyed concern. "Is your mother all right?"

Josh, startled by the gruffness of Zade's voice and the look in his eyes, could only nod and point toward the doorway. Zade's eyes followed the direction Josh indicated, his eyes lighting on Lindy, who stood just inside the doorway, her hands thrust into the pockets of a short-sleeved summer robe of brilliant turquoise seersucker.

The look in his eyes and the notably concerned sound of his voice when he asked Josh about her sent Lindy's heart sprinting forward in double time.

"Why did you—"

"Are you—" they both began at once, then stopped at the sound of the other's voice. They exchanged smiles.

"You first," Zade said, pulling Josh into a loose embrace between his legs and dropping a distracted kiss to his cheek as the child wrapped his arms around Zade's neck.

"Josh woke me up and said you were in the living room and he couldn't wake you up. He thought you were dead," Lindy told him, a half smile quirking the corner of her mouth and dancing in the depths of her eyes.

Reciprocal laughter shimmered on the silvery surface of Zade's eyes. "I was so tired, I think I was dead—dead to the world," he confessed. "When Josh woke me up, shaking me and hollering like that, I thought you were sick..." his voice trailed away as his eyes dropped to her stomach, "...or something."

The touch of his gaze on her body brought back half-remembered feelings that his kiss had evoked the night before. Feelings she should try to forget, not foster. "I'm sorry," she apologized. "He was so frightened, he barreled in here before I could stop him."

"So everyone's okay?" Zade looked from her to the boy in his arms for confirmation of his statement.

"I'm not okay. I'm *hungry*!" said Josh, who was always ready to eat as soon as his feet hit the floor in the mornings.

Lindy mentally held her breath, crossed her fingers in her pockets and asked, "Can you stay for breakfast?"

Glancing at the cypress wall clock, whose hands stood at six thirty-seven, he replied, "I have time, if you're sure it isn't too much trouble. I'm supposed to meet my lawyer at the courthouse at ten."

Lindy shook her head, the riot of curly red hair brushing against her shoulders. "I have to fix something for us. It's no trouble."

"Then I'd love to stay. Thanks."

Lindy accepted his thanks with a smile. "Feel free to use the bathroom. The towels are in the linen closet, and I think there's a new toothbrush on the top shelf of the medicine cabinet."

Zade ran his hand over the twenty-four-hour growth of beard shadowing his lean features and cocked an inquiring eyebrow. "I don't suppose you have a disposable razor?"

"No, but there are new blades for my Schick on the bottom shelf. Just make yourself at home. Josh, you use the little bathroom and then come with me."

"I wanna stay with Zade," Josh whined, looking up at the man who had become so important to him in such a short time.

Zade saw the combined dismay and reluctance on Lindy's face. After her statement last night, he knew she was afraid that Josh would become too dependent on him. He stood, holding the boy in his arms. His eyes glowed with a gentle understanding as they met hers. "Let him come with me," he offered. "I'll teach him how to shave."

Lindy's auburn brows drew together in a frown. "You're sure?"

"Positive."

"Okay, then." She glanced over at the clock and announced, "You have twenty-five minutes until it's ready. If you aren't through by then, I'm throwing it out!" Her smile was wide, beautiful and rooted in a happiness she was afraid to trust.

Almost twenty-five minutes to the second later, Zade and Josh entered the kitchen, which was redolent with the smell of sizzling bacon and freshly dripped coffee. Josh was ready for the day, clad in a pair of jeans and a striped T-shirt, his hair neatly parted and brushed. Zade's efforts, Lindy thought with a sudden sense of *déjà vu*. It almost seemed like old times—like it was before the accident. Randy usually took care of getting Josh ready. The fact that Zade saw to his needs this morning made it almost seem as if she and her son were part of a family once more—except there was no similarity between Randy's rugged, blond good looks and Zade's polished handsomeness, a handsomeness apparent in spite of the ravages of the night before.

His shirt was still jam-stained and wrinkled, but he had buttoned it and tucked it into the waist of his close-fitting slacks, and his loafers resided once again on his feet. His damp hair—he must have showered, she thought randomly, feeling another blush creep to her hairline at the picture it brought to mind—was neatly combed and his clean-shaven jawline invited a woman's touch.

Lindy, still in her gown and robe, hadn't had time to do anything more than give her teeth and hair a hurried brushing. She felt grungy, frumpy and worst of all…pregnant. Well, she thought, eyeing Zade with a jaundiced eye, not everyone could look like a million bucks when they first got up.

He caught her look and flashed her a heart-wrenching smile. Disconcerted at being caught staring, she asked tartly, "How do you like your eggs?"

"Basted," he said easily, reaching into the cabinet for a cup and pouring his coffee while Lindy broke two eggs into the hot bacon drippings. She was concentrating so hard on sloshing the hot grease over the tops of the eggs and testing their doneness from time to time that the sound of his voice caught her by surprise.

"How do you know when they're done?"

She jumped, gasped and turned toward the sound. Zade stood directly behind her, peering down over her shoulder at the skillet. He was so close she could see the tiny lines fanning out from his gray eyes and could smell the slightly flowery fragrance of the soap he'd used in the shower, a scent that was totally at odds with the masculinity oozing from every pore of his male body. Her flustered gaze dropped to his chin, and she gave a small cry of dismay when she saw a cut left by the razor's sharpness. Before she could think of the imprudence of her actions, she reached up and touched the place with tentative fingers.

"It's nothing," he said dismissively at her obvious distress. "It's just one of the hazards of shaving with bar soap instead of shaving cream. I'll live."

"Momma can kiss it and make it better," Josh said, pausing in his job of buttering the toast long enough to offer the piece of sage advice.

Zade flashed the boy a smile. "Can she do that?" At the child's emphatic nod, Zade smiled. "Good idea, Josh." His eyes locked with Lindy's, and a teasing, tender light entered his when he saw the rush of rose to her cheeks. "Just a tiny kiss is all it will take…it isn't a big cut," he explained with commendable seriousness. "Right…here." His finger pointed to the spot.

"Zade…" she began in a trembling voice.

"Don't you want it to be better?" he asked, mock disappointment in his gaze.

Knowing she was being manipulated because of her son's presence and excited by his suggestion in spite of herself, Lindy gave in with a sigh of defeat, raised up on tiptoe and, steadying herself by placing her hand on his chest, pressed her lips to the raw place on his chin. His hands came up to grip her upper arms in a gentle vise.

His skin was smooth and slightly cool against the warmth of her mouth and, like the rest of him, smelled of soap. Without thinking, the tip of her tongue touched his flesh. She heard the sudden intake of his breath; felt the instant acceleration of his heartbeat beneath her palm. He even tasted like soap, she thought, and his face, though freshly shaven, felt the slightest bit rough to her tongue's touch. Her own breath caught in her throat at the sudden longings spinning through her, longings that—even though it was crazy—he seemed to feel, too.

She pulled away, her eyelashes drifting upward with lethargic slowness. His gaze caressed each feature of her face gently, thoroughly. A masculine finger pointed to the underneath curve of his bottom lip near the corner. "I think I nicked it right here, too," he said softly.

Lost to everything but the man before her, and seeing nothing to mar his sexily-shaped lower lip, Lindy nevertheless helplessly rose up on tiptoe once more and pressed her mouth to the exact spot he indicated in a kiss that wasn't quite a kiss. The soft brush of his mustache was an erotic stimulant to her pulsing libido. She wanted more...wanted him kissing her back...

Josh called out an impatient, "Momma!" that neither Lindy nor Zade heard.

Right now she'd give twenty-five-thousand dollars *not* to be pregnant, she thought. Then she might at least have a fighting chance to pursue this thing that seemed to have sprung up between them. Lowering her heels to the floor, she ended the touch of mouth to mouth.

"Thanks." His voice held a breathless quality, almost as if he'd been indulging in some sort of physical activity—almost as if he might be as affected as she was.

She nodded and swallowed the lump of emotion choking her.

"Momma! Zade!" Josh yelled loudly.

Two pairs of eyes broke contact and focused on the child at the table, whose obvious need for attention finally penetrated the mood of the moment. "What is it, Josh?" Lindy asked, her mind still on the taste and feel of Zade Wakefield's flesh.

"I think you're burning Zade's eggs," the boy said soberly, pointing to a spot behind Lindy. She whirled around and saw that the eggs were a crispy brown around the edge and that the centers were almost completely hard. She'd have to fix him some more.

As she stared at the ruined eggs, Lindy faced the sudden realization that if she didn't get away from the flames of attraction blazing between her and Zade she would wind up the same way—burned beyond salvaging—or consumed completely by the conflagration. She wished it could be the latter, but at that moment would settle for just being scorched.

Thirty minutes later Josh and Lindy walked Zade to the door. He bent and swung Josh up into his arms, planting a kiss on his cheek before setting the child's feet to the ground once more. Lindy smiled. "I really appreciate all you did for us last night," she told him. "I don't know what I'd have done without you."

"No problem," Zade assured her, reaching out in an absent gesture to touch the curls gleaming like burnished copper in the early morning sun. "What do you have planned for this evening?"

Lindy shook her head in a negative motion, mesmerized by the look in his eyes. "Nothing special."

"If you can find a sitter, how about dinner…just the two of us?" he asked. "Something casual. Maybe catfish or Mexican."

A date. It was a date, wasn't it? Why was he doing this? For Josh? For himself? Why? At the moment, Lindy didn't care. He wanted to spend time with her and for now, that was all that mattered. She nodded with a smile of pure happiness. "I'd like that."

"So would I." The words were delivered seriously, soberly. Then, without any warning, and no fuss, he leaned down and brushed her mouth with a kiss so soft that if it hadn't been for the sudden racing of her pulse, she might have thought it was just her imagination. She watched him walk down the sidewalk to the Jaguar, get in and roar off into the bright spring morning. For the first time in a long while, Lindy felt the stirrings of springtime in her heart.

"It's got to be a man!" The bizarre, but true, observation was made by Amy's nurse, Phyllis, as she stood leaning against a filing cabinet, a can of soda in one hand, a sandwich in the other and a considering look on her pleasant features as she regarded the woman seated at the typewriter.

Lindy blushed, embarrassed at having been caught in the throes of a rather scandalous daydream in the midst of her lunch break.

"Aha!" Phyllis straightened and pointed a finger at Lindy, giving Joan, the bookkeeper, a wink and an I-told-you-so look. "Guilt. All over her face."

"Those are freckles, Phyllis," Lindy said with saccharine sweetness.

"C'mon, Lindy, 'fess up. Only a man can put that kind of look on a woman's face. So you might as well tell the truth."

Lindy sighed. She might as well give in and tell them *something*. This close inner-office teasing was part and parcel of the job, and she wouldn't get a moment's peace until she satisfied at least a portion of the rampant curiosity. "Okay, okay! So I was indulging in a little daydreaming."

A dual chorus of "Aaah…" followed the statement.

"C'mon, girls! Give me a break! Daydreaming is about all I'm allowed at this point," Lindy said dryly.

"Who was it about?" Phyllis asked. "I mean we know *what* it was about, but we don't know who with."

Lindy felt a blush rising. "Phyllis Jones, did anyone ever tell you you have a dirty mind?"

"Once or twice a day," the buxom blond said without a trace of contrition. She rested her palms on the edge of the desk and leaned toward Lindy. "Now are you gonna tell us about the guy, or are we gonna have to resort to torture?"

Lindy grinned. "I don't know. What's the torture?"

Phyllis glanced at Joan and wrung her hands together. "Well, I know this mad scientist who could tie you to a chair and give you a shock treatment to scramble your brain—thus robbing you of your daydreams."

Lindy shrugged and managed to keep a straight face as she said, "He'd have to catch me first." This brought a hoot of laughter from Joan.

"Okay," Phyllis said, "you leave me no alternative. I'll put the coffeepot under lock and key."

"Aaagghh...not that!" Lindy said, throwing up her hands in mock horror. "You win! I'll tell you everything."

Phyllis planted her ample bottom on the corner of the desk. "Who is he?"

"Anything but that," Lindy amended, her voice and attitude going immediately from teasing to serious.

"Why don't you want us to know who he is?" Joan asked.

Lindy toyed with the crust of her sandwich. "I'd just rather not say." Her eyes begged for understanding. "Just in case it goes nowhere. You understand, don't you? I don't want you all feeling sorry for me." Her worried gaze moved from one woman to the other.

"Sure." Phyllis reached out and patted Lindy's hand affectionately. "So tell us what he looks like. Or is that confidential, too?"

Laughing, Lindy succumbed to the temptation to spread her happiness and good fortune with the world. "He's gorgeous! Tall, dark...gray eyes, a wonderful build...and he's so good with Josh it's unbelievable."

Phyllis and Joan exchanged smiles at the enthusiasm and joy in Lindy's voice. If anyone deserved a break, they knew she did.

"So how do you feel about him, besides wanting to jump his bones?" Phyllis asked with her usual bluntness.

A look of wonder stole across Lindy's features. "I think I'm in love," she told them dreamily. "I really think I'm in love." Her smile was bright, happy, a typical Lindy smile as she confessed, "And the funny part is, he seems to have a penchant for pregnant ladies. Isn't it crazy?"

The Mexican restaurant was typical of the popular southern chain; white plaster walls, tile floors, clusters of dried chili peppers and piñatas. The menu was as varied as individual tastes, for one price entitled customers to eat all they wanted of just about anything Mexican. Lindy, whose platter looked as if she'd tried at least one of everything, had just spread her napkin out when a feminine voice said, "Zade! What are you doing here?"

Lindy's gaze lifted to see a petite and stunningly beautiful blonde—one whose name escaped her but whom she had seen several times in the office over the past two years—standing beside their table, holding hands with an attractive but slightly overweight man. The woman and her male friend were obviously friends of Zade's. Lindy gave an inward groan. She really didn't think she was up to this.

Snatching a quick glance at Zade she saw a smile of welcome brighten his handsome features. He rose from his seat and gave the woman a hearty kiss on the mouth in spite of the half-hearted threats from her escort.

"Lindy Scott, I'd like you to meet Paul Matthias and his wife, Tammy. Paul, Tammy, this is Lindy, a friend of mine."

Paul and his wife were the epitome of social politeness as Lindy smiled and acknowledged the introductions with what she hoped was the proper response. What must Paul Matthias and his wife think? What *could* they think but the truth? For some unknown reason, their long-time friend had asked a pregnant woman out for dinner. Lindy wanted to crawl into a hole. If only she weren't pregnant. If only she could meet his friends in a few weeks....

"Sit down and have a drink," Zade suggested. "The sitter won't leave the little demons until you get home with the money...no matter how badly she wants to," he teased.

"Low, Wakefield, low," Paul said, grinning. "But true." He and his wife settled themselves at the table amid a burst of laughter. They ordered drinks and Lindy and Zade continued their meal, while the newly arrived couple eyed Lindy covertly.

"Lindy is Amy's receptionist," Zade said, as if the statement—totally unrelated to the real issue—cleared everything up satisfactorily. It didn't. Lindy didn't miss the still-unanswered questions lurking in two sets of eyes.

"I know Lindy from the office," Tammy said, offering Lindy a friendly smile in spite of the reservations she seemed to be feeling over this unexpected turn of events. "How are you?"

"Fine." Lindy did her utmost to conceal the embarrassment gripping her.

"When is the baby due?" Tammy asked, a look of genuine interest in her blue eyes.

"Less than a week, now."

Tammy moaned. "I can't believe it! You look great! I looked like a miniature blimp by the time I was as far along as you. It must be nice to have all that height."

"It does have its advantages," Lindy said, trying her best to loosen up in the face of the woman's friendliness. She found it hard to do, however, since she still felt the scrutiny of the woman's husband, who somehow managed to carry on a conversation with Zade and look her over at the same time.

"Haven't we met before?" Paul asked suddenly, his piercing blue eyes probing Lindy's with an intensity that left her more than a little disconcerted.

Zade and Tammy looked at each other and moaned at the clichéd question. "That line went out with corsets and hoopskirts," Zade observed dryly.

"Come on!" Paul said with a grin. "I'm serious. I think I know the lady." He turned to Lindy once more. His smile was friendly, teasing. "Do I know you?"

Lindy raked back the forever-loose strand of hair in a gesture that betrayed her nervousness and regarded him thoughtfully for a moment. There was something familiar about him. Something she couldn't put her finger on. "No," she said at last, "I don't think so." She offered him the smile that had first captivated Zade. "Maybe I just have one of those common faces."

Paul, astounded by the transformation, said huskily, "Lady there's nothing common about your face."

Zade heard the sincerity in his friend's voice. It seemed that Lindy had made another conquest. He was glad. Approval by his best friends was important, although even if Lindy hadn't won them over, it wouldn't have made any difference. His lif was so intricately bound up with hers, that nothing short of death could alter the course fate seemed to have set them on. "So how do you feel about the case?" he asked Paul, feeling that Lindy and Tammy were hitting it off well.

Lindy, who was just beginning to feel a bit more comfortable with the situation and was telling Tammy Matthias about Josh, felt her heart skip a beat at Zade's casually posed question. Her eyes moved from one man's face to the other. Whatever Tammy was saying was completely lost by the unease sweeping through her. Case? What case?

"Summations are tomorrow. We'll get what we want, no doubt about it. We have the law on our side."

A lawyer, Lindy thought. Paul Matthias was Zade's lawyer. He was trying the case Zade told her about. The case about the faulty wiring. It was nothing, yet the very fact that Paul was a lawyer made Lindy uneasy. And as nice as Zade's friends seemed, she wished they would hurry with their drinks and leave.

"Money isn't the real issue here," Paul was saying to Zade. Absorbed with her thoughts, his voice jolted Lindy back to the present with a statement dredged from her past. A statement whose very tone, cadence and innuendo had been indelibly printed into her mind...a statement that caused a frisson of fear to scamper down her spine as she knew suddenly and without a doubt why Paul Matthias seemed familiar to her...and why he thought he knew her. Paul Matthias wasn't just a lawyer. He was *the* lawyer who had talked to her the day Amy called. His was the voice threatening her with a lawsuit if she didn't comply with the terms of the agreement to give up the baby.

From a distance, Lindy heard the undertones of talk and laughter and clinking china. The combined scents of tobacco and spices assaulted her. She forced down a bite of enchilada and reached for the cool moisture-beaded glass of tea. The room felt suddenly stuffy...it was closing in on her...smothering...Her head began to spin.

"Are you okay?" Zade's voice, coming from the center of a vacuum, sounded concerned and caring.

"I—I'm not feeling well all of a sudden," she answered truthfully, barely able to focus her gaze on him. *Oh, God! Just get me out of here!*

"She is awfully pale," Tammy said to the two men before turning to Lindy. "Is there any pain?"

Lindy gripped the napkin in her lap and shook her head, her mind whirling with a whole barrage of new realities. If this was the lawyer representing the father of her baby, then *he* could be anyone. Anywhere. It had never really crossed her mind that she might possibly pass him on the street or, like tonight, could be sitting beside him at a restaurant without knowing it.

"Is it another headache?" Zade asked, regarding her pale features with a worried frown.

Lindy grabbed the proffered excuse thankfully. "Yes," she lied.

"Damn!" he swore. "She has these terrible headaches," he explained to the couple.

"Look, Zade, you take Lindy on home. I'll pick up the tab," Paul suggested, concern etched into his face.

"Good idea." Zade rose and pulled out Lindy's chair, draping his arm around her shoulders and guiding her from the restaurant, leaving the explanation to his friend. Once out the door and into the comparative sanctuary of the outside, Lindy drew in a deep breath of the warm evening air.

"Better?" he asked, leading the way to the Jaguar.

"A little," she said. Then, because he looked so worried, she added, "Maybe I just got too hot or something."

"It was pretty stuffy in there, not to mention all the cigarette smoke," he said, glancing at Lindy as he unlocked her door. He helped her in, shut the door and, rounding the hood of the car, got in beside her. The engine purred to life as her head drooped onto the back of the seat.

"Close your eyes and rest until I can get you home," he commanded softly. "And tomorrow you tell Amy about these headaches. I don't like the fact that you're having so many of them."

"I'll be all right," she protested.

"But you aren't! I want you to tell her," he pleaded, reaching out and taking her hand in his. Their gazes met and melded. Something powerful flowed from hand to hand, eye to eye. "Please."

The single, low spoken word was Lindy's undoing, coupled as it was with his obvious concern. Her eyes filled with tears she couldn't hold back, tears that welled and spilled over the dam of her long lashes. It had been so long since anyone had been concerned about her. So long since anyone cared. It seemed as if she'd been single-handedly holding the whole world together ever since the accident. The tears cascaded down her cheeks in an ever increasing torrent, even as she tried to console herself with one thought. Zade was here now. She could count on him...just as she had last night.

He swore at the sight of her tears. Whipping the car into a nearby parking lot, he pulled her into his arms, covering her wet cheeks with kisses and blanketing her fear with soothing words whispered into her ear.

What am I going to do? The question, as it usually did when she asked it of herself, found no answer. But this time was different. The encounter with the lawyer had been just a little too close for comfort. The unknown man was no longer a nebulous threat. Recognizing Paul Matthias as the voice on the phone had altered the threat of discovery from a possibility to the realization that it could very easily become reality.

Zade held her trembling sob-racked body, his heart aching at what she must be feeling. It had all finally gotten to her, he thought. Her husband's death, Josh's surgery, the responsibilities that grew greater and greater each day. He wanted to keep her from hurting, wanted to protect her from worries, wanted to hold her like this forever...and longer.

He finally acknowledged the newly discovered fact that had been hovering on the fringes of his mind and emotions. Not all women were alike. Deep down, he'd known it all along, and knowing Lindy only reinforced the fact. He knew something else, too. Some women were born with the ability to master corporate matters, some were born with all the fortitude and courage to face life and death every day, as Amy did, and some were born with the inherent traits that made them perfect candidates for the home and family. Lindy was one of those women. She was a woman who breathed the essence of home into a structure of wood and brick. She had the enviable capacity of making motherhood look easy. Neither were small feats when you considered the love and dedication both jobs entailed.

He wondered suddenly about the woman carrying his baby. Was she anything like Lindy? Her attitude suggested she was. Thinking of the unknown woman dragged up the question never far from his consciousness the past few days—the question that rose up and demanded an answer. Had he acted selfishly to expect the woman to give up a part of herself? He was beginning to think so. He knew now that asking a woman to give up her child was asking a lot, even if there was the exchange of money.

So where do you go from here, Wakefield?

He didn't know. He had to think, and he couldn't sort out his own feelings while helping Lindy struggle with hers. He didn't know where he would go from this point, but he knew without a doubt that he wanted Lindy Scott to go with him.

The whispered endearments and words of comfort spoken by the man holding her so tenderly in his arms finally began to ease Lindy's anguish. She wiped her streaming eyes with a tissue and snuggled deeper into the solace offered by Zade's arms...arms that held her tenderly, possessively. Strong arms that belonged to her savior in a starched shirt.

Chapter Eight

Zade rolled over onto his back, dragging the sheet with him. The bold navy-maroon-and-brown striped fabric twisted around his lean hips, molding his lower body intimately. He smothered a yawn, and folding his arms behind his head, stared unseeingly up at the ceiling.

Lindy. He smiled as he thought of her. He would see her soon. It was her day off, and he was taking her and Josh on a picnic. An historic event for several reasons.

He laughed, the sound ringing with masculine joy as he bounded naked from the bed and headed for the shower. As the hot water sluiced down the hard planes of his body, his mind was filled with her…the graceful way she moved despite the fact she was in the final stage of pregnancy. The curly vibrancy of her red hair. The way the honey-colored freckles marched across the bridge of her nose. The way it crinkled when she laughed.

She entranced him totally, and for the life of him, he couldn't figure out why or how. He'd courted scores of women more beautiful, more sophisticated, more the type of woman he'd always been drawn to. So why did he find his heart racing when she walked into a room? Why did he want to keep her from any more hurt? And why did he find himself just wanting her so badly?

Even more amazing was the ease with which he'd confided to her about his mother. It was strange, this mesmerizing effect she had on him. Unbelievable, the way something in her seemed to whisper that he should tell all his secrets to her, lower all the barriers he'd erected around his heart. Not even Margot knew of his loneliness as a child and how starved for love he had been after his mother left him and his father. Feelings that had only intensified over the past years with the help of his ex-wife's duplicity. Feelings Lindy was eradicating as he learned to trust again, to show his feelings, and to believe in the possibility of love. He was learning that not all women cheated and lied. He was quickly finding that those who did represented the minority, not the majority, of the women of the world.

And, as his knowledge of Lindy and womankind grew, so did his uncertainty about the wisdom of his carefully planned campaign to get his child. He suffered twinges of doubt about it all from time to time, in spite of his vehemence about seeing justice done and getting what he had bought and paid for. And all the twinges of uncertainty could be traced back to the first time he'd set eyes on Lindy Scott. She wanted and loved the child inside her—that much was blatantly obvious. That she would be destroyed if she lost it, equally so. Knowing how she felt made him wonder about the mother of his baby. Would she be devastated if it was taken from her? He seriously questioned the advisability of carrying through his self-imposed vendetta. And on a Thursday morning in early April when he was about to take Lindy and Josh on a picnic, he was ninety-nine percent certain that Lindy Scott had somehow managed to change his mind about the whole thing.

She was all women, he thought, turning off the water and reaching for a large bath sheet. He rubbed it briskly over his firmly muscled body, recalling the soft pliancy of her mouth when he had kissed her the night of her headache. Her response, like the kiss, had been unplanned, as was the lightning response of his body just now at the memory of that same kiss. And, the next morning at breakfast, when she had kissed his chin at Josh's suggestion to make it better...

She could destroy a man's resolve with just a touch. For all that she had been married and had a child, there was still a certain shyness when it came to being physical. A shyness that, knowing her as he was beginning to, he felt certain had a lot to do with the pregnancy and the fact that she was bound to feel uncomfortable trying to establish a new relationship with one man, while expecting the baby of another.

He groaned and willed his body to normalcy even as he wondered just how it would be without the pregnancy between them. He had a feeling there was a lot of passion hidden behind the domestic, motherly facade she presented to the world. And by damn, he intended to taste it. The intent was so strong within him that Zade didn't even stop to wonder if she felt the same. She had to.

He dressed hurriedly in white tennis shorts and a striped knit shirt, slipping his bare feet into battered Topsiders. He couldn't get ready fast enough. Lindy and Josh were waiting for him, and he couldn't wait to be with them because he loved them so much.

He stopped dead in his tracks. What he had suspected for several days finally struggled to the surface of his consciousness, demanding recognition. He hadn't planned on this when he had begun seeing her. As a matter of fact, it was the furthest thing from his mind, but nevertheless, there it was.

He loved her. Zade let the acceptance fill his mind and soul. With his mind's endorsement of what his heart had known for a long time, Zade was filled with a sense of peace he had never experienced before. Lindy. He wasn't certain how it happened, but somehow, a red-haired, freckle-faced woman who saved soup labels had —in just three short weeks—in·

sinuated herself so firmly into his life he couldn't imagine living without her.

The changes she had wrought in him were nothing short of miraculous. She had given him a new outlook on the world. Old, common things were seen through the excitement mirrored in her eyes. The humdrum became fun as he found himself drawn into her web of domesticity—and loving every moment of cleaning the kitchen, and getting Josh ready for bed. She made the impossible things of life look within reach as he watched her faithfully enter every contest and sweepstakes that came along with a gleam of excitement twinkling in her eyes as she fantasized about how she would spend her money. After all, someone had to win, didn't they?

It was the same every day. He couldn't wait to just be with her, to feel the soothing balm of her personality as it worked to take away the frustration of his work at the day's end. He didn't even mind telling her about the problems he encountered. Something about her actually encouraged his confidences. Perhaps, he thought, pursing his lips in a considering manner, it was the way he felt she really listened. Or maybe it was the gentle understanding of her smile.

Her smile. The smiles Lindy bestowed upon him were as varied as the facets of her personality. The tender smiles soothed him. Her saucy smiles taunted him. Her self-deprecating smile infuriated him, and the slight, half lifting of the corners of her wide mouth teased him with the promise of passion.

He sighed. Somehow, in less than one month, this one woman had turned his world upside down and put all his distrust and insecurities to rout, filling him instead with a new zest for life and its offerings—good or bad. The realization made him feel almost giddy with relief that she had rescued him from becoming a hard, insensitive tyrant—the future that had stretched before him before the advent of Lindy Scott into his life.

The important thing, he knew, was to make certain she was always there for him. And he intended to do just that. He couldn't wait to see her face when he told her how he felt. And that moment would be soon.

But first things first, he thought, reaching for the receiver of the bedroom extension and dialing the number of Paul's office.

"Reynolds, Matthias and Cope."

"Kitty? Zake Wakefield. Is Paul in?"

"Oh, I'm sorry, Mr. Wakefield. Didn't he tell you? He promised Mrs. Matthias a long weekend when he finished up your case. They've flown to Vegas for a few days."

"He did mention it to me, but it completely slipped my mind," Zade said. "Thanks, Kitty. I'll give him a call Monday."

Zade replaced the receiver. Damn! He needed to talk to Paul, but a few more days shouldn't matter one way or the other. He raked his hand through the thickness of his hair and rose from the side of the bed.

He could still go ahead with the rest of his plan. He could still ask Lindy to marry him this afternoon.

He loved her.

Fact. Plain and simple. He wanted and needed her in his life, and he thought she was feeling the same thing he was. At least, all indicators seemed to point in that direction. The most sensible thing to do, the logical thing to do in a case like that was to marry. Having her and Josh to care for and to have care for him, would more than make up for the fact that he wouldn't have his own child by the surrogate mother. The driving need to find out who she was and persuade her to give up his baby had lost its importance with the prospect of having Lindy for his wife and having the chance to father Josh and the new baby. Of course, he would always wonder... But then, he and Lindy could have a baby of their own one day.

He rose from the side of the bed and headed for his car. He'd take care of today, and first thing Monday morning, he'd call Paul and drop the pursuit of the woman who carried his child.

* * *

The Family Park, just off Airport Road, was all but deserted when Zade pulled into the parking lot.

Josh, always glad for a day away from the day-care center, was primed and ready for the day's outing, barely letting Lindy get the door open before he was crawling over her, his sneaker-clad feet hardly hitting the asphalt before he was racing out across the large expanse of grass to the huge, covered pavilion.

"Slow down, Josh!" she cautioned, before turning to Zade and rolling her eyes upward in exasperation.

He offered her a lazy grin. "Let him go. He'll be okay." He uncoiled his long form from the car's interior and stood, leaning one forearm on the gleaming top as he let his contented gaze take stock of his surroundings. Spring was in full swing, as was evidenced by the light green of new leaves, the mauve-pink blooms covering the otherwise naked branches of the redbud trees, and the lacy-looking dogwoods whose white-petaled blossoms danced in the soft breeze, their faces turned upward toward the warming rays of the sun. It promised to be exceptionally warm for that time of the year if the nine o'clock temperature outside the bank and the weatherman's predictions could be counted on.

Lindy got out of the car and stood staring across the shiny silver top at the man who meant so much to her and Josh. A slight wind ruffled the ebony blackness of his hair and his eyes mirrored an inner serenity, a softness not there before. He looked relaxed, happy. Nothing at all like the man she'd first seen in Amy's office. That man wouldn't have dreamed of going on a picnic with a pregnant woman and a small boy. He would have been too busy worrying about his motels.

As if he felt the touch of her gaze, Zade turned and looked at Lindy, a slow smile tugging at the corners of his mouth and causing the appearance of fine lines at the corners of his eyes. "You actually glow," he told her in a husky voice.

The unexpected compliment caught her by surprise. She wrinkled her nose at him. "Is that supposed to be a compliment?" she teased.

"I guess it is," he said with a nod. "The sun makes your hair look on fire."

"Yeah?" she queried with a skip of her heartbeat and a lift of her auburn brows. "Well unless you want to see my skin look on fire, I suggest we move out of this sunshine."

The warm sound of his laughter sent ripples down her sensitive nerve endings as he reached inside for the keys and, going to the trunk, began to unload the picnic trappings.

"Want me to take something?" she asked, her long legs hurrying to keep up with his even longer strides as he carried a large picnic basket and an ice chest toward their destination.

"You can take your sweet little tush and park it at one of the tables," he tossed over his shoulder, along with another heart-stopping grin.

Lindy halted dead in her tracks. Sweet tush? Oh, Lordy! Did he really think she had a sweet tush? How could he even tell?

"Coming?" he called, startling her out of her thoughts. The sight of him standing in the sunshine regarding her with a quizzical expression drew Lindy toward him like metal filings to a magnet. She stepped beneath the cooler shadows of the open wooden structure, determined to act normally if it killed her. And it just might. How could she act normally when every time he looked at her, she quivered like a bowl of Josh's favorite raspberry Jell-O?

"I wanna play on the swings," her son moaned plaintively.

"I want a snack," Zade said.

"A snack?" Lindy's voice and eyes reflected her disbelief. "It's only ten o'clock. You just had breakfast."

"How 'bout it, son? Want a snack?" Zade asked.

"Yeah!" Josh hollered, jumping up and down. "I wanna grape soda."

Son? Funny he should call Josh that, Lindy thought, because that's exactly how she was beginning to think of them. Father and son. Zade was wonderful with Josh. Loving, helpful and stern when necessary.

"Mom! I wanna grape soda!" Josh cried, tugging on the

leg of her bright-yellow shorts. Lindy bestowed equally disapproving frowns on the man and the boy at their strange cravings.

Undaunted, Zade offered her a beguiling smile and said softly, "Loosen up, Mom. This is a picnic." Then before she could respond in any way, he leaned forward and brushed her lips with his before retracing his steps back to the car for the rest of the picnic gear.

"Zade!" Lindy wailed moments later as she watched him unloading one of the sacks. "Three kinds of cookies! That's ridiculous!"

A stricken look crossed his features and he jerked his head once in the direction of a nearby tree. "Ssssh. Don't let those little guys in the tree hear you. Old Ernie tried to get me to buy five."

Josh's eyes rounded at the mention of the famous cookie elves that lived and worked in a hollow tree.

Laughter spewed from Lindy's peach-glossed lips. Unbelievable! Zade Wakefield actually teasing...joking...and doing it very well. It promised to be a wonderful day.

And it was. After their snack—consisting of a sampling of all three kinds of cookies, a few potato chips and a soft drink each—Zade and Josh played on the swings while Lindy sat in the shade and watched, laughing at their antics and listening with pure enjoyment to the boyish squeals of pleasure and the deep, masculine sound of Zade's laughter. They slid down the slide, then dabbled at the water's edge, looking for tadpoles while Zade bemoaned the fact he hadn't brought along a fishing pole. With a smile, Lindy assured him the small body of water couldn't possibly harbor any fish.

She watched, her heart filled to overflowing with a love that grew greater with each passing moment. Love and an ever increasing sadness. If only things could be different. If only she wasn't involved in this mess...

"We're hungry!" Josh announced, running up to his mother and plopping at her feet on the tender shoots of new grass.

Her eyes widened with amazement. "You've got to be kidding!"

"Do we look like we're kidding?" Zade asked. He raised the bottom of his shirt and sucked in the hard flatness of his abdomen. "See? Nothing but skin and bones."

Skin and bones, indeed! Lindy thought. His stomach was tanned, firmly muscled and covered with a downy whorl of fine, black hair that trailed invitingly downward before disappearing into the waistband of the shorts. He was all muscle and man...deliciously masculine man.

Josh raised up his shirt and tried to suck in the roundness of his tummy. "Yeah," he nodded in sober imitation, "skin and bones."

"Does this mean it's lunchtime, guys?" she asked dryly.

"Suits me," Zade said, reaching down and offering her a hand up. "This playing is hard work."

They feasted on grilled hamburgers and all the trimmings before Zade and Josh made another round of the playground equipment. Then they took a walk, with Lindy accompanying them as they picked wild flowers and tried to identify each kind.

When Josh began to get cranky Lindy suggested that they spread out a quilt under a tree and take a nap. Only when Zade announced that he was sleepy, too, did the boy acquiesce.

They all stretched out on the quilt, Josh situated on the outside edge so "nobody would squash him," putting Zade and Lindy side by side. Which suited them both just fine. It was only a matter of minutes before Josh was sound asleep.

Flat on his back, Zade lifted his head, turning to see if Lindy was awake. He encountered her warm, sherry gaze. He smiled and whispered softly, "Hi."

"Hi," she whispered back, rolling to her side and raising herself up on one elbow. There was happiness glowing in her eyes, along with the warmth of gratitude. "You're wonderful with him. Thank you."

Embarrassed by the praise and the thanks, Zade shrugged. He hadn't spent the time with Josh for either. "You're pretty wonderful, yourself,'' he told her, turning on his side so that they lay facing each other—thigh to thigh, heart to heart. Reaching for some of the wild flowers they'd picked earlier, he tucked them behind her ear, then cocked his head sideways as he considered his handiwork.

"Me?" she asked breathlessly. The tender petals felt cool against her temple. He was so close she could feel the warmth of his body. So close the crisp hair of his bare legs tickled the smoothness of hers. Close...so close. Her eyes caressed the bold bone structure of his face before finally meeting his.

"You."

"Why?"

"Oh," Zade said musingly as he reached for a dandelion that had fallen from behind her ear, "because you're bright and sunshiny and happy all the time."

"I'm not."

"Well, most of the time, then." He smiled. "You've got to remember that I haven't seen that temper you're supposed to have."

"Stick around, bud," she said with a lift of her brows.

He nodded slowly. "Oh, I intend to. Forever." Then, as if he'd just commented on the weather instead of making such an earth-shattering statement, he commanded softly, "Tilt your head back. I want to see if you like butter."

Her emotions reeling from his comment, Lindy was helpless to do anything but obey. As he lifted the dandelion beneath her chin to initiate the age-old childhood ritual, she reached for his wrist. His flesh was warm to her touch. Their eyes tangled. Breath tangled. Their heartstrings, so long in tune with each other, reached out and tangled.

Determinedly, Zade moved the flower beneath her chin. The yellow of the dandelion petals was reflected onto the creamy flesh of her neck. His eyes met hers. "You like butter."

She nodded.

His free hand came up to rest against the hollow of her throat, his fingers brushing the sweet, curving line of her jaw, his thumb caressing the side of her neck. His head began a downward scent as he breathed the words, "So do I."

Lindy's breath caught in her throat. His lips, warm and gentle, touched the underside of her chin, then inched upward in tender, tiny kisses toward her mouth. Her lashes lowered helplessly, her breath slowly escaped from her body and her heart revved to life once more.

He covered her jawline and chin with kisses, then opened his mouth and bit its soft roundness gently, perpetrating a subtle hunger that had nothing to do with food, as his teeth began a slow nibbling over her face.

She wanted him to kiss her, wanted him to... "Zade?"

"Hmmm?" he answered distractedly.

"What did you mean?"

His mouth moved to the corner of hers. "Mean? When?" His tongue touched the corner of her mouth, and traced the underside of her bottom lip.

"A few...minutes...ago." His mouth covered her bottom lip, drawing it into his mouth with a gentle suckling. She whimpered. "A-about..." Continuing its journey, his tongue slipped across her top lip. "Ohhh..." she moaned softly, struggling to finish the question before her thoughts flew completely from her mind, "...hanging...around forever..."

He lifted his head to look at her. Her hair straggled in curly disarray, her full lips were wet from his kisses and her eyes were hazy with the same desire racing recklessly through his veins and setting up an uncomfortable throbbing in the most masculine portion of his body. "Any objections?"

"Objections?" Lindy mouthed, so rattled by his nearness that she wasn't even certain what they were talking about.

"About me hanging around. Forever."

"How can I have objections when I don't even know what you're suggesting," she said breathlessly, hopefully.

His voice was a low rumble as he said, "I'm suggesting marriage, Lindy-love. My marriage to you. I'm suggesting that I adopt Josh and become a father to him and this baby." His large, warm hand came to rest on the rounded swell of her stomach.

Lindy's heart lurched. Marriage! Zade wanted to marry her! Surprise held her captive. As much as she might have wanted this, not even in her wildest dreams had she believed it would actually happen. He wanted to marry her! She'd like nothing better, but she had to know what motivated him to offer marriage. Was it just for Josh? "Why?"

"Why?" He smiled, his eyes crinkling in the corners. "Because you're 'sugar and spice and everything nice,'" he told her. Then when the seriousness of her expression registered on his mind, the laughter drained from his eyes and he spoke in a voice that trembled as he said softly, wonderingly, "Because I love you."

Lindy couldn't swallow for the lump of emotion clogging her throat. He loved her. He loved her! How had it happened? And again, why? The joy of the moment was suddenly overshadowed by the resurrection of her old insecurities.

"Why?" she persisted. "I'm not beautiful."

"You damn well are!"

"My mouth is too big."

"The better for kissing, my dear," he misquoted huskily.

"I have these freckles all over..."

He grinned wickedly. "I had noticed. And I'm dying to take an inventory of every single one of them. I'm going to mark each one with a kiss."

His teasing made it harder to pursue her interrogation. "I'm not well-bred."

"I'm not buying a horse. I'm marrying a woman."

"You don't even know me!" she argued, determined to clear up all her doubts. "I might be a terrible person." Her voice faltered. "I might have some deep, dark secret..."

He laughed. "That's another reason I love you. Your honesty and your sense of humor. You know, I'd almost forgotten how to laugh until you came into my life and reminded me how."

"Oh, Zade!" she cried softly, tears shimmering in her eyes.

Her teeth clamped down on her bottom lip as she realized the futility of it all. Why couldn't she have met him before? Why now, when her life was in such a mess? How could she tell him about being a surrogate mother? It wasn't the sort of thing you could mention in casual conversation. And he thought she was honest, for goodness' sake!

And what would he think of her if he did find out? And, even if he wasn't completely turned off, if he could somehow accept her folly, she would have to leave when the baby got here, and that would be the end. After all, she could hardly expect him, or any man, to give up all they'd worked for to follow her as she ran from her mistakes—as she ran for her life.

"Why the tears, Lindy?" his voice rumbled softly. "I didn't mean to upset you." He laced their fingers together and carried her hand to his lips.

Because I can't marry you. I love you, but I have to leave soon. She sniffed. "We hardly know each other, Zade, and marriage isn't something to go into lightly."

"You don't even have to love me back," he told her. "Just be there for me."

She stopped and swallowed. "I—I do love you back. But there's a lot more than my feelings and needs at stake here. There's Josh…and the…the new baby to consider."

"I have considered them," he assured her. "All I want is to take care of all of you, and to be able to come home to you every night. I've never felt like this before, Lindy—such contentment, such peace—as when I'm with you."

"Feeling peace and contentment isn't love, Zade," she reminded gently.

A note of impatience entered his voice. "I know that. There's more, so much more I wouldn't know where to begin." His lips curved up at the corners in a mocking smile. "Besides, I've got the hots for you so badly I'm about to go insane." He moved her hand to the evidence of his arousal straining the bonds of his snug-fitting shorts.

"Zade!" she admonished, shocked at his actions, yet secretly excited by this newly discovered power she wielded over him. She jerked her hand away, a bit alarmed at the passion careening heedlessly through her. Her cheeks burned with the dusky rose of embarrassment.

He chuckled softly. "Prude!"

"I'm not a prude! I'm pregnant."

"God, I know," he groaned. He placed his hands on her belly, smoothing over its full hardness. "I can't wait until there's nothing between us but a millimeter of air…and I can look my fill of you…touch you." His hands inched up to brush lightly over her breasts. Then, as if the touch crumbled the last vestiges of his restraint, he cupped their heavy fullness and rubbed his thumbs over their sensitized tips. His eyes closed, and with a groan of frustration, he released her and rolled onto his back, flinging one forearm across his face.

His voluntary nullification of the passion building between them was as stressful for Lindy as it was for him. She reached out and laid her hand on his chest, feeling the rapid pounding of his heart beneath her palm. Slowly, slowly, its rhythm returned to normal, and with the cooling of their need, came the return of reality.

She couldn't tell him about this baby's father. He might leave her and Josh without a backward glance. She couldn't imagine life without him, and knew she couldn't give him up until she was forced to. It was selfishness, the simple need to have him near as long as possible, that prompted her to make a deliberately misleading statement. "I'd like to think about it. Maybe…after the baby is born…"

Zade smiled, and reaching up and grasping the back of her neck, drew her face down until their lips met in a kiss of sweet promise.

Lindy's kiss held the warmth of her love and the still-simmering heat of her desire. The emotion, dampened somewhat, left behind the cooling ashes of sorrow as she confronted the fact that as much as she wanted what he did, it could never be. There was no way she could keep this baby and have Zade without explaining her unexplainable actions.

* * *

Dusk was drawing the gauzy veil of twilight over the end of the fantastic day when Zade pulled into Lindy's driveway. After his proposal they had both done their best to keep the mood between them light. Talk was open and easy, and they shared things they hadn't shared with anyone before. Zade learned about the accident that had taken Randy and forced Josh to have his three operations. Lindy learned of Margot and her destruction of her baby, along with the destruction of her marriage. Hearing the tale made her understand more clearly why Zade and Josh had taken to each other so quickly. Each met a mutual need of the other.

When Josh roused from his nap, they loaded the picnic gear and headed out Highway 270 West toward Lake Oauchita. Josh wanted to stop at the Mid America Museum, but Lindy insisted that they wait until another day. They drove to Crystal Springs on the lake just to look. The popular campgrounds wouldn't open until May, and Zade promised Josh they would camp one day soon, some time after Lindy had the baby and could go with them. Her heart grew heavy with the knowledge that the day would never come. They would be gone.

She was beginning to dream of a bath and bed long before Zade headed the car back toward Hot Springs. When he looked over and saw her head drooping tiredly against the back of the seat, he suggested, "How about a hamburger before I take you home? That way you won't have to cook and clean up the kitchen." Thankfully, Lindy agreed.

Hamburgers had been a wonderful idea, she thought as she preceded Zade and Josh into the house. She was bushed and she had been plagued off and on all day with irritating little pains. Her back and legs ached—probably from lying on the ground, she reasoned.

Zade saw how tired she was; guilt for putting her through such a long day swamped him. "I'm sorry," he apologized, pulling her up against him, and dropping a kiss to the top of her shining head. "I shouldn't have kept you out so long."

She smiled wanly at him, happiness in the depths of her eyes. "I wouldn't have missed it for the world."

"You go ahead and have your shower and get to bed, and Josh and I will unload the car. I'll get him to bed and wait until he falls asleep before I go."

Lindy was too tired to even pretend that the idea was anything but wonderful. "You're on," she said. A smile quirked her lips as she looked from one to the other. "But no bubbles, huh, guys?"

Zade feigned a wounded look and shook his head. "Rules, rules." He brushed her mouth with his. "Go on, babe. I'll check in on you before I go."

Lindy felt pampered, protected, loved. Hugging the feeling to herself—all the more precious because she knew it couldn't last—she headed for the bathroom.

While waiting for Josh to fall asleep Zade put away all the picnic supplies; no mean feat, considering he had to work around stacked egg cartons, empty coffee cans, and stacks of paper grocery sacks. He wondered why she saved it all, then decided to ask her at the first opportunity. That chore done, he swiped over the bathroom, and then went to check on Josh.

The child slept peacefully, his sheets kicked down around his ankles. Zade bent and dropped a kiss to one sleep-flushed cheek before stopping to peek in at Lindy.

She, too, slept, one hand beneath her cheek. As he watched, she stirred restlessly, then settled back once more as a soft sigh fluttered from her lips. He smiled, and closed the door. He let himself out of the house when all he really wanted to do was crawl into the double bed beside her and hold her until he fell asleep.

She wanted to think about his proposal. In a way, he couldn't blame her. They hadn't known each other long. But he knew she was what he wanted, what he needed.

He got into the Jaguar and turned the ignition. The expensive motor purred into life. She loved him, he thought, hanging on tightly to that thought. That was the important thing. The rest—their marriage—would all come sooner or later. Even considering her caution, he didn't doubt it for a moment.

Chapter Nine

When Lindy awoke Friday morning, a good thirty minutes later than she was supposed to, she should have had at least an inkling of what the day held in store for her. She wanted to linger in bed, reliving the day before—especially the moment Zade asked her to marry him. Some things deserved to be savored minute by minute, second by second. And yesterday had been one of them. She wanted to replay the scene in her mind, giving him a different answer. Unfortunately, the alarm had failed to go off, depriving her of those few, precious moments spent in that dreamworld somewhere between sleep and wakefulness.

The mumbling of unladylike curses under her breath neither revived the faulty alarm clock, nor gave back the lost time. The morning slipped another notch when Josh didn't have any clean jeans, and horror of all horrors, was forced—amid screaming refusals—to wear shorts to nursery school. And, when Lindy looked up briefly from pouring his juice and accidentally ran the glass over, puddling the sticky, orange liquid all over the table and floor, she began to wonder just who had perpetrated the conspiracy to make this the most miserably memorable Friday of her life.

"What's the matter?" Amy asked later that afternoon. She had just finished Lindy's weekly examination and was rapidly jotting down her findings in a bold, indecipherable scrawl.

"It's nothing." *Nothing except a misplaced file, a child who got sick in the waiting room, and this dull ache in my back.*

"Come on," Amy prodded, "tell me. Is it the boyfriend?" When Lindy's eyes widened in surprise, Amy shrugged. "Office gossip. You know Phyllis couldn't keep a secret if her life depended on it."

A bitter smile, one that somehow looked out of place on Lindy's face, twisted one corner of her wide mouth. "Good old Phyl." She met curiosity in her boss's blue eyes head on. "Life isn't fair!"

"True," Amy nodded sagely. "Be specific, please."

"Your gossip is right. There is a man." Lindy longed to confide to Amy that it was her handsome cousin who had turned her world upside down, but thought better of it. It wouldn't do to get anyone's hopes up over her soon-to-be-over relationship with Zade.

Amy's eyes gleamed with pleasure. "Aha! The plot thickens! So what's the problem?"

"What's the problem!" Lindy cried, scooting off the examination table and pacing the length of the small room. She pinned Amy with a disgusted stare. "How can *you*, of all people, ask such a question?" She stopped beside the table and struck the padded surface with a tightly clenched fist. "Damn!"

Amy rose from her chair, placed her arms across her breasts and leaned against the pale blue wall. "Come on, now, simmer down," she soothed.

Lindy continued to pace, her breasts heaving with the force of her impotent fury. She looked at Amy with angry, yet sorrow-filled eyes. She lifted her hands imploringly. "Why? Why did I find him so late?"

Amy was silent, helpless to offer any acceptable answers.

"He says he loves me. Can you beat that? And I know I love him." Shoulders drooping, she sagged against the examining table, losing the battle with her tears as her anger spent itself and sadness surged to the forefront of her seesawing emotions.

Two fat tears rolled down her cheeks. "He wants to marry me, and just look at the mess I've got myself into! Why did I have to meet him now? Why couldn't I have met him months ago when I first needed the money for Josh, before I committed myself to having a stranger's baby? If I'd met him sooner, I could have a home, a husband, and a new baby. *His* baby."

"Maybe—" Amy began in a consoling tone.

"No," Lindy said with a negative shake of her head. "I can't deal in maybes. I have to be realistic. And reality is that most men would find it hard to believe any woman would do what I've done." She sniffed and wiped at her eyes with trembling fingers. "And if he did believe it, and accepted it, then what? Could I ask him to give up his life and run away somewhere with me?"

Seeing the skeptical look in Amy's eyes brought a short, mirthless laugh from Lindy. "No. Of course I couldn't." Her fragile hold on what was left of her composure slipped away, and she dissolved into the relief of more than a year's worth of crying.

Amy's heart went out to the younger woman. As she held the sorrow-racked body in a comforting embrace, a line of poetry from her high school days flitted through her mind. "Oh what a tangled web we weave, when first we practice to deceive...."

Lindy turned the key in the lock of the apartment door and put her hands at the small of her back, arching her aching spine and trying to ignore the recurring twinges of pain that had plagued her from time to time all afternoon. Her day, off to a rotten start from the moment she realized she'd overslept, had progressed steadily downhill. Once or twice, she had wondered if she'd last, especially after her crying jag, which left her wrung out physically and emotionally. But she had made it, and now, she thought with a wistful sigh, there was only dinner and baths to get through before she could go to bed and hide her anxieties for awhile beneath the comforting blanket of sleep.

Josh raced ahead of her, making a beeline for the television with a burst of energy that irritated her. She couldn't remember ever feeling so energetic. She followed him inside, dropping her purse onto the sofa and kicking off her shoes. "What'll it be, Josh? Soup? Or a ham-and-cheese sandwich?"

The television blared loudly, interrupting her question and grating on her tautly strung nerves. Butter squawked his displeasure, and he and Lindy rasped an almost simultaneous, "Turn that thing down!" Lindy's mouth edged upward at the corners in spite of her weariness. Good old Butter had a lot of sense.

"Joshua Scott!" Lindy yelled over the sound of the Rifleman's shooting.

Josh turned, his attention obviously divided somewhat unequally between his mother's words and the draw of the television as he sneaked a peek over his shoulder. "Huh?"

"Ma'am," Lindy corrected sharply, automatically, while silently wondering if she would ever teach him any manners. "Do you want a ham-and-cheese sandwich or soup?" she asked more quietly.

"Both," he said unhesitatingly, flopping onto his stomach and propping his chin on his hands.

"Both," she muttered tiredly under her breath as she dragged her aching body toward the kitchen, the television blaring in the background. She was halfway there when the phone rang. Zade! He had promised yesterday to call as soon as he got back from his trip to Little Rock. A feeling of pleasure suffused her, reviving her weary body the tiniest bit. She lifted the receiver to her ear, a wide smile bringing the glow of happiness to her face. "Scott residence."

"Lindy? This is Amy."

Something, some inner radar, warned her that her miserable day was readying itself for another nosedive. Her voice was the merest thread of sound as she said, "Yes?"

"It came."

It came. Two short words. Blood pounded in a surge of panic through her veins. IT came. She knew what "it" was. Still, in a voice reedy with breathlessness, she asked, "What came?"

"The subpoena."

Lindy flinched as if she'd been struck, pain ripping through her—body, heart and soul.

"They brought it by the house about the time I got home." When there was no answer from the other end of the phone line, Amy asked, "Hey! Are you all right?"

All right? I'll never be all right again. My world is falling down around my ankles for the second time in my life, and you want to know if I'm all right.

"Lindy?"

"I'm fine, Amy."

"I don't have any choice now," Amy explained, almost apologetically. "I'm supposed to go to the courthouse next week and give the judge your name."

"I understand," Lindy said, her gaze moving around the cheerful kitchen like someone trapped and looking for a way out. "I really do."

I understand, but I can't bear this. Not today. I just can't. Her eyes filled with tears. God, she was so tired of tears. She'd cried enough today to last a lifetime. "Uh…look, Amy, I have to go," she lied. "Josh's soup is about to boil over."

"Sure." Amy was silent a moment, then said, "If you need me, give me a call, huh? Steve will understand if I need to come over for a while."

"I will."

"Promise?"

"Promise."

"Okay," Amy said, hesitant to sever the connection. "Take care."

Lindy replaced the receiver with amazing calm and without a goodbye. From the living room came a low montage of common, everyday sounds—the too loud television, Josh's delighted laughter, Butter's occasional squawk, demanding the boy's attention. Sounds whose very normalcy seemed blasphemous on a day that wasn't normal at all. Sounds that contrasted her safe, sane world against the catastrophic day she'd just experienced—was still experiencing. She became slowly aware of another, closer sound. The sound of slow, heavy pounding she somehow finally equated with the painful beating of her heart.

"I'm hungry!" Josh's voice roused her to the immediate need to fix him something to eat. She reached into the cupboard for a can of vegetable beef soup, automatically peeling off the label and adding it to the growing stack in the coupon drawer. *It came.* Her movements were steady, mechanical as she opened the soup, dumped it into a small saucepan, added the required amount of water and turned on the burner.

Subpoena.

She went to the refrigerator and took out the sandwich makings, smearing mayonnaise on the bread quickly, efficiently, layering ham and cheese and tomato and lettuce. Lettuce?

Next week.

Josh doesn't like lettuce.

Courthouse.

She took the lettuce from one sandwich, tossing it into the sink, and picked up a knife to quarter Josh's sandwich.

I don't have a choice.

She wasn't even aware that the knife had slipped, wasn't aware that she'd cut herself until she saw the blood oozing from her finger. She stood staring at it, unable to think of what she should do as it dripped onto the cutting board.

It came.

"Momma! Your finger's bleeding!"

The alarm in Josh's voice sliced through her numbness, and

her gaze flew from the concerned look on her son's face to her finger. It *was* bleeding. She turned on the faucet and stuck her hand beneath the cold running water. The coldness helped to erase the last of the blankness she experienced only seconds before. Thankfully, it was only a small cut. She wrapped a paper towel around it, urging a smile to her lips for Josh's benefit. He returned her smile, the small exchange restoring his normal equilibrium.

She glanced at the pan and saw that the soup was simmering around the edges, just hot enough. "Okay, kid, time to eat." The words were barely out of her mouth when a pain slashed through her, robbing her of her breath and forcing her hands to the countertop in a knuckle-whitening grip.

Oh, God! The baby! She wilted against the cabinet, dragging a deep draft of air into her oxygen-starved lungs as the hurting faded into nothingness. What a fitting finale to her day, she thought with a hint of her usual dry humor.

"Are you all wight?" Josh lisped, his eyes wide with unease.

A wavering smile trembled on her lips. "I'm fine. I'm going to dish up your soup. You eat while I go and see if Mrs. Hancock can keep you tonight."

"Why? Are you going someplace?"

Lindy nodded. "I'm going to the hospital later. To get our new baby."

"And your tummy won't be fat any more?"

Lindy reached out and ruffled his blond hair, her heart filled with love for the earnest-faced child gazing so hopefully up at her. "Nope. I'll be all skinny again."

He accepted her statement about the baby with an enviable insouciance, smiling up at her and climbing into the chair to wait for his dinner.

Luckily, Mrs. Hancock was at home and agreed to watch Josh when the time came. Lindy straightened the kitchen, then went to the bedroom and started packing a small overnight case. She was just closing the top when another pain, this one rooted deep within her, tried to claw its way out. She caught her bottom lip with her teeth and closed her eyes, wishing she'd taken the natural childbirth classes after all.

The sound of Zade's voice, breathless with panic, preceded him as he burst through the doorway scant seconds later. He found her doubled over the bed, her palms pressing into the softness of the mattress as she waited for the labor pain to subside. Pushing herself slowly upright, Lindy straightened and managed a weak laugh. "Your timing is fantastic."

He hurried to her side, drawing her into a loose embrace and brushing her lips gently with his. "You okay?" he asked, resting his chin on the top of her gleaming red head.

She nodded and laid her cheek against his chest. His heart sounded remarkably solid, stable, secure. Her arms crept around his hard middle. She nuzzled her nose in the soft hair emerging from his open-throated shirt, content to rest in his embrace and breathe in the spicy, masculine scent of his cologne now that the pain was gone and her mind was assuring her that everything would be okay now that he had come. "You smell good."

"I smell good?" he repeated disbelievingly, pushing her away a little and tilting her chin up so he could look in her eyes. "Is this it?"

"I think so."

"What are you going to do with Josh?"

"The landlady is going to watch him."

"Shouldn't I take you to the hospital now?"

Lindy shook her head. "No. They'll make me go to bed, and I like to walk."

"You like to..." Zade began, then shook his head in wonder. "Never mind... Look, I really think we'd be better off at the hospital."

"Not yet." He heard a bit of steel creep into her voice, the hint of the temper she was supposed to have.

His forehead wrinkled in concern. "What if we don't make it?"

Lindy laughed, a thin thread of a sound. "We'll make it. I promise. It doesn't take any time to drive to the new hospital."

"Famous last words..."

"Stop worrying," she said, her eyes smiling up at him before she loosened his hold on her and turned toward the suitcase.

"Don't touch that!" he bellowed.

She whirled in surprise.

He had the grace to look sheepish. "It's too heavy," he explained in a more normal tone.

"Look," she said, sighing, "why don't you go in and see about Josh?"

"What are you going to do?" Zade asked, having the distinct feeling that, like a child, he was being banished from the presence of the big people.

"I'm going to walk in the back yard and look at my flowers...pull a few weeds..."

His expression was one of disbelief. "You've got to be kidding!"

"I'm in no pain right now. The contractions are a good twenty, twenty-five minutes apart. I feel fine."

At the skepticism etching his features, she clutched his hands in hers, an earnest expression molding her features. "Please, Zade. Take the suitcase. Put it in the car, and go take care of Josh. Please."

"Okay," he agreed, obviously unhappy with the suggestion, but willing to do whatever would make her happy. He lifted her hands, pressed a soft kiss to the back of each and released them with a sigh before scooping the small suitcase from the bed and stalking from the room. Lindy watched him go, a half smile on her lips, an ache in her heart and tears in her eyes.

Two hours later Zade was speeding down Central Avenue, his emergency lights blinking. His tires squealed as he rounded the fountain near the Majestic Hotel, the convention center was nothing but a blur as he sped past, and he ran the red light at the corner of Malvern and East Grand. Lindy found herself praying a policeman would stop them before he got them both killed. Then she forgot his reckless driving, forgot everything as another contraction enveloped her, pulling her into pain.

Once through the emergency room doors, the hospital began the usual, efficient, no-nonsense routine she remembered from Josh. She was helped into a wheelchair and asked to fill out the usual admittance forms. She could see Zade pacing back and forth, his hands rammed into the pockets of his slacks. Zade pacing this time instead of Randy and looking every bit the part of the prospective father with a frown turning down the corners of his mouth and his eyes wild with concern. She told him not to worry, and they shared a brief, dispassionate kiss before Lindy was whisked down the hallway by an orderly. She glanced over her shoulder at him for a final look and saw a nurse put her arm around him. He didn't even correct her when the woman said encouragingly, "She'll be all right, Mr. Scott. Don't worry."

Mr. Scott. They thought he was her husband. She started a smile that twisted into a grimace as another contraction captured her breath. The next half hour was a blur of faces, sensations and a sort of ordered confusion as she was bundled into a hospital gown, treated to the usual pre-delivery procedures and trundled into the labor room where, at the telephoned request of Dr. Fedders, she was given an injection for pain. Breathing exercises or not, there would be no natural childbirth for Lindy Scott. She accepted the medication gratefully, happy to learn that Amy was on the way.

Lost in the restful world of the medicine and unaware of the passage of time, Lindy didn't know if it had been three minutes or three hours since she was wheeled into the labor room before she heard Amy's voice saying, "It's been a helluva day one way or another, hasn't it?"

Lindy opened her eyes and tried to focus on Amy's face smiling down at her. She offered back a woozy smile before the foggy feeling swirled around her once more, wrapping her in a cocoon of cotton. She drifted out of reality again to the muted murmur of chatty feminine voices....

She must be in the delivery room, she reasoned groggily,

because it was cold, so cold. There was the sound of voices and she heard a baby crying, heard Amy saying something, then the doors burst open and a man…a faceless man stormed in—accompanied by a police officer and Paul Matthias—demanding his baby. He couldn't have her baby…he couldn't…

"Nooo!" she screamed, bolting into an upright position, her eyes opening to the familiar surroundings of the labor room. Immediately, three sets of hands and three soothing voices that belonged to women in white uniforms and caps were urging her to lie back. "…That's right…just rest…" and Amy's voice saying, "Only a dream…only the medicine…it's going to be okay, Lindy."

"I want Zade," Lindy said to the fuzzy-edged Amy who stood leaning over her.

"Zade!" Amy's voice quivered with shock. Shock that, even in her state of unreality, Lindy could see in her boss's eyes. For just a moment, Lindy was surprised that the simple request should bring that look of surprise to the obstetrician's face. Then some lucid part of her brain remembered. Amy didn't know Zade was the man she was seeing.

"Zade Wakefield?" Amy asked, her tone hesitant… disbelieving. "Why would you want to see him?"

Lindy could hear the question in her voice. "Please, Amy," she begged through gritted teeth as another contraction struck. "I need to see him. I have to tell him not to let that man take away my baby."

Amy entered the hospital waiting room. Zade stood with his back to her, staring out the window at the night. Zade Wakefield. Obviously the man in Lindy's life. Zade, the real father of Lindy Scott's baby. Amy's mind filled with questions…and she didn't like the answers she was coming up with. Oh, she knew *why* he had insinuated himself into Lindy's life, but how had he found out who she was?

His shoulders slumped wearily as he stood staring out at the night. As well they should, she thought bitterly, her surprise at last giving way to the fury rising within her. Concocting a scheme this convoluted just to get his baby required a lot of thought and work to pull off. Dear God, how... Amy's anger faltered at a new thought. *If he'd known who Lindy was all along, why had he gone ahead with the subpoena?* It didn't make sense...

Then, as if he sensed someone was in the room, Zade turned and saw her poised in the doorway. He crossed the short distance of the room, his long stride eating up the space until he stood directly in front of her. His face was pale, his eyes shadowed with concern.

"How is she?"

"Fine. She's asking for you." Amy's sharp gaze probed his with a burning intensity.

"Can I see her?"

Amy nodded. "She's in the labor room now. I'll have the O.B. nurse fix you up later and you can go into delivery with us."

She thought his color paled another degree. Angrier at him than she could ever remember being, Amy turned and began walking briskly down the hallway, Zade matching her pace for pace.

She stopped abruptly in the middle of the long corridor and plunged her hands into the pockets of her smock. "How did you meet Lindy, anyway?" she asked, looking up at him and waiting for the preposterous tale he would likely spin.

Surprisingly, soft laughter spilled from his beautifully shaped lips. "Would you believe we shop at the same grocery store? I thought she looked familiar that day I came to your office. Then when I saw her at the market the next day, I realized why. I spoke to her. She was so friendly, so happy...and I was so damned miserable." He shrugged. "It sounds corny to say I felt drawn to her, but that's exactly how I did feel. I decided it was because she was pregnant, and I knew there was someone out there carrying my baby. Someone who didn't want to give it to me. The next thing I knew, I was spending more time at her house than I was at mine." His eyes held a faraway, reminiscent look.

"I think in the beginning I thought of her as a sort of consolation prize. If I couldn't have my baby, at least I could experience some of the joys I was missing secondhand."

Amy's considering gaze razed her cousin's features, delving into the depths of his silvery eyes. Eyes she knew well. A face she was long familiar with, one that had never been able to fool her when they were children. What she saw there left her limp with relief, her anger and doubts about his ethics fading in the face of these new revelations.

It was one of life's strange coincidences, she thought. One of life's jokes. Or more likely the caring hand of God who wanted to see things come aright. As crazily impossible as it seemed, fate, God, *something* had brought Lindy and Zade together. Zade didn't know who she really was. That much Amy was certain of.

Should she say something, or let it go? The love they shared for so many years and her compassion at his predicament, urged her to tell him it was all right. *Lindy is the woman, Zade.* Five words that would make everything right in his world. But common sense told her she might be opening up the proverbial Pandora's box. Best to leave things alone. Maybe, just maybe, he would forget about finding this other woman. Maybe she could even ask him to give up the quest before Monday. Maybe...

She took his arm and ushered them both through some double doors, pointing toward a room. "She's in there." They exchanged smiles, and Zade brushed a kiss to Amy's cheek.

He approached the bed hesitantly, uncertain he wanted to see Lindy hurting more than he already had. Her red hair sprawled untidily across the stark whiteness of the pillowcase, and her hands clung to the railings. He lifted one of those hands, covering it with the warmth and strength of his.

Her eyes, glazed with the residual effects of whatever Amy had given her, flew open instantly. She smiled up at him, that beautiful Lindy smile. "What are you doing here?"

"I came to see you," he said, reaching out and brushing

the moist curls from her forehead, aware that the drug had muddled her memory.

"Where's Amy?"

"Scrubbing up, I think."

"The baby." As she spoke the words, her eyes widened and filled with a sort of panic, almost as if she'd just remembered something. Her hand gripped his, the tips of her nails digging into his flesh.

"What is it, Lindy-love?" he asked, bending and brushing his lips across her sweat-dampened forehead.

"The man! The man without a face."

Zade couldn't help but smile. He'd never seen anyone so affected by medication before, but figured the best way to calm the drug-induced fear was to go along with whatever she was saying. His voice was calm, soothing. "What man, Lindy?"

She ignored his question and said earnestly instead, "It isn't Randy's baby."

Zade couldn't help the shock that rocked his peace of moments before. Not Randy's baby? Dear God, what was she saying? Was it the truth, or was it the medicine? It *couldn't* be the truth. Lindy, his Lindy, wasn't the type to play around...was she? Telling himself to be calm, not to jump to conclusions, he forced evenness to his tone. "Of course it's Randy's baby."

Her head moved back and forth on the whiteness of the pillow in negative motion. "It—" Her confession was cut off as she was gripped with another contraction, this one seeming hell-bent to rip her apart as she closed her eyes and sank her teeth into her bottom lip, stifling a low moan. Zade felt the blood rush from his face. He pried her fingers from his hand and raced toward the door, bellowing, "Amy! Get the hell in here!"

Amy came hurrying into the room, followed by two nurses who went immediately to Lindy's side. Sparing a glance at her patient, Amy took Zade's elbow and escorted him to the door.

He glanced toward the bed. "Is she going to be all right?"

"She's fine," Amy assured him, an indulgent smile curving her mouth. Zade was too upset to notice. "Go on and get ready; I'll meet you in the delivery room." She pointed him toward a door and called for a nurse to come and help him. Then she disappeared behind the doors that held his very life. Lindy.

Zade sat with his head leaning against the back of a vinyl-covered chair. It was over. Thank God, it was over. It was an experience he was glad he'd had, but something he thought no one should have to go through more than once. He hadn't liked seeing Lindy in pain, knowing there was nothing he could do to help. There had been consolation, though, when Amy had placed the squalling, kicking infant on Lindy's abdomen and said, "You have a beautiful baby girl." Consolation and...the strangest, almost overwhelming sense of pride.

He'd been with her so much the past few weeks. He'd helped with Josh, helped when Lindy herself wasn't well, felt the baby moving inside her body. He'd even felt his own body stir with passion for her and longed for the time that same passion could be assuaged—just as any husband would. So, it seemed only natural that he feel that sudden dizzying surge of pride when he'd first seen the baby. Pride that had intensified when the nurse wrapped her in a soft cotton blanket and held her out for his inspection.

She looked like most babies, he supposed, except perhaps for the soft fluff of red hair covering her head. But to Zade she was special, perfect. He couldn't wait to hold her, couldn't wait... Then she had opened her eyes—dark blue eyes—and blinked against the bright lights of the delivery room. He had spoken to her, softly, lowly. Her bottom lip, which was shaped just like Lindy's, had begun to quiver, and the comparative silence of the room shattered in the wake of a loud wail...

Zade jumped when a door slamming somewhere nearby brought him momentarily back to the present. A six-pound, eight-ounce baby girl. He wondered what Lindy would name her. Then, for the first time in days, weeks, maybe, his mind turned to thoughts of *his* baby. Had that other woman given birth yet? And if she had, was his baby a boy or a girl? He might never know the answer. The realization brought a sense of sadness and regret. Even though he would be more than content with Lindy, Josh and the new baby he would always wonder....

"Mr. Wakefield?" The questioning, feminine voice transferred Zade's attention from the past hour's events to the nurse standing in the doorway of the waiting room.

Zade's eyes met sparkling brown eyes smiling out of a plump face. "Yes?"

"Mrs. Scott is in her room now. You can go in if you like."

"Thank you".

The nurse smiled and walked away, her crepe-soled shoes whispering over the highly polished floor. He looked at his watch. Only forty-five minutes since they had wheeled Lindy from the delivery room to recovery. Forty-five minutes since he'd seen her. He stood up and headed toward the room Amy pointed out to him earlier. Too long to be without her smile. Too long...

Unlike the time spent in the labor room, Lindy now lay resting on her back, one arm across her now-flat middle, the other bent at the elbow, her slender, ringless hand resting on the pillow beside her, the fingers just brushing her cheek. Her color was better. The extraordinary length of her lashes fanned out, brushing the dusting of whiskey-colored freckles, both contrasting against cheeks blushed with health.

Zade watched the slow rise and fall of her breathing, fighting the tightness in his throat and the burning beneath his eyelids. As they had in the delivery room, his emotions swerved from high to low and back again. From agony to exultation. Agony as he suffered right along with her, hurting with her pain. Exultation at being a part of the birth, something he thought he'd never experience. There was fear that something might go wrong, and wonder that a simple physical act could lead to such a wondrous miracle.

He replayed the scene in his mind and felt again the thrill

as Amy said, "You have a beautiful baby girl." He remembered repeating the words to a tired Lindy who'd smiled such a beautiful smile that his heart felt close to bursting with the love filling it and overflowing into his entire being. A love so powerful, so intense he could feel it sweeping the last, lingering vestiges of bitterness from his heart and leaving him filled with an unparalleled contentment. The same feeling washing through him now.

He leaned over the bed, his mouth touching hers in a kiss bordering reverence. Her eyes opened groggily; she lifted the hand resting against her cheek to touch his.

"Hi," he whispered, smiling down at her.

"Hi," she said softly and a bit thickly. "Is it over?"

"Yes."

"What did I have?"

"A girl," he told her, dutifully answering the question she'd already asked in the delivery room. The drug, he thought, remembering that Amy said she might be talkative and confused until it wore off.

She gave him a weary smile. "Is she okay?"

"She's perfect," Zade assured her. "Beautiful. She has hair just like yours." He reached out a finger and looped a lock of fiery hair behind her ear. "And a mouth like yours." His finger moved to her top lip, tracing the curvaceous outline with a gentle touch.

"Mmmm..." she said groggily, fading out again.

Zade watched her for a few moments, an indulgent smile wreathing his boldly masculine features. As he stood counting the freckles dancing on the bridge of her nose, Lindy's eyes fluttered open and she said sleepily, "You won't let him take her away from me, will you?"

Zade frowned. "Take who away?"

"My baby." Her eyes, suddenly and without warning, filled with tears. "I have to tell you. But I don't...didn't want to, because you'll leave me."

Zade felt a heaviness begin to descend on the happiness in his heart, a smothering sensation of foreboding that he wasn't going to like what she was about to say. She was going to tell him about the other man. The man, not Randy, who had fathered this child. And he didn't want to hear it...didn't want all his newly found trust in women to die with her confession. He didn't think he could go back to his cold existence after knowing the sunshine of her love.

"Lindy...just rest," he urged, for her own good—and his.

"I—I can't. I *have* to tell you!" She drew in a deep breath and sniffed, tears balancing on the fringe of her lower lashes. "I did it...not for me...Josh. I had to. Don't you see? Needed the money..." she said in a rush of unrelated statements.

A coldness swept through Zade's heart with the suddenness of a blue northern, leaving him cold...numb... Inside and out. His Lindy... He felt tears stinging behind his eyelids at the freezing death of something good and precious he'd held close to his heart for a brief time. Trust. And maybe even his love.

She rambled on, unaware of the defeated posture of his shoulders, unaware of the hurt inside him, unaware of the single tear that fell from his dark lashes onto her hand. "Man...wanted baby...Amy told me...he'd pay. For Josh, Zade...I said I would."

The words were run together and almost incoherent. Zade wasn't certain if it was from her need to get it all out, or from the lingering effects of the anesthetic, but he did know the garbled sentences were suddenly making sense in some strange way.

"He didn't want to get married..." Lindy continued, "...Josh's...surgery. I said...okay. I'd have...baby, then Josh could...have...operation." She stopped abruptly as Zade's head jerked upward in sudden realization, his tear-silvered eyes finding hers.

"What are you saying, Lindy?" he demanded huskily, shock and a feeling of disbelief replacing the numbness of what he thought was her betrayal.

Two crystalline tears slid from her sherry-hued eyes down her temples and into the froth of brilliant-colored hair that made a curly halo around her face. "I needed...money...for

Josh…his operations. Amy signed…papers for me. I said I'd have a baby…give it to him, but I can't give her up, Zade. I can't!''

Zade stood by the bed absorbing what Lindy was telling him. It couldn't be coincidence, could it? How many men in Hot Springs, Arkansas, paid someone to have their baby?

"You have a beautiful baby girl." Amy's words, spoken just as the baby was born, flitted through his mind. And for the first time, he realized that when she spoke them, she had been looking directly into his eyes.

Chapter Ten

"Zade?" Lindy's voice, filled with the worry reflected in her eyes, jolted him back to the present. "You won't...let him take her, will you?"

Let him take her? Zade heard the words, but his mind—a maelstrom of half-formed questions and nebulous answers—was unable to form a response. The suspicion rising with each syllable of her garbled confession had to be true. Lindy must be the woman Amy had chosen to be the mother of his child.

"Zade!" The single word held the fine edge of panic, and her hands reached up toward him in supplication when he didn't answer.

He couldn't think clearly, and though he heard her, he was too weighed down with the realization of her identity to respond to her plea. Lindy was the woman he'd been fighting all this time. She was the woman he'd spent the happiest three weeks of his life with. And she'd given birth to his daughter just over an hour ago.

The sound of a harsh sob drew his distracted gaze to the

bed where she lay staring up at him through a pool of tears. "I...knew you wouldn't...want me...us...anymore if you knew. I told Amy..."

Her anguish at his continued silence finally penetrated his confusion and shock. She was afraid. He took her hands in his, bringing them to his lips. "Shhh. Don't cry," he crooned softly. "It's going to be all right, I promise. No one, *no one* is going to take your baby away."

She drew in a shuddering, sobbing breath. "B-but the money. H-he wants the m-money."

"I'll take care of everything." Zade's hand moved to her tear-streaked face, his thumb brushing the moisture from her lashes. She was the mother of his baby. It was unbelievable. What had he done to deserve such a surprising and undeserved gift after the way he had unknowingly made her life so miserable these past few weeks? He blinked away the treacherous burning beneath his own eyelids. "Sleep," he urged in a low tone, brushing the bright tangle of her hair from her flushed cheeks. "It's going to be all right."

"Amy..."

"I'll talk to Amy."

"A-and you aren't...going to leave me?"

"Leave you?" He smiled, his heart swelling with the sweet healing love he felt for her. "I'll never leave you."

She smiled back, a wobbly, teary smile that glowed in her eyes. "I love you——" she whispered, her tear-spiked lashes drifting downward as she drew his hand to her cheek "——so very much..."

Zade lowered his mouth to hers in a kiss that, to him at least, was the sealing of some unspoken bargain. A kiss that promised he would never deliberately hurt her again.

Her lips curved into another smile, and her grip on his hands tightened, then she drifted away again on a sea of dreams, leaving behind a man whose whole world had been turned upside down, shaken, then righted to a position of solidity and security and joy he'd imagined only in his most ambitious longings. He loosened her grip on his fingers and left the room, a hundred unanswered questions still tumbling through his mind.

Amy was waiting for him just outside the door. She smiled. "I was just coming to get you. There's no sense in your staying with her all night. She'll be fine."

He nodded and raked a hand through his hair, his gaze meeting and holding hers as he asked point-blank, "She's the woman, isn't she? The woman I paid to have my baby?"

A sigh hissed from Amy's lips. How had he found out, when only an hour ago she would have sworn he was ignorant of the situation? Was he a better actor than she gave him credit for? Relief that things were out in the open at last warred with a sense of surprise at the unvarnished bluntness of the question. She tilted her chin and looked him directly in the eyes. "How did you find out?"

He perched his hands on his hips. "She told me just now. It was a lot of incoherent ramblings about not letting some man take her baby away…some man paying her and her taking the money for Josh, but I pieced enough of it together to make an intelligent guess. Besides, how many men in a city this size pay a woman to have their baby?"

Amy smiled tiredly. "You really didn't suspect anything until she told you?"

Zade shook his head. "I knew there was something on her mind, but she's pretty good with getting on with life in spite of what's bothering her."

"I know." Amy's hands went to the pockets of her smock. "So where do you go from here?"

"I asked her to marry me yesterday."

"And?"

"She said she loved me, too, but she wanted to wait until the baby was born to decide about marriage because we haven't known each other very long."

"You know why she really wanted to wait, don't you?"

Zade shook his head. "No."

"She was planning on having the baby and then leaving

town so the baby's father couldn't find her...so you couldn't find her."

Zade swore, unable to stop the brief dart of pain that came from knowing she'd misled him, even though it was for a good reason. Close on the heels of the hurt came the even more painful knowledge of how close he'd come to losing her.

"Are you going to tell her you know?"

One tanned hand came up and scrubbed over his face that bristled with a day's growth of beard. "I don't know. I think I'm still in shock. I have to go home and think things through. I have to decide how to handle this so no one gets hurt anymore."

Amy nodded. "I just want to tell you one thing. She's special, Zade. I think you know that. You don't know how many times I wanted to tell you about her so your mind would be easier about the whole thing. Just make certain you do whatever you can to keep her in your life. You need her and what she can give you."

Zade smiled, a tired smile that reflected the glimmer of hope in the depths of his gray eyes. "I know."

Three hours later, at home in his own bed and wide awake, he still couldn't believe the twist his life had taken. Just when he decided to give up searching for the woman carrying his child, he learned she was right there under his nose. It all fit. Even without verification by Amy, it fit. Lindy was perfectly capable of acting as that "unknown" woman had. She would do anything for her children. Or at least try to.

Gradually, a subtle change began to take place inside him. The surprise began to give way to pleasure...happiness. He loved Lindy, wanted to marry her, and she was the woman who'd just had a baby he thought he'd never see. How much more could a man want?

His daughter. God, he wanted to see her...hold her. It was hard to believe that the moment he'd longed for, waited for, had arrived. Hard to believe the room he'd decorated would soon be filled with the sounds of the rocker whispering across the carpet, of baby laughter, baby cries. And Lindy. A smile curved his lips in the darkness of the room. Lindy sitting in the rocker, holding his daughter. No. Their daughter.

He and Lindy had a child. The wonder and exhilaration he experienced in the delivery room returned twofold. It was almost more than he could believe to realize they had a baby, and he'd never made love to her. But he would. There was no doubt in his mind that he still wanted to marry her. No doubt at all. That topic had never been in question. The real question was, should he tell her who he was? The fair side of his nature told him he should, but his practical side whispered that telling her would raise more problems, more conflict. After all the threats he'd made, would she believe he really loved her? His stomach felt queasy, just remembering how he must have hurt her, how much mental agony he must have caused.

Don't tell her.

He wouldn't, he decided. After all, it would be better if she didn't know. Telling her would only cause more heartaches. and he didn't want her to ever hurt again. She deserved happiness. Deserved a lifetime of someone taking care of her for a change. A sentence he would accept gladly. It seemed more than a fair exchange for what he would be receiving from her in return. Besides the joy of her personality, he had a feeling Lindy Scott held a fire inside her that would make the color of her hair seem tame in comparison. It was a fire that lured him. A fire he wanted to try to put out. He wanted her by his side for all their tomorrows. It was as simple as that. It was as simple as being deathly afraid she wouldn't be able to forgive him if she knew the truth.

With a smile of satisfaction at his decision, Zade rolled over onto his side and closed his eyes. He drifted off into sleep, Lindy a glowing memory in his mind, her sweetness branded in his heart, her name the lullaby falling from his lips.

Zade's trip to Little Rock had been made as fast as the Jaguar and his fear of the law would allow. The last thing he needed was to be detained by a state trooper when all he wanted to do was hurry to the hospital and see Lindy and the baby.

The hospital corridors were relatively quiet since it was a good thirty minutes before visiting hours officially started. He planned to see the baby first, then spend the rest of the time with Lindy. Unfortunately, the fact that he wanted to see the baby didn't make the task any easier. He found the nursery had rules and schedules, and the only way he finally got to see her was by telling the head nurse she'd been born the night before, he'd just come in from Little Rock, and hadn't even set eyes on her yet. When accompanied with his heartbreaking smile, the tale succeeded. The Oscar-merited performance even rated him a small private room where he could spend a few minutes with her privately.

He sat waiting, garbed in green throw-away garments, his leg crossed ankle to knee, the steady shaking of his crossed foot swinging the tassel of his expensive loafers. He pushed back his sleeve and looked at his watch. What was taking the nurse so long? Heaving a disgusted sigh, he threw his head back to stare up at the acoustic ceiling tiles and began to count the rows of dots.

The barely perceptible swish of a door closing brought his gaze to the doorway where a white-clothed nurse stood holding a small bundle wrapped in a pale pink seersucker receiving blanket. His breathing came to a shuddering stop, then hissed from his lips in a long, slow expiration.

"Here's your daughter, Mr. Scott," the nurse said, assuming, as the one had the night before, that he was Lindy's husband. She came nearer, a smile on her pleasant, middle-aged face. The closer she got, the paler Zade grew.

The nurse, whose name tag read Mrs. Michaels, R.N., laughed at the look of fear on his face. "You don't have to be afraid. Babies are a lot tougher than people think. Is she your first?"

Licking lips gone suddenly desert-dry, he nodded, incapable of speech now that the moment he had waited for nine long months was upon him. The moment he had waited for a lifetime.

"See how I'm holding her?" Mrs. Michaels went on, an indulgent smile twinkling in her blue eyes. She leaned down with the softly spoken command, "Hold out your arms."

Zade obeyed wordlessly, automatically. He could smell the scent of the woman's perfume as she lowered the miniature parcel into his arms and cautioned, "Be sure you support her neck."

Zade found his voice long enough to ask, "Like this?"

Mrs. Michaels, completing the transfer of the child from her arms to his, met his worried eyes and smiled. "That's great. It won't be long until she tries to hold her head up. But until she can control it, it's best to give her some support."

"Thank you," Zade said.

"I'll leave you alone with her now. I'll be back to get her in a few minutes."

He nodded, wanting her to go so he could look all he wanted at his daughter, yet longing to call her back as he watched her disappear through the door with eyes suddenly filled with panic. What if he needed her? What if the baby began to cry? What if...

The tiny bundle wriggled, and a noise, something between a grunt and a snuffling sigh assailed his ears. His eyes dropped to the baby in his arms and he shifted her weight slightly, cradling her against him with his left arm while he pushed back the pink blanket that had somehow slipped up around her face as she shrank down into it.

The wispy caplet of reddish-blond hair he remembered from the delivery room was the first thing to catch his eye. Lindy's hair. His silvery gaze drifted in loving awe down over the smooth forehead, tiny, button nose, and the perfectly shaped baby lips. Dear God, but she was beautiful! Perfect! Moisture collected without warning beneath his eyelids, and he swallowed twice in an attempt to rid his throat of a sudden obstruction.

His tear-misted gaze caressed the round, infant cheeks and

his finger moved to touch the miniscule hand resting against her tiny, shell-like ear. He reached out to stroke the petal softness of her cheek, fighting the piercing shard of pain stabbing his heart as he realized just how close he had come to never knowing about her. The realization was sobering, humbling.

She was a special child for so many reasons. He stared down at her, fighting the gathering tears. Where was he when she was conceived? In the prohibitive confines of the world he had constructed to keep out the pain of the real world? Wheeling and dealing on a multimillion dollar deal, or in bed with some woman whose name or face he wouldn't recall now? Where was he when Amy planted his seed in the fertile valley of Lindy's womb? And why did it seem so important to him now that he hadn't been the one to do the planting?

He wanted to be involved with living in the real world now, thanks to Lindy. He wanted to be there to share all the things this child would experience growing up. He could see her wearing ribbons in her strawberry-blond hair and dresses bedecked with lace and ruffles. Someday she might paint those fingernails you could barely see with that god-awful blue and black nail polish he saw on the teenage girls in the mall. He would watch her leave for her first date and dole out the money for her cheerleading outfits and prom dresses. And one day a boy would kiss that perfect mouth, would put a ring on that tiny finger. One day she would have babies of her own and he would be a grandfather, for goodness' sake! Through this tiny scrap of humanity he would live forever.

Would she have his disposition, or Lindy's sunshiny personality? Would she be as clever as Josh? As loving? She squirmed in his arms. Her miniature mouth pursed and puckered and began flexing in an involuntary sucking motion that brought a wide smile of pleasure to the grim set of his features. He couldn't help the delighted laugh that tumbled from his lips. Raising her up, he pressed a gentle kiss to her soft, smooth cheek, getting high off the very scent of her and the knowledge and pride that she was his, and would remain his. It suddenly seemed imperative that he be there to put the fairy money under her pillow when she lost her first baby tooth. And mandatory that he hold her when she cried over her first broken heart. Zade held her as close as he could for fear of crushing her, rubbing his lips against the incomparable silkiness of coppery hair. Holding her so close, smelling the sweet, baby smell of her, and touching her, he now understood why Lindy had fought so hard to keep her, why she would never have been able to have given her away...

"Mr. Scott?" The soft voice of Mrs. Michaels interrupted his total absorption with the baby.

He lifted his head. "Yes?"

"How did you do?" she asked, noting the extra sparkle in his eyes.

His wide smile was an obvious answer. "Isn't she beautiful?"

"She is, indeed. Don't you hope she has your wife's disposition? She's such a sweetheart."

"I know." He stood and placed the baby in the nurse's arms.

She winked at him. "You just throw that outfit in the trashcan there, then go on in and see your wife. It's a bit early yet, but we can bend the rules a bit from time to time."

"Thank you." Zade's heart somehow felt both lighter and heavier. He watched the nurse leave the room with the baby in her arms. Two things were certain. He loved Lindy and, like her, he couldn't give this baby up. She had to marry him. She just had to.

Lindy parted her lips slightly, an old trick to keep from blinking as she applied the dark mascara to her long lashes. Her hands trembled with nervous anticipation. Zade would be here soon. He'd called earlier in the day and told her he had to go to Little Rock and it would probably be evening visiting hours before he could come and see her. Which was just as well, she thought, because she was still uneasy about her confession the night before.

She remembered telling him about being a surrogate mother,

but she didn't remember much after that, except his assurance that everything would be okay. He hadn't seemed angry, but then, she really hadn't been the best judge of emotions at the time. When she told Amy what she'd done, her boss added her assurances that everything would come out all right. She also told her that the anesthetic had been the catalyst spurring her confession. Lindy sighed. However things turned out, it was too late to call the words back. She'd just have to live with them.

Lindy regarded herself in the mirror, hoping Zade found her attractive. Not that she thought her looks would sway him on any decisions or any feelings he might have for her, it was just…she wanted to be pretty for him. Her makeup was perfection—the freckles hardly showed at all, she noted thankfully. Her eye shadow, a subtle blending of three shades, made her sherry-colored eyes stand out and echoed the tint of the aqua gown and peignoir ensemble she wore. A peach blush highlighted her cheekbones and pearl studs pierced the lobes of her ears. Her hair was loose, caught back with a matching aqua ribbon and hanging in a jumble of soft curls to her shoulders. Not bad for someone who weighed fifteen pounds more the day before, she thought with a smile of satisfaction curling the corners of her mouth.

Would Zade think she looked good, or would his reaction to what she had told him overshadow the love he professed just two days ago and leave him polite and reserved, as he'd been when they first met? She moaned softly. Why had she told him? Her stomach quivered with the stirrings of a battalion of nervous butterflies, and her legs felt weak, possibly a reminder that she'd just had a baby instead of a case of nerves. Time to get back into bed and fluff up her pillows so she could meet him prepared, looking cool and unconcerned when he arrived.

"Lindy?"

She whirled at the sound of the masculine voice calling her name, the sudden action making her feel decidedly light-headed. Or was it the sound of his voice disturbing her equilibrium? Zade's voice. "In here!" she called, flicking off the bathroom light and stepping through the threshold to the bedroom area.

He stood beside the bed, a huge sheaf of red roses in his arms and a definitely pleased smile on his face as he stared at her. Lindy wanted to cross her arms in front of her breasts, or run back to the bathroom and hide. She felt exposed even though she knew the semi-sheer gown and matching robe were opaque enough for decency in the evening shadows of the room.

"Hi." *I want you Lindy—you have no idea how badly I want you.*

His voice was a deep, pleasant rumble, the intimacy in it causing desire to flicker hotly through her veins. Her voice, shallow and breathless, whispered a soft, "Hi," in return.

"Should you be up?" he asked, aware suddenly that she wasn't flat on her back as he'd expected. *She's so thin!*

She reached up and caught a curl brushing her shoulder, twisting it around one finger. "I was just getting ready for visiting hours." *Just waiting for you.*

He nodded, his eyes devouring every move she made. She was twisting her hair. Was she nervous? "You look fantastic!" *Damn, but she looks sexy in that thing. I'd like to...*

The words sounded sincere enough. And the look in his eyes... "Thank you." *I wanted to look fantastic for you.*

He held out the roses. "For you." *I want to kiss you, Lindy.*

Her bare feet moved over the coolness of the flooring. She took the roses, cradling them in her embrace the way she'd cradled her new daughter throughout the day at feeding time. She buried her face in the sweet-smelling moistness of the fragrant blossoms, drawing the heady aroma of their perfume deeply into her senses. The thick veil of her lashes lifted and her smoldering gaze met his. "They're lovely. Thank you. We should get them in some water."

"I love you."

The words had nothing to do with roses, but pierced straight to the heart of what each of them was truly concerned with.

"Do you?" Lindy's eyes were wide with uncertainty. *I want you to kiss me.*

"So much you wouldn't believe it," he said softly. Reaching out, he took the roses from her, tossing them with callous unconcern onto the bed before grasping her gently by the shoulders and pulling her nearer. He dipped his head to close the gap between their mouths, his warm lips meeting hers in a gentle contact. She was sweet...so sweet, and she tasted like peaches and cream, he thought as she took the initiative, rising up on tiptoe to deepen the kiss, responding to the touch of his lips with lightning quickness. A low growl of pleasure and desire emanated from Zade's throat as he broke the contact of their mouths and pulled her more fully into his embrace. A deep, soul-shuddering sigh rippled through him at the feel of her sparsely clad body next to his, closer than they'd ever been to each other.

Her arms went around his waist and she melted against him—no, she melted almost into him. Soft, full breasts flattened against his broad, masculine chest, a much flatter stomach pressed closely to the rock hardness of his middle, slender thigh clung to the firmness of his and her deliciously aching womanhood cradled the undeniable proof of his arousal as she fit all her feminine curves into his corresponding male counterparts. His arms held her tightly, possessively. God, what if he had never found her, he agonized. Never known her? He couldn't imagine life now without her.

For long moments they stood there, content to rest in each other's arms, basking in the full realization of their love. Now that the baby was born, and while she stood in the shelter of his embrace, Lindy could almost picture them having a future together. But even though Zade seemed unconcerned with what she'd told him, her nature wouldn't allow her complete happiness until she had slain all the dragons that might keep them apart. When she could stand it no longer—when she became so afraid that the unspoken thing between them might still rend them apart—she whispered, "Zade?"

"What is it, Lindy-love?"

"A-about last night." She lifted her head from its resting place against his chest and met his eyes with a look of complete candor.

He lifted a finger and placed it against her peach-glossed lips. "You needed money for Josh, so you agreed to become a surrogate mother. Then, the closer the time came to give it up, the more you realized you couldn't do it. No big deal."

Lindy caught at his wrist, freeing her lips. "But the money…"

"I've taken care of everything. So just put it from your mind," he said with soft insistence.

"But, Zade, how can you love me knowing what I've done?"

His voice was low, husky as he gazed tenderly down at her. "You've got it all wrong, Lindy. The question isn't how can I still love you, but, how can I not love you for what you were willing to do for Josh?"·

"I think I'm going to cry again," she said with a sigh as he pulled her close once more. "I don't know what I ever did to deserve you."

What she'd done to deserve him? His eyes closed in sudden pain. He felt a stab of guilt to his conscience for the nine months of hell he'd put her through, and for the deception he was perpetrating now, even though it was for her own good. "Don't cry. You'll mess up your makeup," he coaxed in a teasing tone, wanting to see her smile and pushing the guilt away simultaneously. "What are you doing Tuesday?"

Lindy pulled back and looked up at him. "Going home from the hospital, I think. Why?"

He shrugged, his shoulders straining the knit of the shirt he wore. His attitude and voice combined to create a perfect picture of insouciance as he said, "I just thought if you weren't doing anything afterward, we could get married."

Lindy's eyes widened. "Married?"

He smiled. "Married. You know where two people live together legally, have a bunch of kids, buy a station wagon and take vacations to Disney World. Married."

The tears Lindy had battled against and won victory over only moments before, shimmered in her eyes once more. "Oh, Zade! I'd like that very much, but are you sure? Very sure? You can have any gorgeous woman you want."

"I want you." His hands went to her hair. He pulled the ribbon from the shining curls and buried his hands in its rich fullness. "I want the redhead with the—" he paused to drop light kisses to the bridge of her nose, her cheeks, her chin "—freckles, the..." He became sidetracked by her mouth, stopping to kiss one corner briefly before continuing in a voice that wasn't quite as steady as it had been, "...smiling mouth." He sucked in a deep breath. "And whatever else goes with the package."

Lindy looked up at him with shining eyes. "One small boy who needs a father."

Zade shrugged again. "What the heck. I could use someone to take out the trash."

"And a baby girl who needs a father."

"Since she looks like you, why not?" The teasing gleam in his eyes sobered momentarily.

Lindy panicked. "What?"

"The baby! I can't believe I've been so caught up with seeing you, I forgot to ask if you've named her yet."

"I did. I called her Gillian Renee—Jill."

"Jill Wakefield," Zade said consideringly, cocking one dark eyebrow at her. "It has a ring to it, don't you think?"

Lindy's heart felt close to overflowing. He actually wanted to adopt Jill. "It does sound...right, somehow," she agreed, smiling up at him through her lashes.

Zade's mustache inched upward at the corners. "Then we have a date Tuesday afternoon? My house at the lake?"

Lindy nodded. "Yes. We have a date."

At eleven o'clock on Tuesday, as he unloaded the last of Lindy's "saved" things from the pickup he'd borrowed from one of his job foremen, Zade began to wonder if he'd made a grave mistake. Lindy had insisted he go to her apartment and bring the things to his house, just as she had insisted that each of the people she saved them for should come to the wedding and get them. His lips twisted in a wry smile. He'd probably have to add on a room just to accommodate her milk cartons and coffee cans! A silly grin spread across his face.

She was actually in his house. In his bedroom. Their bedroom, now. She was in his bed, resting for the wedding that would take place at seven that evening—if he lived that long. And he just might not if he didn't get a sandwich and the chance to see her soon. The smile widened, and he headed toward the bedroom. First things first.

Thoroughly tired of the bed, Lindy had showered and washed her hair before pulling on a pair of shorts and a cool cotton top, bemoaning the fact that though her stomach was flatter, she still had a way to go before it returned to its normal tautness. She had checked on Jill who rested peacefully on her stomach, the morning sun glinting off the soft copper color of her hair as she slept contentedly in the secure confines of the bassinet. Then, succumbing to the lure of the outdoors, she stepped through the French doors leading to the flagstone patio that ran the length of the house.

She was sitting at a glass-topped table, letting the sun dry her hair and polishing her nails when she heard Zade calling her.

"Out here!" She watched him leave the house, shielding his gaze against the glare of sunshine greeting him. She waved the hand holding the brush at him. "Did you get everything?"

"I hope so! Woman, do you realize just how much junk you had in those cabinets?"

Laughter gurgled from Lindy's lips. She held up her left hand, inspecting her handiwork. "One man's trash is another man's treasure," she quoted saucily.

"Why, *why* would anyone need a three-foot stack of egg cartons?" he asked, casting her a jaundiced look from the corner of his eye as he sprawled in the chair across from her.

Lindy, intent on the application of coral polish to her thumb nail, looked askance at him and said, "Mrs. O'Kelly sells eggs. I save them for her."

"Two dozen plastic milk jugs?"

"The milk jugs and the coffee cans are for Mr. Lowery who used to take Josh and Randy fishing." Her hand stilled and her features clouded briefly at the mention of Randy's name. Resolutely, she began to brush on the glistening color again. "He catches and sells catfish. He freezes them in the containers I save."

Zade straightened and leaned toward her, placing his hand on her bare knee. Their gazes locked. "Are you okay?"

"I'm fine."

"Are you worried about what Randy would think?"

"No. Randy would be happy for me. Truly." A look of pensiveness clouded the sunshine of her features momentarily. "I just got a little sad there for a moment. I guess I always will from time to time. Will it bother you?"

Zade shook his head. "As long as I know you love me I'll never begrudge your memories of him."

It would go down in the annals of Wakefield history as the most unconventional wedding of all time, Zade thought dazedly as he made a thorough survey of the guests who, now that the brief ceremony was over, were indulging in the cake and punch Tammy thoughtfully arranged for the impromptu reception.

Besides the minister, he'd invited Paul and Tammy and Amy and Steve. Mrs. Hancock, who had kept Josh while Lindy was in the hospital, now shared the sofa with an elderly man in a pin-stripe suit whose cut was reminiscent of the forties. Josh sat on the man's lap, his arms outstretched in a measuring gesture. Ah, Zade thought, the fish man. The woman in the floral cotton dress and the straw hat sitting in the wingback chair must be Mrs. O'Kelly who sold eggs. Or was Mrs. O'Kelly the plump woman in the knit pantsuit and Miss Harper the woman in the floral dress? It was too hard for him to remember, especially when all he wanted was for the entire lot to clear out and leave him with his new family.

He saw Lindy across the room, chatting happily to a prim and proper type he remembered as Josh's Sunday school teacher, the one who used the toilet tissue and paper towel rolls and the lids from hairspray and deodorant. Or had that been his nursery school teacher who also collected the soup labels? He smiled. What the hell! They were Lindy's friends, people she cared about, and who obviously cared about her and Josh, even if they were a strange social mixture.

He recalled the casualness of the wedding ceremony itself. It had been almost time for the ceremony to begin when Tammy had hurried into the room and motioned for Zade to join her. "We're running a bit behind," she said. "Josh decided he wanted something to drink, and he spilled punch all over his clothes. I rinsed them out and they're in the dryer. It shouldn't be too much longer."

Zade had felt panic rising. "What do I tell the preacher?"

Tammy patted his hand. "The truth. He'll understand."

Ten minutes later, Zade was listening to Mr. Lowery's theory about purple worms as bass bait on Lake DeGray when a muted whisper from Steve announced that the wedding was about to commence.

He had turned then, his attention focused solely on the woman coming through the door, clad in a dress of soft, creamy yellow. The dress, a cool, summery confection of eyelet and lace had a scalloped neckline and cap sleeves. The full skirt and matching yellow high-heeled sandals complimented the slender grace of her legs. Her hair, piled on top of her head in the usual tumult of red curls, was adorned with a bit of baby's breath and a solitary yellow rosebud. A single strand of pearls—his wedding gift to her—rested against the delicate hollow of her throat and matched the pearl drops at her ears. A bouquet of rosebuds and daisies was clutched in her hands as she approached him with a tentative smile, her graceful carriage bringing her to a spot mere feet from where he stood.

The dress and the color suited her. She'd never looked so

beautiful, so full of sunshine and life. If there were any last traces of hurt and bitterness still lingering in some dark corner of his heart, they were swept away by the love-glow shining in her eyes. As he held out his hand, and she placed hers in it, he knew that this one moment of his lifetime would be forever engraved in his memory. With a smile that embodied all the love he felt for her, he had drawn her close to his side, close to his heart.

What followed was nothing but a jumble of impressions, the stereotypical comedy of errors: Josh, stretching up on tiptoe and then lowering his heels to the floor, over and over again, his hands clasped behind his back. Josh tugging on Paul's slacks and whispering loudly that his clothes were still damp. Jill choosing the exact moment Lindy was to repeat her vows to wail in Tammy's arms, drawing the attention from the couple being united in holy wedlock toward the baby and the woman trying to comfort her. A softly muttered, "Damn," came from Lindy and a disapproving look from the Reverend Turner.

When Jill began to wail harder and louder, and Lindy excused herself to go to her, Zade thought the minister would have a stroke—if the color of his face was any indication of his blood pressure. Three weeks ago, Zade thought, he would have been in the same shape as the minister. As it was, he couldn't remember ever feeling such a desire to laugh in his entire life. It was a wedding to be remembered. It was soon over, Amy holding Jill just long enough for him and Lindy to exchange rings, and then he was kissing her, trying not to squash the baby while everyone had talked and laughed and Josh tugged at his pants leg, wanting to know if he could call him Daddy now.

"Why are you wearing that silly grin?"

Zade's silly grin broadened at the sound of the voice interrupting his memories. His wife's voice. The knowledge that Lindy was his forever was a welcome balm to his heart. He slid an arm around her shoulders and drew her against his side, leaning down to whisper in her ear. "I was thinking about the ceremony."

Her lips twitched with suppressed laughter. "What a fiasco! Zade, what are you doing?"

"Nibbling on your ear. Do you mind?"

"I don't, but Reverend Turner might. Did you see his face?"

Zade's chuckle was sexy and warm in her ear. "Yes. Do you see mine?"

She drew back and saw a decidedly lecherous leer on his attractive features. "Shame!"

"Get rid of all these people."

"Zade!"

"I want to be with you and Josh and Jill."

"I guess I could show everyone where their stuff is on the carport. Maybe they'd take a hint."

"Maybe. You get rid of your guests; I'll get rid of mine. Deal?" His silvery eyes glimmered with mischief.

Lindy looked skeptical, but agreed. "Deal."

Zade was in the bathroom an hour later when Lindy called, "How'd you do it?"

"How'd I do what?" he asked, scraping the razor over his lathered cheeks.

"Get your people to leave so fast?"

"I told them all to get the hell out of here!"

"Zade! You didn't!"

"Didn't I?"

He heard her laugh, then heard her talking softly to the baby. It was a wonderful feeling knowing they were both so close. When he entered the bedroom a few moments later, drying his hair with a small hand towel, the first thing he saw was Lindy leaning against a mound of pillows, nursing Jill. He stood transfixed in the doorway, his throat tightening with a sudden surge of emotion, awed by the beauty of the picture the two made.

His wife and his daughter. Lindy's profile held a purity of

line as it contrasted against the curtain of her hair that was gilded with gold light from the bedside table. One arm held Jill close, the other hand was busy touching... One slender finger smoothing the baby's silky red-gold hair, moved to the fragile shell of her ear, then caressed the finely shaped line of her soft brow.

A memory of the woman in Amy's office a few weeks earlier came back to Zade. How had he ever been shocked by the sight of a woman nursing her baby? It was natural, beautiful. Or was it just Lindy who made it so? He wished fervently that he possessed the talent to capture them on canvas for all the world to see. *The Titian Madonna.*

She glanced up, suddenly aware he was watching her. The sight of him standing in the doorway with nothing but a towel around his lean hips brought her breathing to a halt and a rush of rose to her cheeks. The baby in her arms was forgotten under the onslaught of the purely sexual feelings Zade's powerful male body stirred to vibrant life. He was so beautiful. So perfectly beautiful. How could she ever hope to hold him...

"You're so beautiful," he said huskily, a smile of exquisite tenderness lifting the corners of his mouth and climbing to illuminate the smoky depths of his eyes. He moved to sit at the side of the bed and, leaning across the baby, found her mouth with a soft kiss.

Nose rubbing nose, mouth to mouth, Lindy smiled against his lips while her heart battered against the cage of her ribs in helpless response to his utter maleness. "I was just thinking the same thing about you," she confessed.

"Yeah?"

"Yeah."

He moved away from her, completely at ease with the situation, as he watched Jill feeding eagerly at her mother's breast. "Greedy little thing, isn't she?"

Lindy laughed softly. "Very."

"Does it hurt?"

The question, accompanied by one tanned finger that reached out and traced a delicate vein in the creamy fullness of her breast, caught her off guard. Another blush burned Lindy's cheeks. "At first, but not now."

"Does my bluntness embarrass you?" he asked, entranced with the bit of naïveté she still retained after being married and having two children.

"A little."

"Are you nervous?"

"Yes." The concession was made breathlessly, softly.

"About what?"

"You. Me. Us."

"No need to be nervous," he said reassuringly, stroking Jill's head with the gentle brush of one finger. "We can't do anything for—what is it—six weeks?"

"Zade," she groaned.

His laughter was low and pleasant to her ears. Their eyes met, his teasing, hers troubled. "I love to see you blush. And I love to touch you. I can touch you now, you know."

"I know."

His glance fell to the baby who was breathing with the evenness of sleep, the tiny bow of her mouth open, allowing milk to run out one corner. "She's conked out on us."

Excitement mingled with embarrassment as Lindy moved Jill away from her breast and placed her on the bed, dabbing at the milk on the baby's cheek. The heat of Zade's gaze as he watched was almost tangible. She reached to draw the bodice of her gown over the rounded globe of her breast, but her wrist was caught and held by hard fingers. His free hand moved up, up, his fingers skimming the outer side of her breast while his thumb rubbed the sensitive tip that hardened instantly beneath his ministrations.

She saw him move and drew in a sharp breath at his intent, just seconds before he leaned nearer, lower, his mouth capturing the nipple so recently abandoned by her daughter. His tongue curled hotly around the pebble hardness, the gentle tugging freeing her breath in a slow hiss. Desire blazed instantly, raging rampantly through her body and settling in the throbbing heart of her femininity.

She gave a small whimper of despair. Six weeks... She reached out to hold his dark head close, but he lifted it, his eyes burning with a passion to equal hers. Without a word, he lifted the sleeping baby and carried her carefully to the bassinet.

Lindy watched him, her eyes bright with excitement, yet hazy with a slumbering sensuality that jerked Zade's already pulsing libido into a higher gear. He stood by the bedside, staring down at her, then slowly, deliberately, pulled the towel from his love-ready body.

There are any number of ways to make love without disobeying the doctor's orders. Together, and often, during the weeks to come, Lindy and Zade tried and perfected each and every one.

Chapter Eleven

Lindy clutched her overnight bag in both hands and regarded Mrs. Hancock and Josh with a worried frown. "Don't forget to call me if Jill gets fretful."

Zade took her by the shoulders, propelled her into the Jaguar and shut the door, a look of tender indulgence on his handsome face. "Jill will be fine," he said encouragingly. To Mrs. Hancock he added, "I'll call later and let you know we got there."

"There" was the secret place he'd chosen for them to spend their long-awaited weekend honeymoon. A place he described as having a beautiful view of a lake, yet not too far from shops and eating places if—he added with a lecherous grin—Lindy got tired of looking at the ceiling. Never a man to waste precious time, he had made some sort of arrangements for a weekend together as soon as he learned the day of Lindy's six-week checkup.

"We'll be fine," Mrs. Hancock assured them with a benevolent smile. She tousled Josh's hair and said, "Let's go start those oatmeal cookies."

Lindy watched them disappear into the house and heaved a deep sigh.

"We don't have to go," Zade said, sliding into the seat beside her.

Her head jerked toward the sound of his voice. She smiled. "I want to go. I'm looking forward to it, but I've never left Josh before."

"Then it's high time you did, because I want you to take some business trips with me from time to time."

Surprise widened Lindy's eyes. "You do?"

"Of course I do, silly. Besides, it'll be good for Josh to be away from you, too. He'll be going to kindergarten soon, and if he gets used to being with different people, it won't be nearly as hard on him." He pulled the car out onto Lindy's old street and was soon guiding the car through the city's downtown area. "And stop worrying about Jill, will you? She took to the bottle like a duck to water. Mrs. Hancock is the equivalent of a grandma and a nurse rolled into one, so there's nothing to worry about."

"I know you're right," she admitted. Then, when Zade continued in the direction of their house instead of turning on Grand Avenue and heading out toward Lake Ouachita as she expected him to do, she asked for perhaps the dozenth time, "Where are we going?"

He glanced over at her, his eyes twinkling. "It's a surprise," he said, offering her his stock answer. He visually measured the distance she was sitting from him and gave a wry smile. "I think it's time for that station wagon."

"Why?"

"Because you'd be able to sit closer to me. How's a guy supposed to get fresh if he can't even reach his woman?"

Laughter glimmering in her eyes, Lindy held out her hand, which was instantly wrapped with the warmth and strength of his. He responded with a slow, sensuous smile. "I love you, Melinda Wakefield."

The look in Lindy's eyes was more eloquent than mere words as she brought his hand to her lips.

In less than ten minutes, Zade reached the outskirts of Hot Springs and was pulling into the Holiday Inn on Highway 7.

She frowned. "Why are we stopping here?"

"This is it," he said, maneuvering the Jaguar into a parking space and killing the engine.

Her expression was one of total bewilderment. "It?"

"Our honeymoon spot."

Lindy's jaw dropped in surprise.

He chuckled and tapped the bottom of her chin with his forefinger. "It's terribly unattractive to go around with your mouth hanging open like that, babe," he teased. Lindy's mouth snapped shut immediately. "Look, I knew you'd be on pins and needles away from the kids, so I thought—why not? The purpose is to get away together. Where we get away is unimportant. This way, if Jill does give Mrs. Hancock any kind of trouble, you can be there in fifteen minutes."

Lindy felt a curious thrill of joy at his thoughtfulness, a trait she'd been aware of almost from the first. "You think of everything. I did want to be with you, but I couldn't help being a bit uneasy."

"I know you were torn about this weekend. I'm new to this fathering business, but I'm trying," he said earnestly.

"Actually, you're a natural," she told him truthfully, thinking of the way he handled Josh, tempering the obvious love he felt for her son with just the right dosage of authority.

"How about husbanding? Am I a natural at that?"

Lindy held out her hand, ticking off points with her fingers as she pretended to recall his husbandly traits. "Well, you make a pretty good cup of coffee, you're getting better about remembering to save things, and you run a mean vacuum cleaner…"

"That isn't what I'm talking about," he grumbled, leaning over and reaching one hand out to capture the back of her head and pull her nearer.

"Oh!" she said, nodding as if she'd just comprehended his

meaning, her heart sprinting forward at his touch. "*That*. Ask me again tomorrow—you know—afterward."

"Redheaded brat!" he growled, giving her a hard, dispassionate kiss as a reprimand.

"Once more with feeling," she quoted with a dramatic sigh.

"I'll give you once more with feeling just as soon as we get into that motel room," he said, his mouth finding hers again. The kiss began as light and playful, but quickly surpassed the bounds of fun as Zade's mouth slanted over hers in more thorough possession, his tongue sliding into her mouth, filling the warm cavern as his body ached to fill hers. Her lips softened, parting easily, accepting the poor substitution for the release she knew her body would soon be yearning for. He tore his lips from hers and pressed a moist kiss to her throat. His voice trembled unsteadily as he confessed, "For some insane reason I feel like a teenager hoping to make out on his first date. Let's get out of here."

Without a word she followed him into the motel.

Lindy couldn't have said what the room looked like, though it did look out over the lake as he'd promised. She was suddenly irrationally nervous. This was the real thing. She didn't know why it should seem so important after all they'd meant to each other these past six weeks— after all the ways they'd made love so beautifully, successfully—but it was. Like Zade, she felt young, gauche, untried.

She was admiring the style of the dressing table, barely able to digest her impressions in the chaos of her mind, when Zade set the suitcase on the floor, grabbed her around the waist from behind and pulled her against him, rocking her back and forth while his lips nuzzled beneath her hair, searching out all the places that sent desire surging through her, places he now knew by heart.

"I'll give you an hour to stop that," she said lightly, in an effort to ease her building nervousness, lowering her head and brushing the hair aside to give freer access to his marauding lips. She caught sight of them in the mirror—a slender red-haired woman held tightly by two masculine arms around her waist. The top of his dark head was all that was visible as he feasted on the delectable softness of her neck. Her hands went to his forearms, delighting in the feel of the crisp hair against her palms.

He lifted his head then, his eyes meeting hers in the mirror, no hint of teasing at all in their silvery depths. They glittered brightly, recklessly as his hands moved to the thin straps of her sundress and he slipped his fingers beneath the straps, easing them down her freckle-dusted shoulders. His lips grazed their bare softness, inching toward the curve of her neck while he worked with maddening slowness at unfastening the three large buttons holding the front of the dress closed. That accomplished, he folded back the two sections of the bodice and unhooked the front catch of her strapless bra.

Lindy's breath, suspended in the heartbeat of eternity, whispered from the glossy fullness of her lips as her eyes drifted shut. Her head dropped back onto his shoulder in utter surrender as her breasts, ripe and heavy with the fullness of maturity and recent motherhood, spilled into the waiting warmth of his hands. High, round and full, their rose-tinted tips thrust forward pertly, proudly, swelling into his hands with an eagerness all their own. He lifted them tenderly, testing their weight as one might that of precious jewels, while his thumbs brushed the plumpness of her nipples that tautened to tight pink buds at his lightest touch.

He pressed a kiss behind her ear, his breath coming shallowly, unevenly against her cheek as his eyes devoured the scene reflected back at him. "Beautiful," he muttered, his hands peeling the dress downward in sudden impatience.

Lindy wriggled her hips and the watermelon-red cotton dress and the bra fell to the floor, a bright splash of color against the neutral tone of the carpet, leaving her clad only in a gossamer wisp of underwear with lace inserts that did nothing to hide her femininity. His hands skimmed her rib cage and fastened on her hip bones, pulling her closer and making her thrillingly aware of his reactions to their love play as her bottom came fully into contact with his throbbing manhood—confirmation of the extent of his arousal.

His hands slipped easily over the silky fabric, gliding over her hips and stomach, cupping and caressing the aching mound of her femininity. Heat raced through Lindy with the speed and intensity of a brushfire, and her soft gasp of pleasure pierced the quiet of the room. The searing warmth of his touch left her nerve endings so sensitive, so raw, that the whisper softness of his breath against her throat sent them into an agonized clamor for relief—relief she sought by arching against his touch when his fingers dipped beneath the fragile barrier of elastic. The ploy failed as his tentative, searching fingers carefully, almost as if he were afraid of hurting, fanned the glowing embers of the passion licking hotly through her.

The heat building inside her spiraled upward.

She burned.

With a cry born of desire and desperation, she turned in his embrace, wanting more, wanting to be closer, wanting...

Zade scooped her up and carried her the short distance to the bed, placing her in the center of the king-sized square, then lowering himself until he rested on her, his lower body pressing firmly, intimately to hers.

She looped her arms around his neck and drew him down, driven beyond reason, beyond caring, beyond the fears plaguing her only moments before—driven by need, by love, by lust—by feelings as old as time, as lasting as eternity. The soft pliancy of her lips fused to his, welcoming the mastery of his kisses, the slight abrasion of his mustache, the invasion of his tongue that ravaged the soft inner recesses of her mouth, stroking, stroking...

Moving of their own volition, her hands swept the breadth of his shoulders, skimmed the firm planes of his chest and glided over the hard musculature of his belly. She tugged his shirt free of his slacks and began to work with an almost feverish frenzy to undo the buttons, whimpering deep in her throat as he lowered his hair-roughened chest to rest against the nakedness of her breasts. His mouth left hers momentarily,

moving to the hollow at the joining of her collarbone while
he raised his hips and fumbled single-handedly with the buckle
of his belt.

"Let me." The plea was soft, slurred. Zade acquiesced by
simply rolling to his back and waiting. Lindy found that, in
her haste, she fumbled, too. The hook on his slacks wouldn't
come undone, and the zipper stuck. She muttered a mild oath
at the frustration tormenting her and then, finally, he was free
of all bonds of clothing and her lavender excuse for underwear
dripped like a cluster of wilted wisteria from the shade of the
bedside lamp where they landed when she tossed them away.

Her eyes, slumberous with the desire ravaging her slender
body, charted the hard slopes and planes of his body—from
the smooth roundness of his shoulder and biceps to the crisp-
curling hair springing from his chest and diminishing to a silky
line that meandered in subtle invitation down the hard ridges
of his belly. Something akin to a sob escaped her throat. Why
couldn't she be beautiful, seductive, gorgeous? He was so perfect, so beautifully masculine and virile, how could she ever
hope to hold him when other women threw themselves at him,
as they were sure to in the coming years?

Willpower? Love? Optimism? A combination of everything? A giving of everything inside her—a fusion of heart,
mind and soul that would bind him to her for all eternity?
Would it work? It had to. So vowing, Lindy lowered herself
to sprawl atop him, feeling the tumescence of his manhood
hard against her abdomen as she pressed her lips to the flat
brown nubs nestling in the downy hair covering his chest. Her
tongue laved them softly. He groaned and shifted beneath her,
his hands gripping the roundness of her bottom and holding
her urgently to him, forcing her to the full realization of his
need.

"Now, Zade, please," she begged softly.

His arms held her with a fierce tenderness. "God, I want
you, but I'm so afraid I'll hurt you…" She began to scatter a
trail of tiny, moist kisses over his chest and his hard stomach.
"I…are you sure it's okay?" he rasped. Then, when her

tongue delved into the miniature crater of his navel he chanted huskily, "You're driving me crazy...crazy..."

"Good. I intend to." Her voice was husky, teasing as she moved back up until they were eye to eye. Her generous mouth was swollen, bruised from the roughness of their kisses, but it smiled that beautiful smile that now bordered on naughty as she reached down, her fingers warm and eager as they closed around him, guiding him into her. Zade's heart literally stopped as she lowered herself onto him slowly, slowly...until he rested fully within her.

"Is it okay? Does it hurt?" he asked, concern lacing his voice.

She bent to kiss him again, touched by his tenderness, the tears threatening as a result of his caring attitude roughening her voice as she whispered against his mouth, "No...it's good...so good..." His heart began to beat again, pounding out a pagan rhythm that matched the pace of her movements as she executed the ancient rites of love.

Hands touched, smoothed and kneaded tender flesh gently, oh, so gently. Mouths lingered, tasting, nibbling, sipping, savoring the taste of each other in a wedding feast of unsurpassed delectation as Lindy sacrificed her heart, her soul at the altar of her love.

When he could stand no more, Zade rolled over and was still, pinning her to the mattress, his body buried deeply inside her while he rested his perspiration-damp forehead against hers and drew in deep breaths of air in an attempt to slow down the pace of their union. His breath was hot on her cheek, and she pressed her lips to the corner of his mouth, her own breathing reedy with exertion and excitement.

"I love you," she whispered, her hips resuming motion while her teeth closed ever so softly on his bottom lip.

His answer was to move away from her, an action that wrung a cry of dismay from her lips. Then he half lifted her, adjusting his body and moving against her, resuming the dance as hip moved against hip—together, apart, together...ever faster and deeper, deeper and faster.

Zade was the quintessence of her desire, the heart of her body, the newly found focus of her life. He was her salvation, saving her from a life of running from herself and her mistake. He was her hope for all her tomorrows as the love he professed manifested itself day to day in the acts of caring he performed. He was her joy, bringing her ever nearer the zenith of the delicious insanity screaming for release each time his superbly fashioned male body moved within the warm, moist sheathing of hers.

She wanted to give as she had never given before, longed to pay him back for all the happiness he'd give her, needed to destroy him as he was slowly, inexorably destroying her with his mouth, his hands, his...

They cried out simultaneously as they both found their release—Zade in a paroxysm of fulfillment greater than any he could ever remember, quenching the sexual fire blazing out of control as he showered Lindy with the proof of his desire, filled her with his love. Her nails dug into the bareness of his sweat-slickened buttocks as one delicious shudder followed another in a diminishing ripple of wonderment until she lay replete, sated, the weight of his body a pleasant reality as it rested heavily on hers.

Long, long moments later, Zade lifted his head, gazing down at her with a sleepy sensuality in his eyes and a smile of supreme satisfaction arcing his beautiful mouth. "Am I too heavy?"

Lindy smiled wearily, shook the tangled red mop of her hair and pressed a halfhearted kiss to his damp shoulder.

"Are you okay? I wasn't...too rough?" His voice held a note of concern, and his dark brows drew together in a sudden frown.

Lindy's smile broadened and she slanted him a teasing look up through the dark tangle of her lashes. "Was I?"

He chuckled, the sound deep and warm and unbelievably sexy. "Oh, I may have a few bruises tomorrow, but I think I can take it," he said facetiously. He appeared totally intrigued with the way one of her auburn brows winged out at the corner as he said casually, "You're a very satisfying lover."

Lindy's heart rate increased a fraction. "I am?"

His eyes found hers. "Love," he said, his silver-gray eyes suddenly serious, "the word and the act take on new meaning with you. I've never experienced anything quite like what we just shared."

"But, what about..." she began.

His fingers moved to press gently against her love-swollen lips. He propped himself up on one elbow and cupped her head with his free hand, pulling her closer and claiming her mouth with a kiss of near reverence. "Never."

Lindy's heart swelled with emotion.

His hand moved to caress her shoulder, and one hair-sprinkled leg insinuated itself between hers. "You're really something, Mrs. Wakefield. So warm, so sweet, so incredibly sexy you take my breath away."

"Sexy!" Lindy scoffed. "I've never been sexy in my life. I'm the wholesome type, you know, the freckle-faced girl next door?"

"I deny anyone to look at you as you are right now and say you aren't sexy," he told her, his fingers skimming over the slope of her breast.

"No one but you will ever see me like this," she reminded him.

"A fact that makes me very thankful," he told her softly. "Because you're a redheaded witch who gives and gives and gives. And waiting six weeks for what I just sampled was well worth it," he added with a smile.

"Oh, yeah?" she taunted, the smile wreathing her features proof of how deliriously happy she was.

"Yeah."

Zade pulled her flush against him, and they laughed for the sheer joy of being together and in love. A state of mind and body both hoped would last far into eternity. Then he kissed her, and there was little doubt, Lindy thought as she pressed closer, that it was a state that would last at least into the foreseeable future. The look in his eyes and the timbre of sincerity in his voice couldn't be faked, could they? He said he'd never been so happy, never felt what she made him feel. Not even Margot had satisfied him so well.

Zade pulled back and looked at her flushed face, the laughter still glinting in the depths of his eyes. "Once more?" he asked. "With feeling?"

Giggles bubbled from Lindy's throat; she was surprised he remembered her corny line from the car. He was alive now, and able to experience all life had to offer, both the joys and sorrows, because he was now involved with living life instead of divorcing his emotions from it. It just went to show, she thought as she felt her own emotions quickly getting out of hand once more, that love could indeed change people.

The weekend didn't last nearly long enough, but the short time Zade and Lindy spent at the Holiday Inn was at least uninterrupted. Both Jill and Josh had been "angels" according to Mrs. Hancock, who promptly offered her services any time Lindy and Zade needed a baby-sitter.

If Lindy thought the first six weeks of her marriage had been perfect, then there was no word to describe the closeness she and Zade reached after their weekend together. Marriage to Zade was like living a dream. Each day brought new discoveries, new plateaus of harmony—both emotional and physical. He was a far different man from the stranger who had looked so out of place in Amy's office less than three months ago. He smiled. He laughed. He wore his newly found joy with an ease reflected in the more casual look of his clothing, the lilt of happiness in his voice and the relaxed demeanor he presented to the world.

Lindy, still disbelieving that life should hand her such happiness a second time, carefully wrapped her memories of Randy with a thin tissue of nostalgia and tucked them away into a corner of her heart, tossing away the last shreds of her grief. Randy would never be forgotten by his son; Lindy would see to that. Together, she and Josh would periodically take out the memories that, like the shoebox full of pictures tucked away on a shelf of the closet, chronicled their time together and lovingly examine each one in an effort to keep Josh's remembrances of his father clear and vivid in his mind.

Nor would Lindy forget him. He'd been her first, true love and Josh's father, but he was now delegated to that special place in her heart where all good and treasured things were hidden from the realities of life. Randy was her past; Zade was her future.

With Zade as her husband and more maturity sitting on her slim shoulders, Lindy's personality, always glowing, took on a new brilliance. Or, perhaps the love he brought to her life only brought back what Randy's death had dimmed for a while. Whatever it was, she exuded an enviable radiance of physical and mental well-being to everyone she came into contact with.

Only one thing clouded her sky, and that was the Memorial Day get-together Amy and Steve were having at their house. It would be Lindy's first official appearance as hotel-tycoon Zade Wakefield's wife. A prospect that made her unbearably nervous.

"You're going to be just fine," Zade, propped against the headboard of the bed, told her the night before Memorial Day.

"I'm scared," she confessed, pulling her nightgown over her head, its soft folds sliding over her hips to the floor.

"You're silly. And take that thing off."

"Silly and scared," she said, obeying his off-handed command mechanically, and slipping beneath the sheets into his arms.

He laughed. "What are you so afraid of?"

"These people are society, for goodness' sake!"

"Society? Good Lord! You know Steve and Amy, and Paul and Tammy. Their opinions are the only ones important to me, and they all adore you. Forget the rest. Once you smile that Lindy smile, you'll have them eating out of your hand."

"What Lindy smile?" she asked, moving closer and throwing one leg over his as she nestled closer against his hairy chest and inhaled the clean, male scent of him.

"The one that's comparable to the sun coming out after a three-day rain," he said seriously.

"That's crazy. Everyone smiles."

"True. But you glow when you smile," he explained, lifting her chin with one finger, his own eyes tender as they looked down into hers. "I think that smile is one of the things I found so irresistible about you."

"Irresistible?"

"Irresistible. The smile and your freckles."

"Oh, sure. They're absolutely stunning!" she said wryly, tugging at a wisp of hair on his chest as a minor punishment.

"No, not stunning," he corrected, pushing her down against the pillows and reaching to turn the lampshade so that the bareness of her upper torso was bathed in the warmth of the lamplight. "Interesting. And irresistible."

Lindy's breathing quickened and her pulse raced to catch up. She knew exactly what that wicked gleam in his eyes meant. She was in grave danger of losing a night's sleep. The thought triggered her desire, which seemed to be stuck in overdrive since her marriage to Zade. "Explain," she whispered, her breasts swelling in the warmth of his hands that captured their willing heaviness.

"I can show you better," he grinned, dropping a kiss in turn to each pouting nipple. His finger began to move over the upper swell of her breasts, moving fractionally, straying upward in a straight line.

"What are you doing?"

"Writing 'I love you.'"

"What?"

"I'm connecting the dots—freckles to you. I always did love dot-to-dot when I was a kid." His finger trailed slowly, tracing a crooked I on her flesh, then moving to an L.

"There isn't enough room," she said. "You'll have to write 'you' on my back."

"Uh-uh. The good part is that I can erase what I've started and begin again."

"Yeah? How?" she challenged.

"Like this." His head bent and his lips began to move slowly over the place his finger had been "writing." He raised his eyes to hers triumphantly. "See. All gone. It's a continuing mystery to me just how it works," he said in mock-serious tones.

"You're crazy!"

"Hmmm. I don't doubt it," he said a bit distractedly as his finger began to spell out another word. "And tired, too. Marriage to you has me fitter than I ever was before."

Lindy laughed softly, the soft sound sending a ripple of desire skittering down Zade's spine. "And what are you writing now?"

"Sexy," he said unhesitatingly.

Lindy's laughing, love-filled eyes smiled up at him. "I love you."

His heart skipped a beat. Would he ever tire of hearing her confess her love for him, he wondered as his finger suddenly trailed lower, across one pouting nipple. "Uh oh."

"What happened?" she queried, raising her head and peering down at her chest.

"My finger slipped. I got out of line on the Y," he explained, while that same finger traced small concentric circles around the pink aureole of her nipple, an action that had absolutely nothing to do with writing "sexy."

"Oh. Well, maybe you'd better erase it," she suggested, her eyes glowing with barely concealed excitement.

He grinned wickedly, winked at her and nodded. "Good idea." His head lowered, and his mouth touched the hard tip of her breast, opening over it and drawing it into his mouth.

Lindy drew in a sharp breath that hung suspended on a thread of pleasure as his tongue bathed the sensitive peak, curling around it and drawing that same pleasure up from deep within her with the slow flexing of his mouth. Her hands came up to rest on the shining blackness of his hair, and her fingers wound through the glossy thickness, holding him to her. His lips gradually moved up slowly over the upper fullness of her breasts, before he finally lifted his head. There was no laughter in his eyes now, eyes whose silvery light reflected the look of wide-eyed anticipation on her face.

"Did you…erase it?" she asked breathlessly as a bolt of sexual electricity flashed through her at the unleashed hunger in his eyes.

He nodded. "Now it just says 'sex.'"

Lindy's hands moved to cup his lean, whisker-stubbled cheeks. "Sounds like a winner to me," she murmured, half raising herself to press her lips to his. Zade's warm, open mouth covered hers with something akin to desperation as he pushed her back onto the bed with the power of his body. Her legs moved to accommodate him, parting eagerly as he lowered himself to rest heavily against the cradle of her body.

His breath came out in a long sigh, and his mouth softened against hers as he began a series of slow, drugging kisses, his teeth nibbling at the fullness of her lower lip, drawing it into his mouth with a sensuous suckling. His tongue traced the curvaceous shape of her upper lip and delved into the honeyed cavern of her mouth, mapping out each place that brought a sigh or a moan, and marking it in his mind.

His hands, never still, moved over her breasts, palming their fullness and caressing her with a controlled urgency that whipped Lindy's senses into a frenzy of longing. Then, slowly, inexorably, his hand moved over her now-flat abdomen and lower, seeking out the readiness of her body.

She whimpered and arched nearer. Zade moved slightly, easing the pulsating fullness of himself into the haven of her, finding within the soft tunnel both contentment and excitement. He edged deeper and stopped, kissing her gently, tenderly, reverently, while one hand brushed the hair from her face and he sought to control the emotions threatening to swamp his normal equilibrium. Only Lindy out of all the women in his life had this effect on him. Only she had the power to wipe his mind free of all past pain, making him live only for the moment but with a gaze staring eagerly into the future.

His eyes locked with hers as he began to move against her, his body stroking hers with a building need as her reciprocal need transformed the sherry hue of her eyes to the dark warmth of port. Her breathing quickened with each sensual surge of body to body, and her mouth, parted and wet from his kisses, lured him back for more, a temptation he couldn't refuse as his mouth took hers again, hungrily, greedily and with a desperation born of the fear that somehow having her for his wife—having her love was all too good, too perfect, too fantastic to last. A fear that haunted him daily, forcing him to take all she so generously offered as often as he could. It was never enough, nor would it ever be.

Zade didn't know Lindy faced the same fear. A fear too terrible to think about. But a fear that plagued her daily, forcing her to take all he so generously offered, as often as she could.

Chapter Twelve

"Do I look okay?" Lindy's words, rife with uncertainty, were accompanied by a quick pirouette. Dressed in a Hawaiian print blouse and matching wrap skirt in yellow, purple, red and green and with her vibrantly polished toenails peeking from strappy red sandals she looked cool, summery and very stylish.

"You look great!" Zade assured her, planting a quick kiss on her forehead before he snapped and zipped his white tennis shorts then sat down on the bed to pull on his socks and shoes.

"I feel wretched," she groaned, peering into the mirror to check her makeup.

"Nerves?"

"Hmmm," she nodded, "and a headache."

"A bad one?"

She shrugged. "At this point it could go either way. I think it was the night we had last night."

"It did go downhill in a hurry, didn't it?" he offered wryly.

She smiled. "When I thought about being awake all night,

it certainly wasn't because I thought Jill would have a bout of colic."

Zade gave her a sympathetic smile that told her he was sorry their night of loving was interrupted, too. "Is she okay this morning?"

"Sleeping like a rock. She hardly woke up when I bathed and dressed her."

"Good. What do you think caused it?" he asked, tying his shoes.

Lindy heaved a deep sigh and laughed shortly. "It's hard to say. She's had a bit of a problem ever since I switched her to formula. Thank you for helping with her. It made the night much easier."

"Isn't that what fathers are supposed to do? Help?"

"I've always thought so, but a lot of men feel like their job is finished when the woman gets pregnant."

Zade's eyes held a combination of pleasure and peace as he told her, "I don't want to miss out on anything, good or bad, that Jill does."

His statement seemed true. Lindy had never seen anyone take to parenting as Zade Wakefield had. From the moment she walked into this house with the intention of marrying him, she had been amazed at his involvement with Jill, especially since she was someone else's daughter. Oh, she'd expected him to pay a certain amount of attention to her since he enjoyed Josh so much, but she'd never expected the utter devotion he seemed to feel for her daughter.

The first surprise was the nursery. A mother and child's delight, the capricious clowns made the time spent in the room cheerful and pleasant. She couldn't believe how quickly he had redecorated the room after she agreed to marry him. The nursery was the first place he went each evening after he kissed her and Josh hello. She had watched him more than once as he leaned over the bassinet just watching Jill sleep. He always took his turn walking the floor, and once Jill switched to the bottle he appeared to delight in feeding her and watching her blow milk bubbles.

Lindy leaned against the dresser now, her pleasure-filled eyes tracking him as he went to the closet and pulled out a knit shirt. Last night had been above and beyond the call of duty. At 3:00 A.M. she had been ready to cry with weariness and frustration. Every time she tried to put the fitfully sleeping baby in her bed she woke up screaming. She had rocked, rubbed, patted and prayed until she reeled with exhaustion. She'd been sitting with her head thrown against the rocker's high back when she felt Zade's warm touch on her shoulder.

"Let me take over for a while," he said softly.

"Oh, no. I'll be fine."

"You're worn out, and we're going to have a big day tomorrow."

"I know," she sighed.

"Come on. Up."

With a sigh, Lindy rose and thankfully handed the baby to him. Jill promptly roused and fussed the prerequisite five minutes before succumbing to sleep once more. Lindy, alone in the big bed she shared with her new husband, had heard the baby's wails and imagined she could hear Zade's low murmurings of comfort as she had tumbled into a restless sleep herself.

"Earth to Lindy. Earth to Lindy. Come in please."

Lindy jumped, her startled eyes meeting Zade's at his reminder to come back to the present from wherever her thoughts were wandering. She gave him an embarrassed smile. "I'm sorry. I was woolgathering."

"I thought you were sleeping with your eyes open," he teased, crossing to her and dropping a kiss to her poppy-red lips.

"Well, you're disgustingly alert for a man who was up from three o'clock until dawn and claims to have only slept in bits and snatches before that," she said with a touch of mock asperity flavoring her voice.

Pulling her closer and rubbing noses with her he said, "That's because I wasn't awake from three on."

Lindy's brows drew together. "You weren't?"

"Uh-uh. Once you got to sleep, I carried Jill in here, stretched out with her on my chest and we both slept like babies," he said.

Lindy's mouth fell open. Why hadn't she done that herself? She'd resorted to that numerous times with Josh, but for some reason it had escaped her bag of tricks last night. Maybe she was more out of practice than she thought. Or maybe she was just afraid she might bother Zade's rest. "How did you know to do that?"

"I moonlight as a nanny," he quipped lightly, then held up a protective arm when Lindy raised a menacing fist. "Okay. Okay. Necessity is the mother of invention. I was as pooped as you, and I thought if she wouldn't let us put her down, I'd go down with her. Simple."

"You're amazing."

"I know."

Her eyes laughed up at him. "And conceited."

"I like to think of it as being positive about my image," he told her in pseudo-serious tones.

Lindy's laughter was soon joined by the low rumble of Zade's. He held her in the circle of his embrace, hugging her tightly in a celebration of life and love.

The entire back end of Amy and Steve's three-acre estate was a kaleidoscope of ever shifting colors, sounds and impressions. The shimmering heat of the late spring day was rent with the squeals of children splashing in the small above-ground pool erected just for them. The sound of a group of wildly yelling men engaged in a game of water volleyball in the huge tiled pool reserved for the grown-ups mingled with the childish laughter. Zade was participating in a tennis tournament. Lindy, still sleepy and plagued with a headache that grew progressively worse in the noise and heat, played a desultory game of croquet, while Tammy watched Jill, who was content to lie in her playpen cooing.

Savory-smelling smoke wafted through the air from silver barbecue pits created from fifty-five gallon drums, an aromatic promise of chicken, sausage and ribs coated with Steve's famous honey and brown sugar barbecue sauce. A Cajun cooker held a smoking turkey and baking potatoes. Tops popped from sweating cola cans, ice clinked into throw-away glasses, and potato chip bags rustled and crinkled as everyone nibbled and munched, waiting for lunch to be ready.

Lindy sat down on a lounge chair, sipping a glass of tea, watching the dappling of sun and shade through the leaves of a huge oak tree and willing her headache to go away. She should have taken something before she left the house, she thought, especially knowing that she had such a long day in front of her. She massaged her temples and held her cool palms to her warm cheeks. What was it they said about hindsight?

"Mrs. Wakefield?" The voice of Casi, Amy's daughter, interrupted her thoughts and misery.

"Hello, Casi," Lindy said, forcing a smile to her lips. "How's it going?"

"Pretty good. Josh fell down and cut his chin chasing the cat. Mom wanted me to find you and let you know."

Lindy had leaped to her feet as soon as she heard the words, "fell down." The pounding in her head increased with the rush of anxiety and adrenaline through her body. "Where is he?"

"In the house."

Lindy asked Tammy to watch the baby again and followed Casi to the large replica of antebellum splendor that the Fedders called home. By the time she reached the back door, Josh and Amy were already coming out, both wearing smiles, and Josh carrying a Fudgsicle.

"Hi, Mom!" he said nonchalantly. "Dr. Amy fitzed my chin. And I didn't even cry…much," he amended.

The relief that swept through Lindy was overwhelming and welcome. Her eyes met Amy's in a silent thank you.

"Run on back to the pool with Casi, Josh," Amy suggested. "But be careful not to bump your chin."

"Yes, ma'am," he said obediently, licking the frozen treat and following Casi back toward the children's pool.

Amy regarded her friend carefully. "He's fine. The cut is about a half-inch long and a quarter of an inch deep. I put a butterfly bandage on it. So stop worrying."

"I'm not worrying," Lindy assured her. "I just feel so rotten."

"What is it? Lack of sleep? Zade told Steve you had a bad night with Jill."

"That's part of it, but I have another of those rotten headaches."

"Did you take anything?"

"No. I was so busy getting everything ready for the day that the next thing I knew we were on our way and I hadn't taken a thing!"

"Look, there's no reason to suffer with it. You aren't pregnant, you aren't nursing Jill, and there's a party out there waiting for you," Amy said with a smile. "You know where my study is?" When Lindy nodded, she continued. "There's a key to the middle drawer in that little wooden box on top of my desk. I have a sample packet of Darvon in there. Take one and lie down for a while. You'll be good as new in no time."

A thankful smile relieved the visible tension on Lindy's face. "Thanks. I think I will. If you see Zade, tell him I'm in here resting, will you?"

"Will do," Amy said.

Lindy entered the air-conditioned coolness of the house, admiring, as she made her way to the study, the antique furnishings. The room she sought was dim, darkened by the porch that ran the length of the house and the partially closed shutters at the windows. A massive, rolltop desk, all oak and shiny brass, dominated the room which was flanked on both sides by floor to ceiling bookcases. The room was quiet, the noise of the picnic nothing but a muted hum.

The key was exactly where Amy had said it was. Lindy lowered herself into the swivel chair and inserted the old-fashioned key into the brass-protected keyhole. It turned with no problem, and the drawer slid open with well-waxed ease. There were several papers and folders in the shallow drawer, plus the usual conglomeration of paper clips, rubber bands and pencils. A quick search failed to turn up the small packet, and Lindy pulled out the stack of folders and placed them in her lap. The sample was probably wedged between some of the papers or something, she reasoned, picking up the top folder and placing it on the desk.

Nothing between it and the next one.

Nor the second.

The third folder was on its way to the top of the growing stack on the desk when the name LINDY SCOTT leaped off the tabbed edge at her. A folder with her name on it? Here? At this house? Why?

The reason hit her with the force of a locomotive, draining the blood from her head and leaving her reeling with the realization. Of course the file would be here instead of the office! This was the *secret* file. The file concerning the surrogate transaction Amy had taken care of for her. The file that no one but Amy was supposed to see or know about…ever.

One finger traced the heavy black lettering spelling her name, while her heart and her head beat out a synchronized rhythm. Open it…open it…open it… She lifted the folder's edge, then fearfully slammed it shut. She couldn't. Did she really want to know who Jill's father was? Did it matter? Zade was her father. Now and forever. He was there when she was born. He took care of paying the money back to the real father. He loved her as much as any father could love a child. That was apparent from the attention he gave her. There was absolutely no reason to look inside the folder.

Except the natural curiosity born within all mankind.

She picked up the folder and held it to her breast, fighting the urge building within her and knowing it was a losing battle. *Don't!* her mind screamed, but her hands were already lowering the manila folder to her lap and opening it. Her eyes scanned the typewritten pages quickly, urgently, fearfully.

They skimmed her name. Stopped. And stared at the name beside it.

ZADE WAKEFIELD.

Lindy's heartbeat seemed to stumble to a halt, then jerked into a heavy pounding that echoed in her head. Her breath hung in her throat, suspended in disbelief as her beautiful, love-filled world shattered around her for the second time in her life. *Zade!* It made so much sense, really. How simple for Amy to match the two of them up. Lindy's aching head began to throb, and her breathing resumed with a gasp that some part of her mind connected with crying. She continued to stare at the name in disbelief. Zade. Jill's father. That's why he'd accepted her so readily. How wonderful that Jill would know her real father. Wonderful for Jill.

Terrible for Lindy.

The tears burning beneath her eyelids and blurring her vision began to slide slowly, hopelessly down her pale cheeks. *He wants the baby. He plans to subpoena the information about who the woman is.*

Is that how Zade found out? No. They'd been seeing each other for weeks and Amy only received the subpoena the day Jill was born. Amy was his cousin. Had she told him? Lindy's mind refused to think in a coherent pattern, couldn't put all the pieces together, but one fact stood out as if laser-etched into her brain.

Zade didn't love her.

He had married her only to get his child. Zade, who never wanted to marry again, a man who went to great lengths to have a baby without the trappings of marriage, had made the supreme sacrifice in the end, and tied himself to a woman he didn't love. He said he'd do anything to get his baby, and he had.

Humiliation at how easily she'd fallen into his plans, how easily she'd allowed herself to believe all the things he had told her, burned through her body. She had always wondered just what he saw in her. She remembered asking him why he was in such a hurry to get married, remembered the way he had kissed her, telling her how much he loved her and how he couldn't wait to make her his wife. The pain of his betrayal of all that was perfect and good between them clawed at her heart and her mind.

Lies.

All lies.

He didn't love her. Didn't love Josh. Harsh laughter bordering on the hysterical bubbled up inside her and spilled into the room with an effervescence gone suddenly flat. She couldn't remember how many times she had asked him and herself what he saw in her. And now she knew. She was a means to an end. The way to get what he was really after. How could she have allowed herself to be used this way? Simple. She'd loved him. Still loved him.

"Lindy?" Zade's voice. She hadn't heard him open the door, but there he stood—beautifully, vibrantly male. Clad in white tennis shorts and the aura of masculinity that made him the most exciting man she'd ever come into contact with. Her throat tightened with more tears. He looked unbearably sexy, unbearably dear. And it was all suddenly...unbearable.

He moved farther into the room. "Are you all right? It sounded as if you were crying."

Lindy was silent. She couldn't speak, couldn't trust her voice. She was hurting too badly. He came closer. His indrawn breath warned her that he saw the ravages of the tears still rolling down her cheeks.

Without a word, she held out the folder. A flicker of something passed over the silvery surface of his eyes before his lashes dropped to hide them as he stared at the printed pages. No more than a second or two passed, but it seemed like eons before she saw his fingers clench the folder. Her anguished eyes climbed the strong plane of his face to his eyes, hoping she would find solace, peace, denial. Instead, she saw ashen features, a hardened jaw, and eyes filled with pain and pleading that aged him beyond his years.

"Lindy...let me explain..."

"Did you know Jill was yours when you married me?" she

interrupted. She was proud of herself. Her voice was calm, controlled, nothing at all like the emotions seething through her. Hurt at being deceived. Embarrassment that she'd been led so easily to his trap. And anger—her only defense against making a complete and total fool of herself. "Did you know?"

Zade blinked in surprise at the measured fury in her voice. He knew that if nothing else, he owed her his honesty. His eyes bored steadily into hers. "Yes."

She literally wilted. Her head drooped on the slender stem of her neck like a flower left too long in the sun. All the brightness, all the emotion, even the anger fled from her face, leaving it blank, empty and cold, without its usual animation. Zade moved around the desk and took her shoulders in his hands.

"Take your hands off me!" she yelled into the quiet of the room. Startled at the vehemence in her voice, his hands fell to his sides and he took a step backward. From just outside the room, a feminine voice trilled in joyous laughter. Pure mockery, considering the palpably anguished feelings roiling in Amy Fedder's study.

"We need to talk about this," he said huskily. "It isn't what you think."

Flat, sherry-colored eyes lifted to his. "How do you know what I think?"

Determined, Zade pressed on. "You're thinking that the only reason I married you was to get Jill."

"Isn't it?"

Zade's control broke. The foundation of his world was crumbling away beneath him, and there was nothing he could do but try, somehow, to make her see reason. In an instant of perfect clarity he realized that nothing he did or said would change things. God, it was worse than he had ever imagined it would be if she found out. Much worse. "After everything we've shared these past few weeks how can you even think such a thing?" he demanded in a grating tone, warning her that he, too, was perilously close to losing control.

At the mention of their happiness the past few weeks, Lindy

felt the sting of his duplicity all over again. She willed the anger to come back and push the aching knowledge of his betrayal far, far into some corner of her mind where she wouldn't have to think of it. She didn't want to think about it, or talk about it. If she could only stay angry until she was alone, she might at least retain a shred of her tattered dignity and battered pride. Wordlessly, she rose and brushed past him, her back rigid, her head throbbing, longing for nothing more than to escape the room before she made a complete fool of herself.

She was almost to the door when his voice lashed out from behind, swearing with a violence that made her cringe. Then he spat out harshly, "Answer me, damn you!"

Whirling around with a speed that amazed him, she tossed his words of months before back at him, "'I'm going to get my baby somehow. Whatever it takes.' Do you remember saying words to that effect, Zade?" She clung to the bitter pleasure of seeing his face pale once more. "After all the horrible threats you made to me through Paul and Amy how can I believe anything else?"

Futility welled slowly through him. She was right. He had said all those things. He had promised those people involved in the legal transaction he would get his child some way. Those promises—threats—had been passed on to Lindy. He suddenly saw things crystal clearly through her eyes. He also saw how near collapse she was. Saw the pain and anger in her eyes. His heart swelled to the bursting point knowing how much hurt he'd caused her. Dear God! Who would ever have thought it would come to this?

He knew there would be no reasoning with her now. Not until the initial shock had worn off. Tonight, when they got home, he would set her down and make her see reason. Make her understand that he hadn't known until the night Jill was born who she was. And make her believe it. He ran a trembling hand through his hair and heaved a deep, shuddering sigh. Waiting wasn't his strong suit.

Tell me it's a mistake. Tell me you love me. Do something

to make me believe that what we have is as wonderful as it's seemed these past few weeks. Lindy's thoughts screamed silently into the room. Instead, she watched him rake a trembling hand through his already tousled hair and give a great sigh. Then, as if he could take no more, he turned and faced the window, his hand resting on his slim hips.

Silently, and on legs that shook so badly she feared she couldn't walk, Lindy let herself out of the study, to escape to some quiet place so she could lick her wounds, the reason for going there in the first place wiped totally from her mind.

The brief display of anger anesthetized her emotions long enough for her to make some sort of garbled excuse to Amy and Steve. She was still in shock when she found Josh and gathered the baby and her trappings from Tammy, asking her friend to drive her home because of a splitting headache. By the time she reached the house the numbness was wearing off, leaving her with an overwhelming grief and the question of what to do with the newly discovered evidence of Zade's identity and the fact that he married her to get Jill.

She put Josh down for a nap, put the already sleeping baby in her crib and took some long overdue medication for her headache, now a pain of mammoth proportions.

She cried, hurt with the pain of a cut to the heart.

Then she paced. And hurt some more. What could she do? She loved him so much, how could he not love her in return? And finally, just when the headache showed signs of abating, she realized what she had to do.

It was three-thirty in the afternoon when Zade pulled into the driveway of the lake house. He had stayed at Amy's far longer than he actually had wanted to, just to give Lindy time to calm down so they could talk. Amy, too, seemed to think some time and space might put a different perspective on things. She didn't say it, but Zade could feel the "I told you so" in her manner. She had warned him from the very beginning that the surrogate idea of his was one rife with possible repercussions. But he couldn't see the potential problems for the burning desire to have a child of his own. Just as Lindy couldn't see his love for the threats he had unknowingly made to her.

His heart fell to his toes when he saw that her blue Pulsar wasn't in the garage. The set of his mouth was grim as he slammed on the brakes and threw the gearshift into park. He already knew emptiness resided within, waiting to infiltrate the spot in his heart where love lived only that morning. With that same heart hammering inside the cage of his ribs, Zade approached the kitchen door, hesitant now to enter and face his fate.

Surprisingly, the kitchen wasn't empty. Trish Rowel sat at the table drinking a glass of tea and reading a magazine. She looked up with a slight smile in her blue eyes as Zade entered the room. "Hi. You're back sooner than I expected. Lindy said she wasn't certain how long you'd stay at the barbecue."

When Zade made no comment she continued, "It's really too bad about her grandmother being so sick and all. Once she got home and called, she decided she'd better go on to Blytheville and check on her. When someone gets to be seventy-eight you never know. Hey! You'd better sit down. You look like you're gonna pass out on me. You didn't get more bad news, did you?"

"No," he murmured, thankful that Trish's talkativeness relieved the necessity of asking awkward questions. But yes, he'd just received more bad news. Lindy was gone. Both her grandmothers had been dead for several years. *Lindy, Lindy, why did you go?*

"No," he repeated more firmly. "I was just...surprised to find you here. I—I thought she might call and tell me what was going on."

Trish's coral-tinted lips curved into a pleasing smile. "Oh, I was here to watch the baby until you got home."

Blood drained from Zade's face with one huge rush. His voice was barely audible as he repeated, "The baby?"

Trish's curly blond hair bobbed as she nodded. "Lindy left Jill here. She said if she had to sit up at the hospital or anything, she'd just have to find a baby-sitter for her *and* Josh. She said you could get Mrs. Hancock to watch her on Monday if she isn't back by then. Besides, she thought you might like the company this weekend."

Zade nodded, totally incapable of speech. Lindy had left him and had taken Josh. But she'd left Jill. Why? It didn't make sense...or did it?

"Gee, Zade, you look terrible," Trish said, dumping the remains of her tea in the sink and frowning at him. "Why don't you take a nap? I'm going on home to start dinner. Do you want to come over later? We're having fried chicken."

Forcing a smile to his lips, Zade declined. "No, thanks, Trish. Maybe another time. I think I got hold of something at the cookout that didn't agree with me."

She shrugged knit-covered shoulders. "Sure."

"Look, do I owe you anything for keeping Jill?"

"Don't be silly. I gave her one bottle, and she's slept like a log ever since." She moved toward the door. "Look, if you need anything while Lindy's gone, just give us a call, huh?"

"I will," Zade assured her. "Thanks, Trish."

"Any time."

The door began to close, then her head popped back around, her gamine features wreathed with another smile. "I almost forgot. She left you a note in the bedroom." The door closed softly, and Zade's eyelashes drifted shut to block out the pain swamping him. Lindy...Lindy...

His footsteps, slow and heavy, led him to the bedroom. There, propped against the mirror, was a long white envelope. He reached for it with palsied hands and carried it to the bed. Perched on the edge, he opened the flap and drew out several sheets of mauve stationery.

Lindy's decisive, rounded script leaped off the page.

Zade, it began. No endearment, just the shortest of salutations.

> *As you know by now, Josh and I have gone. I don't know where we're going, and I don't suppose it matters*

to you. As Trish told you, I am leaving Jill. Under the circumstances, I feel it is the only possible thing I can do. She is your daughter. You wanted her so badly you paid a lot of money to have her. And I wanted the money so badly I said I would give her up. You upheld your part of the bargain; I didn't. Legally, morally, she is yours.

Emotion clutched Zade's throat. Anguish, sharp, pungent, filled his soul. He read on:

But the real reason I'm leaving Jill with you is because, in spite of your rationale for going into this marriage, my reason was the traditional one of love. Less than three months ago, I couldn't give my baby to a stranger, even though he was the biological father because I loved it and wanted to be a part of its growing up. But now I find that as much as I do love that baby— our Jill—I love you more.

The letter, written with a felt-tip pen was spotted with tear stains, black ink running the letters completely together in places. Zade hardly noticed; he wasn't certain the splotches weren't the result of the tears flooding his own eyes and falling onto the pages. He drew in a deep, soul-shuddering breath.

You need her, Zade, for so many reasons, but mostly because Jill will be your salvation. The Zade Wakefield I first met was hard, unyielding, unlaughing. But watching you with our daughter has made me see the tremendous changes loving her has wrought in you.

Zade threw his head back and stared up at the ceiling through the glaze of tears in his eyes. It wasn't just Jill who had changed him. It started with Josh and Lindy. It was being a part of people who cared back. It was learning that there was meaning to the words "trust" and "love." And people you could trust with your love. He did love Jill. Having her would help to ease the pain of Lindy's leaving, but it wouldn't nullify it. There was no way that all the love Jill would give him through their lifetimes could ever compensate for losing Lindy. The crack in his heart widened. He wiped his nose with the back of his hand and lowered his eyes to the letter again.

And so I leave her with you—not gladly—my heart weeps at the knowledge that I won't see her again—but willingly, because I know how much you truly love and need her. Knowing that, and the love I feel for you, will make her absence in my life bearable.

There was more, something about how to mix Jill's formula and how often to feed her, but Zade could read no further for the tears running without shame down his cheeks and the harsh sobs racking his body. With movements that seemed slow and clumsy, he placed the letter on the bedside table and pushed himself from the bed.

It wasn't far to the nursery, but it seemed to Zade to take forever to make the short journey down the hallway. He stood in the door, looking into the room, imagining he could hear Lindy's voice singing a lullaby as she rocked Jill to sleep.

Jill.

How could simply wanting a baby so badly have caused so much heartache? And how could love cause such joy and such pain? It wasn't fair…. He approached the bed quietly. Jill lay on her stomach, her face turned toward him, one fist pressed against her lips. He reached down and laid his hand on the sweet-curving line of her bottom. She stirred briefly and began a noisy sucking on her clenched fingers. Zade smiled through the curtain of his silent tears. Unable to help himself, he reached into the bed and lifted her into his arms, turning her and cradling her against his chest.

Going from soft comfort to the hardness of her father's chest, combined with the harsh sounds coming from his throat roused Jill from a deep sleep. She stiffened in his embrace and let loose a blood-curdling wail of her own, waving her tiny fists in the air in protest.

He moved to the rocking chair, pushed the bear to the floor and sat down, holding her close as he rocked to and fro, back and forth. His lips brushed softly against the top of her head. A head covered with the incredibly soft, red-gold hair so much like Lindy's.

Together they cried out their misery to the silent, brooding house...each in his own way seeking what comfort they could from the other.

"I know where she is."

Amy's voice spoke the sweetest five words Zade thought he had ever heard. They were certainly the most precious he had heard in the month since Lindy had left him. His hand gripped the telephone receiver and he leaned back against the kitchen counter. "Where?"

"Shreveport, Louisiana," Amy said.

"Did she call?"

"No. I just had a hunch late yesterday evening. Knowing Lindy as we both do, what is the first thing she'd do once she got settled in?"

"God, Amy, I don't know! Let's don't play games. Just tell me."

"She'd find a pediatrician for Josh. She's very conscientious about all that, and more so with him because of the accident."

"You're right."

"So..." Amy drawled, "I just called his doctor here and asked if his records had been transferred, and where. I told them I needed to forward Lindy's records and the girl in the office had lost the address. Pretty quick thinking, huh?"

"Pretty quick," Zade agreed, the first real smile he had had on his face in four weeks lighting up his face. "So give me the address!"

"Patience, patience," his cousin said, laughter in her voice.

Zade wrote down the address and thanked Amy.

"What are you going to do?"

"I'm going to bring her home."

"Just like that?"

"Just like that."

"Good luck."

"Thanks." He recradled the phone and let out a rebel yell that shook the kitchen. Then, his feet barely skimming the floor, he raced into the nursery and began to pull things from the drawer. Three-month-old Jill, who lay on her back totally entranced with the musical mobile hanging overhead, turned her head to look at him when he stood over the bed. Her arms and legs began a furious pumping, and a wide, toothless smile lifted the tiny bow of her lips. Zade picked her up and held her close, his lips nuzzling the soft skin of her neck. "Wanna go get Mommie?" he asked in a low whisper. "Huh?"

Jill's answer was a soft coo of assent.

Lindy lifted the sack of groceries from the car and swung them to her hip. The early July heat combined with the Louisiana humidity was almost unbearable. Still, there was a bounce to her step that had been noticeably absent the past month. Hope did spring eternal, she thought. "Josh, get those panty hose, will you?"

He picked up the package, but not without a frown. He frowned a lot lately. Moody and irritable, Josh was nothing at all like the child she had nurtured for four years. He still cried for Zade every night at bedtime and asked daily when Grandma Scott would be well enough that they could go back home and be with Zade and Jill. Mrs. Scott's sickness was a story Lindy fabricated in lieu of telling Josh the truth—which he wouldn't have understood in the first place.

With no one to turn to, she had gone to Randy's parents, who put them up until she rented a small, two-bedroom apartment. The Scotts had been supportive and sympathetic, but Mrs. Scott, an incurable romantic, seemed to think Lindy should have listened to Zade's side of the story before "up and leaving." Missing Zade as she did, Lindy often found herself agreeing with Mrs. Scott's theory.

And then there was the phone call from Amy early this morning. After recovering from the shock of being located, Lindy found she was glad to hear from her ex-boss. Amy explained how she had found them, then, in a voice that brooked no arguments, proceeded to tell Lindy exactly how and when Zade discovered who she was, how he tried to stop the subpoena before he asked her to marry him and ended by telling her, "He's miserable without you."

She wanted to believe it. Needed to. She had jumped to conclusions. Wrong ones. As usual, her impetuosity had reigned and landed her into another mess. If what Amy said was true—and Amy didn't lie—Zade did love her. He always had. He hadn't married her just for Jill. She should have listened to him. She was grown up, an adult. Unfortunately, the day she found the folder, all her heart had been able to accept was pain, not reason.

What did she do now? How could she go back and just say she was sorry? After all the things she had said, all she had accused him of—after leaving him—would those two simple words be enough? She was so afraid they wouldn't. And what would Zade do now that he knew where to find her and Josh? She'd existed all day in a confused state, half hoping he would come soon, but afraid of what he would say and do if he did.

She unlocked the door and pushed it shut after Josh. "Go put that sack on my bed, honey," she told him, her footsteps already headed for the apartment's small kitchen. He grumbled, but he went.

Lindy had just taken a carton of milk from the grocery sack when Josh's loudly yelled, "Momma!" pierced the afternoon stillness. It was the cry all mothers recognize immediately. Something was wrong. The milk fell to the floor, and Lindy raced toward her room, her heart pounding in fear. Dear Lord! What could be wrong?

She stopped in the doorway at the sight of Josh in the middle of her bed. Josh and something that looked like a doll. Then the doll moved. Josh lifted his bright excited gaze to hers. His mouth widened in a grin that threatened to split his features. "It's Jilly," he told her in an awe-filled voice.

Lindy shook her head, approaching the bed slowly. Jill? Impossible. It couldn't be. She put one knee on the bed and, bracing herself on her left hand, leaned over the baby who, now that she had Josh for an audience, was smiling and blowing bubbles, her chubby legs and her tiny feet—feet covered with white satin shoes—kicking at the air. White satin shoes with a puff of pink on the top. Shoes she remembered vividly.

"Oh!" The word, holding a plethora of emotions, gusted softly from Lindy's mouth, drawing the baby's attention to her mother. It *was* Jill. Jill wearing the beautiful white dress that had triggered the desire to keep her in the first place. Jill, who was gnawing the trailing ends of the single pink bow and her fist with obvious enjoyment as her huge blue-gray eyes stared soulfully up at Lindy who reached out a solitary finger to trail gently over the exquisite softness of the baby's sleep-blushed cheek. Oh, God! Jill. Lindy offered her daughter a watery smile that Jill returned with one of heartbreaking beauty.

Another thought hit Lindy with the suddenness and force of a typhoon. Zade! He must have brought her. Babies just didn't... He wouldn't have just left her... Even as the half-formed thoughts stumbled through her mind, her eyes were busy making a sweeping survey of the room.

And there he was, sitting in the fan-backed chair in a darkened corner, one ankle resting on the other knee, his arms folded across his chest, a cautious, waiting expression on his handsome face. Josh, carefully gauging his mother's reactions to everything, saw his father and friend at almost the same time she did. Leaping from the bed, he hurtled himself into Zade's fierce embrace.

A glow of love, of peace, settled inside her, pushing away the cold lump of pain lodging there. Her wide mouth curved into a smile of singular beauty as she watched the display of love between her husband and her son. She stood and picked Jill up, holding her close to her heart, breathing in the sweet, baby scent of her.

Zade, his chin resting on the top of Josh's gleaming blond head, raised his gaze and saw…a Lindy smile. An answering smile, one reminiscent of those first labored attempts she recalled so well, tugged at his lips. "You forgot something when you left," he told her, his voice hardly more than a husky whisper.

You, she thought. "Yes."

"I've missed you."

She bit her bottom lip and nodded. "Me, too."

There was earnest entreaty in his tone and his eyes as he said, "I swear I didn't know until the night Jill was born when you started telling me—"

She held up a hand to silence him. It didn't matter. They could talk later. "I know. Amy told me."

"Amy?"

Lindy nodded. "She called this morning."

"Then you knew I was coming?"

"No."

"I never meant to hurt you. I'd rather die than hurt you," he told her.

Moisture shimmered in the depths of Lindy's eyes. "I know that now." She pushed back the strand of hair that was forever falling down.

"Oh, Lindy," Zade breathed. "I love you. And Josh and Jill and I all need you."

With a small cry of joy, Lindy rounded the bed and, as Josh had only moments before, launched herself at him. Josh on one knee, Lindy and Jill on the other, Zade held them—his family, his love, his very life. He cradled them close, covering Lindy's beautiful, freckled face with random kisses. Then, when she buried her face in the warmth of the side of his neck, he whispered, "Please, please, come home."

She raised her head and looked into his eyes, seeing there

finally, clearly, the love he felt for her. A look that was mirrored in her own eyes. Tremulously, happily, she murmured, "I am home."

* * * * *

SILHOUETTE® *Desire®*

Do you want...

Dangerously handsome heroes

Evocative, everlasting love stories

Sizzling and tantalizing sensuality

Incredibly sexy miniseries like **MAN OF THE MONTH**

Red-hot romance

Enticing entertainment that can't be beat!

You'll find all of this, and much *more* each and every month in **SILHOUETTE DESIRE**. Don't miss these unforgettable love stories by some of romance's hottest authors. Silhouette Desire—where your fantasies will always come true....

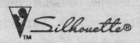

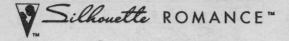

Silhouette ROMANCE™

What's a single dad to do when he needs a wife by next Thursday?

Who's a confirmed bachelor to call when he finds a baby on his doorstep?

How does a plain Jane in love with her gorgeous boss get him to notice her?

From classic love stories to romantic comedies to emotional heart tuggers, **Silhouette Romance** offers six irresistible novels every month by some of your favorite authors! Such as…beloved bestsellers **Diana Palmer, Annette Broadrick, Suzanne Carey, Elizabeth August** and **Marie Ferrarella,** to name just a few—and some sure to become favorites!

Fabulous Fathers…Bundles of Joy…Miniseries… Months of blushing brides and convenient weddings… Holiday celebrations… You'll find all this and much more in **Silhouette Romance**—always emotional, always enjoyable, always about love!

WAYS TO UNEXPECTEDLY MEET MR. RIGHT:

♡ *Go out with the sexy-sounding stranger your daughter secretly set you up with through a personal ad.*

♡ *RSVP yes to a wedding invitation—soon it might be your turn to say "I do!"*

♡ *Receive a marriage proposal by mail— from a man you've never met....*

These are just a few of the unexpected ways that written communication leads to love in Silhouette Yours Truly.

Each month, look for two fast-paced, fun and flirtatious Yours Truly novels (with entertaining treats and sneak previews in the back pages) by some of your favorite authors—and some who are sure to become favorites.

YOURS TRULY™:
Love—when you least expect it!

FIVE UNIQUE SERIES
FOR EVERY WOMAN YOU ARE...

 **ROMANCE™**

From classic love stories to romantic comedies to emotional heart tuggers, Silhouette Romance is sometimes sweet, sometimes sassy—and always enjoyable! Romance—the way you always knew it could be.

SILHOUETTE® *Desire*®

Red-hot is what we've got! Sparkling, scintillating, *sensuous* love stories. Once you pick up one you won't be able to put it down...only in Silhouette Desire.

Silhouette SPECIAL EDITION®

Stories of love and life, these powerful novels are tales that you can identify with—romances with "something special" added in! Silhouette Special Edition is entertainment for the heart.

SILHOUETTE·INTIMATE·MOMENTS®

Enter a world where passions run hot and excitement is always high. Dramatic, larger than life and always compelling—Silhouette Intimate Moments provides captivating romance to cherish forever.

SILHOUETTE YOURS TRULY™

A personal ad, a "Dear John" letter, a wedding invitation... Just a few of the ways that written communication unexpectedly leads Miss Unmarried to Mr. "I Do" in Yours Truly novels...in the most fun, fast-paced and flirtatious style!